TRY A LITTLE TENDERNESS

The Letter Club – Book 5

Elle Wright

PRAISE FOR THE LETTER CLUB

Nothing Else But You

"This was one of my favorites from an author period. It had everything I love in a novel. The characters and plot had me from beginning to end. Highly recommend." ~JuliaBookLandReviews

If Ever I Fall

"The second book in "The Letter Club" series does not disappoint. I have to admit that I am a sucker for an old-fashioned letter, so this story was right up my alley. If the idea of breaking out pen and paper seems archaic to you, then you may want to skip it.....but why on Earth would you want to do that? You would miss a phenomenal love story. Matteo is the love interest that everyone is looking for and Sophia is the girl that makes his heart melt." ~ RomanceReaderHB82

Never Without You

"These Letter Club books are fantastic! This is the third book I've read in the series and this one was just as good as the first two. It feels like you are part of trying to solve a mystery as you look for clues in the letters trying to figure out where each person lives. The love story is full of action, passion and steamy scenes! Highly recommend all of these books!" ~ Midnight Maiden

Anyone Who Had A Heart

"Max is a hair stylist at a ritzy salon in Redwood Falls. She has a difficult past and stays close to family. She keeps her heart even closer afraid she will fall foe someone to be heartbroken when they find out her past. Ryan is the new police chief. In town. He is smitten with Max from the moment he first saw her. After having coffee with her and one

date, he is certain she is the one for him. Wonderful story of one woman's struggle with self doubt, forgiving herself, the anxiety that the un-forgiveness causes, and allowing herself to be loved. And about the man who loved her enough to not give up and to help her heal. Such a great love story. I like the use of letters to break through some of the communication barriers." ~ L. Courter Vine Voice

www.BOROUGHSPUBLISHINGGROUP.com

TRY A LITTLE TENDERNESS
Copyright © 2023 Elle Wright

ISBN 978-1-957295-39-8

For all the sweet nerds who are so much more than they seem

ACKNOWLEDGMENTS

To say that the Covid pandemic put in a kink in my writing schedule would be a statement most authors would embrace. It took a while for life to get back to normal, and a bit longer to get back into the grove. Thank you for waiting for Amy and Jonas's story. It's one of my favorites. I hope you love them as much as I do.

Thanks to my beta reader who always catches the details, and to Boroughs Publishing Group for being there.

TRY A LITTLE TENDERNESS

Chapter One

Happy Happy

Amy

A little more than two years ago

I'm standing next to Sofia's dad, who's holding his three-week-old grandson with exquisite care and jumbo pride as we watch Matteo twirl his wife – Sofia, my best friend – on the dance floor. As weddings go, this one is fantastic. The food is great, the booze is primo, and the vibe is relaxed. There's not more than eighty people, and everyone is having a great time. We're in Theresa and Ethan's – the newlyweds – big backyard under a huge tent. The DJ's been spinning oldies for a while, mostly Motown slow drags. These folks like to dance close.

A huge man named Tommie, whom I've known most of my life, comes up behind Sofia's dad, says something in his ear, and Don Di Caro – yes, *that* kind of Don, not an Oxford scholar – turns to me and says, "Please watch over Alessandro."

"Sure." I hold out my arms, and he places the sleeping baby in them like the kid is made of butterfly wings. He walks away with Tommie, and I'm holding the Don's namesake, cooing at the kid like a total goof.

Of course, that's when a guy who goes to the same school I do – Boston University – comes over and stands next to me. "Hey," he says while looking straight ahead. I think his name is Jonas. He was in my English Lit class last semester, and he might've lived in my dorm, but I'm not sure. He's cute in a California surfer dude kinda way. Tall and lean, broad shoulders, and he has sun-bleached blond hair overlaying his natural light brown. Not my type, but I can see his appeal.

"Hey," I answer back, though I have the courtesy to look at him when I speak. "You a relative?"

He looks down – I'm a little over five-six and not big on wearing ankle-breakers, and this dude's well over six feet – and says, "Nah. My dad's good friends with Ethan, and I've known him since I was little." Not something I usually notice, but this guy has a nice voice. Mellow and soft. "You're Amy, right?"

At this point I'm thinking it's weird he hasn't said anything about me holding a baby, but maybe he's seen a bunch of people holding the kid, who's been passed around all day like a doobie at a frat party. "Right. You're Jonas?

"Yeah. Jonas Vandenberg. I was in English Lit with you last semester."

"I remember. You sat in the back. I figured you were enduring a requirement."

"Nope. I always sit in the back. I'm tall and even in stadium seating, if I sit in the front or the middle, people are behind me and they can't see." He shrugs. "Anyway, I like English Lit. It's not my major, but I read a lot so it interests me."

A guy who's considerate, likes to read, and follows his interests. He doesn't seem the type, but goes to show ya, don't judge a surfer dude by his looks. "You're starting your sophomore year, right?"

"Yeah. You?"

"Uh-huh. You know your major already?"

"Totally." His face lights up. "The future's all about technology. I'm concentrating in nanotechnology. There's all sorts of tie-ins to AI." I must've seemed confused because he goes on to explain, "Artificial intelligence."

Again. Not what I expected. "You want to build a Data?"

He looks at me like I'm a divine oracle. "Have you seen Sophia?"

Odd segue, but okay, I'll go with it. I lift my chin in the general direction of the dance floor. "She's dancing with Matt."

Jonas laughs. "I don't know who they are. I'm asking you about the AI robot Sophia who made the rounds in the media about two years ago."

I chuckle. This guy is a likable nerd. "No."

"Go online. She's the precursor to what's coming. An early Data, to use your example."

"That's your jam, huh?" He gives me a blank look. "Your thing. What you want to do."

"Oh, yeah. Totally."

This guy isn't particularly in tune with popular culture. His looks and his affinity for things outside nerdom don't match the stereotype of a techno-geek living in a cave-like apartment sitting behind a bank of monitors pounding away on his keyboard. But what do I know? I'm so far from declaring my major I might as well be in the fifth grade.

"You interning for a tech company this summer?"

"Nah. Monday I'm flying out to California. My parents are divorced and I'm spending the rest of the summer with my mother. She works in the movie business in post-production and she got me a job at a CGI company."

I have to think for a minute and then – a-ha. Computer-generated imagery they use in the movies. "That sounds cool."

He shrugs. "I'm sure I'll be no more than a glorified gofer, but it pays pretty good for a college student."

Don Di Caro is walking toward me, his steely gaze honed on Jonas. My father is a shit dad, and a worse human. I've never had what the Don is throwing off right now. You know, the protective father who's suspicious of every guy who talks to me. Sofia always complained about how smothered she was, and for a while there, she was right, but I wouldn't've minded one bit if my father took even one quarter the interest in me Don Di Caro shows his daughters.

The Don holds out his arms and I transfer Alessandro. We all call him Alex, but even in my head, I call him Alessandro around the Don. As he nestles the baby against him with a gentleness no one would expect from this man, I say, "This is Jonas Vandenberg. His father is a close friend of Ethan's. Jonas, this is," the Don gives his head a barely perceptible shake and I know what that means, "Mr. Di Caro, the baby's grandpa."

Jonas sticks out his hand then withdraws it when it registers the Don's arms are otherwise engaged. "Nice to meet you, sir." Then Jonas turns to me and says, "See you next semester," then lopes off, heading to a group of men standing together in a loose circle with beer bottles in their hands.

"He goes to Boston University?" the Don asks.

"Yes. Jonas was in my English Lit class last semester."

"Ah," the Don makes the *I see* noise with a tone that says Jonas being in my presence is acceptable.

I squeeze the Don's forearm and say, "Thanks."

What's odd, but isn't, is he doesn't ask "What for?" 'cause he knows I have a shit father and an equally fucked-up mother. Alessandro Di Caro knows everything about everyone who has even remote contact with his family, and since Sofia and I have been best friends since forever, he knows *everything* about me.

He cares more about what I do, what I'm studying, and who I'm dating than my parents do. Side note: I did him a solid during the whole Sofia and Matt long-distance romance thing, even though I was afraid it would cost me Sofia's friendship. The Don told me it wouldn't, and it didn't. Don Di Caro *never* forgets favors done for him.

The caterers are cutting the cake without all the newlywed playacting hoopla. Ethan goes over to the table and takes the plate with the largest piece that has a grouping of beautifully decorated flowers on top, and brings it over to Theresa. He forks up a piece, and she leans forward to take it into her mouth. Before she can swipe a bit of frosting from her lip, Ethan places his mouth over hers and kisses the frosting away.

I look around the tent and it seems everyone is watching them, and the assembled guests all have the same look on their face: Awww.

It's enough to make even me feel all happy happy.

Chapter Two

Awkward

Jonas

Present Day

Two summers ago my life changed. One thing had – maybe still has – the potential to be seriously good. And the other, while it has its rewards, has a downside that sucks so bad it isn't worth it. First, I finally got to talk to Amy – I still don't know her last name – after watching her come and go from our dorm for months. Then I had to switch dorms because of some FBI shit my father couldn't talk about, but he insisted I move, so I did.

The whole time I sat behind her in English Lit I kept trying to figure out ways to approach her and talk to her, but she always had people around. She's totally friendly and talks to everyone. If I'd worked up the nerve, she probably would've talked to me too, but I suffer from terminal awkwardness. Hard to blend in when you're five-nine in the sixth grade.

I was shocked when I saw her at Ethan's wedding, but it was an opportunity I never thought I'd get. There weren't a ton of college students around her, and some guy had passed a baby to her so I saw my chance and took it.

Damn. She's totally great, like I knew she would be. The reason there's always so many people around her all the time is 'cause she's so easy to talk to. I mean, she seemed really interested in what I'm studying and she didn't act all judge-y and shit. We talked for like ten minutes, but then the baby's grandfather came back and gave me the hairy eyeball. I took that as my cue to leave.

But we'd talked and she knew who I was. I figured I'd run into her on campus, or we'd have another class together. It's never happened, but I keep hoping, even though there are around thirty thousand students at BU.

The other thing that changed my life has been weird in the extreme. I was working for a CGI company in Santa Monica that's close enough to my mom's house, I rode my bike to work. One day a woman was driving too fast on Olympic Boulevard and nearly clipped me. I swerved and fell onto the sidewalk. She stopped – unusual for LA especially during morning rush hour – and made a fuss. She wanted to call 9-1-1. I was banged up, but not bleeding or anything. After she calmed down – I was the one who'd been nearly hit, but she was totally shaken up – she kept staring at me like she was taking inventory. Then she asked if she could take my picture. I mean, LA's all kinds of different, what with the entertainment industry and the endless summer, people can be a bit…off.

I'd gone to Santa Monica High School, and as much as anyone could, I'd gotten used to the crazy. I let her take the picture, then she gave me her card with her name on it – Sheree Berman – and the card had a logo I didn't recognize. I stuffed it in my pocket and she asked if she could have my number to check to make sure I was all right. Again, LA. I didn't think much about it.

Four days later she called me and asked if I'd be interested in modeling for her agency. I talked to my mom, who had one of her attorney friends "represent" me, and the next thing I knew, I wasn't working for a CGI company anymore.

I went to a bunch of "casting calls," then bam, I'm doing photo shoots for a famous clothing line. Part of the deal my mom's friend negotiated was I return to BU each semester and only work for Sheree during winter breaks and the summers.

The money is outrageous, especially for a college student. Apparently, I have "a look," whatever that means, and I'm in demand, so I don't have to go to "casting calls" anymore.

I don't mind the work. It's boring and there's lots of waiting around. People are always touching my hair, my face, my clothes, even when they're on my body, telling me to stand this way, move that way, smile, don't smile, pretend to love the women I'm modeling with, pretend to hate the women I'm modeling with... You get the drift. If I took it seriously, it's crazy-making.

The female models are nuts. They're so skinny they look sick. They don't eat and they drink so much water they're always going to the bathroom. Some probably go to throw up – I learned that's a thing in the industry – though I don't know what's coming up since they don't eat. A lot of them take drugs, some prescription, most not, to keep them from wanting to eat. A few of the male models are no better, but some of the guys are all right. They're thin naturally, like me, and are active, like me.

My favorite shoot was for a swimsuit line. We went to Zuma Beach in Malibu and I got to surf for work. I've been surfing since I was little when we lived in Oregon – before my parents split up – and it's the best thing about living in California. There's good surfing on the East Coast, but it's limited – winter weather.

The real downside to this modeling thing is how I'm treated at school. People started to recognize me, and it's not for my intellect. That's why I grow my hair and a beard at the beginning of every semester. It helps some, but not nearly enough.

Some of the propositions are mega outrageous and come from both sexes. Mostly, though, I seem to always have a group around me, crowding me when I'm at a club, or even when I'm standing in a hall outside of class.

Listen, I like to get laid as much as the next guy, and given my terminal awkwardness, it hadn't been happening all that often before the modeling gig started, but at least I'd had some say in the outcome.

These people are tigers and come at me like I'm meat for consumption. Or they're derisive, calling me "sell-out" or "pretty boy."

Truly better to be a nerd nobody notices.

To keep the wolves at bay, I've adopted the California fuck-boy attitude toward dating, and getting laid. It's not a suit I wear comfortably, but it buys me a barrier.

Yeah, the downside sucks so bad it isn't worth it. At the end of the summer after I graduate my contract is up, and I am so not renewing.

In a bid for normal, I joined The Letter Club so I could be me when I "talk" to a woman. Actually, I'm still awkward, but I've learned how to hide it. Writing is an easier way to express myself, and I want to communicate with a girl who has no idea who I am, what I look like in board shorts, and who wants to get to know me as a person, not as a face on a billboard.

The Letter Club has a premium membership where letters are sent overnight. I know it's a bit insta-grat of me, but I don't want to wait a week, answer a letter, she waits a week… You get the picture.

I received about forty responses to my first letter before I found the woman I wanted to talk to. Since we're anonymous, I can't be sure it's a woman, but it sure sounds like one. If it's a guy who has feminine qualities that are coming through in a letter, I'll take it for friendship's sake, but I don't see it going anywhere past that.

Hey, Carly,

I know that's not your name, and if you hate it, change it, but I like the idea of us having an identity unique to here. If you're wondering why I picked Carly, I grew up listening to a lot of music from the 60s and 70s. I used to go to my grandparents' house after school 'cause both my parents worked, and my gran is a hippie like for real. She went to Woodstock, she lived in the Haight for a while, then moved to a commune before she met my gramps, who picked her up hitchhiking in Big Sur. She loves Peter, Paul and Mary, Bob Dylan, the Byrds, James Taylor, Carly Simon, Carol King, Crosby, Stills & Nash, Joni Mitchell, and anything Motown. I know it's retro, but I enjoy that music. It reminds me of Gran and all those years I hung out with her when I was a kid.

She taught me how to play the guitar and we used to sing together. I'm not great, but sometimes I can carry a tune. Gran's talented and is all around artsy. She paints watercolors and her works are sold in lots of galleries. Gramps is the complete opposite. She says she married "the man," which in hippie-speak means a traditional conservative guy. Somehow they made it work. They have three daughters (my mom's the oldest) and they've been married for fifty-five years. Gran says she never wanted to get married, that it's an institution set up to subjugate women, but she wanted my gramps and he wasn't going to live with her without marrying her, so I guess the compromise worked out.

Sorry to say, my other grandparents died when I was little, but my dad says they were really good together, and they were married for forty-six years.

A good track record from both sides.

David

I'm looking forward to this woman writing back, and it'd be great if we got close. I'd like a friend, and maybe something more, but I'm still holding out hope I'll run into Amy.

Who knows, maybe she'll be at this big "secret" party I'm going to next weekend.

Since I've been modeling, I get invited to all sorts of parties I never knew existed when I was a freshman. My roommate, Collin Dineen, is a quiet guy who's studying art history. He wants to be a professor. He never gets invited to anything, so I take him with me.

Most of the time he leaves early, and while I know he's grateful for the exposure, he gets rattled by the noise and the crush.

Really, I do too, but I know if I don't go, I won't ever find Amy.

Chapter Three

My Calling

Amy

I fell into my major by doing what I love. At the end of this academic year, I'm getting a Bachelor's of Science in Hospitality and Communication. What I love is planning and throwing mega parties and events. I know, I know, I gotta back up and explain, but I can't tell you how goals AF getting the degree and having my own biz is.

A few years ago, I met this sweet nerd at a wedding. We didn't chat for long, but man, he knew exactly what he wanted to do with his life and loved talking about it. After the wedding, I went to the Hamptons to hang with my grams, who's the only member of my family I like, never mind love. Basically, she feels the same about me. She's my father's mother, and she doesn't think much of him, and she detests my mom. Grams and I don't bother to commiserate since we know we're rowing in the same boat.

The Hamptons in the summer is *the* place to be if you're anyone with oodles of money or are trying to get with a person with oodles of money. Of all the towns that make up the Hamptons, the village of Sagaponack in Southhampton is the priciest, and it's where my grams lives.

Way back when, in like 1960, my grandfather, who owned a snooty publishing house, married my grams and decided to leave New York City and move out to what is now Sagaponack. Back then, the village was home to writers, literary agents, and folks in the publishing business. Get this, it was where my grams and gramps wanted to live because it was a quiet, *cheap* place near the beach conducive to their bohemian lifestyle.

Gramps found a colonial farmhouse built in 1775 on tons of land, and had it modernized. Over the years, for serious money, he'd sold off all but a little more than an acre. About three years before he died, he had a major renovation done on the house, and had a new pool put in. I sort of think he wasn't feeling well even back then, and didn't tell anyone. I know how much he loved Grams and probably didn't want her to worry about repairing the house, so he made sure she had upgraded and more modern conveniences. The house is now worth *beaucoup* duckets.

He died about five years ago and Grams lives in the big old house by herself. The gardens are amazing. She's been working them since they moved into the house, but now she doesn't get around as well as she used to. She has a woman named Gloria come in to clean twice a week who also does the shopping and errands for Grams on a third day of the week.

This past March was Grams's eighty-first birthday. I came down and spent a long weekend with her. My father, the asshole, sent her flowers and a card, and my mother, the bitch, called. Aside from me and a few of her old friends who still live in the area, Grams doesn't have anyone else. Her daughter, my father's older sister, died of breast cancer when she was thirty-one. She'd been married, but didn't have any kids. Too fucking sad to talk about, but her pictures are all over the house. Every now and again I catch my grams standing with tears in her eyes when she's holding a photo of my aunt, who I never knew. Breaks my heart.

The summer after my freshman year, when I was hanging with Grams, I told her about the sweet nerd and how he knew his life plan while I was still floundering. Aimless Amy Stern was what I called myself.

Grams and I are a lot alike. We're saucy. We're brazen. We don't suffer fools gladly. We don't whine, and we can't stand whiners. My whining about my aimlessness was so out of character, Grams called a meeting of the Old Ladies' Club. That's what she calls them. Now there are only six of them. A couple of years ago there were eight.

Eight women between the ages of seventy-five and eighty-six convened in my grams's salon – similar to the family room, but more formal, though not as formal as most people's living rooms. I gotta tell you, I've known those women all my life and I adore them. Each and every one of them are accomplished in their own right. While they might be old, they're still kickass, have lived long, extraordinary lives, and have plenty of opinions on pretty much everything. Any advice, assistance, or recommendations they have, I'm all ears.

That night we talked for hours, and at the end of evening they decided my problem was I'd withdrawn from the social life that'd pumped me up, and being a homebody made me lose my light.

Looong story, but here's the quick recap: Freshman year I went out clubbing with two friends from BU. I left early to work on a paper and both my friends were roofied and were almost kidnapped. One came back to school a few weeks later, the other had heart problems 'cause she was double dosed, and she left BU.

When I learned what happened to them, I freaked and stopped going out. It took a while to get back to level. Sofia helped with that a lot, but I refused to go clubbing again. I went out only to restaurants and I stopped drinking everything alcoholic except wine and beer, and I only drank them when the server brought the bottle to the table and it was uncorked or uncapped in front of me.

One of the members of the Old Ladies Club, Maddie Simons, suggested I'd get my power back by organizing an event instead of going out to places where someone else controlled the environment. She offered me the job of putting together her Labor Day party – a huge end-of-summer event that was usually handled by super-expensive party planners.

Years and years ago, Maddie and her husband had started a clothing line that defined fashion forward, and still does. Mega money, which meant a seaside party with A-list celebs and tons of paps. Most of that summer I was scared out of my mind because I had no idea what the fuck I was doing. But damn if I didn't pull it off, and got rave reviews.

Surprised the hell out of me, but I found I'm good at it. Six people approached Maddie to find out who did the party. *Bam*. My business and my calling were born.

When I went back to BU for the fall semester, I had two clients, both of whom wanted me to plan huge winter holiday events in NYC.

Most East Coast people with giant money "do" the Hamptons only for the summer. They stay "in town" (that's NYC) in the fall, and once the holidays are over, depending on their lifestyle, they go to Gstaad, Aspen, their ranch in Montana, Banff, Palm Beach, the Bahamas, Antigua, Nevis, or their own private Caribbean island.

They don't come back to "town" until late March or early April and stay until right before Memorial Day weekend when they start the cycle all over again in the Hamptons.

Tough life.

The holiday parties kicked major ass, and my clients were thrilled. I'd gone back and forth to NYC a ton of weekends, which was hell on studying, but I pulled it off. Word spread and I picked up Boston work, including secret parties thrown by kids of super-rich money-to-burn parents.

Yeah, my business took a hit during the pandemic – my sophomore year – but not as much as you'd think. You'd be surprised how many super-rich college kids were throwing parties in the great outdoors no matter the time of year, all showing up with designer masks to match their attire.

Money. It makes people really fuckin' crazy.

Speaking of… Remember the sweet nerd? Let's take a moment to flash back to me running back and forth to NYC, which I did by train for four hours each way. Hello. Where do you think I did my studying?

So, I'm on the train and scrolling IG and there's an ad for a famous menswear company, and who do you think is featured in the ad? My sweet nerd, Jonas Vandenberg. Holy shit.

I mean, he's cute in person, but with the magic of makeup, good photography, and all the filters and manipulations, Jonas looks like Brad Pitt in *Thelma and Louise*.

Problem is: apparently he thinks so too.

Well, that's what I've heard. Total fuck-boy with a California 'tude.

I'm guessing he went from bad to worse when a larger-than-life Jonas wearing bright blue board shorts carrying a surfboard was on a Times Square billboard in the dead of winter.

Such a shame. He had promise.

Between BU having a huge student population, Jonas's and my majors having no intersection whatsoever, and how busy I've been with Big Pond Entertainment – my corporation's name – I haven't seen him since the wedding years ago.

Until right now.

I'm standing with my client – a total douche who goes to Harvard, of course – explaining to him why the DJ has to have a break, and how during those meager ten minutes when the dude is peeing and scarfing, house music will be playing so the party will continue to rock and the dancing will still be mega.

Finally, after saying the same thing five different ways, it sinks in and dumbass, whose daddy doled out millions to get him into an Ivy League school, heads back into the crowd.

Now that my brain is unencumbered with stupidity, I focus on my surroundings and I catch, "Hi, Jonas" gushed in the ooziest voice I've ever heard. The "i" in "hi" is drawn out so it's like fifteen "i's," and the breathiness factor is hitting the needle at ten.

I quarter turn to see if it's the Jonas I know, and sure enough, tall, beach blond and now with a hipster beard and a man bun, he's sorta tilting his head down to a perky brunette whose tits are pushed up so high on her chest they're almost living on her collarbone.

If all that's not bad enough, he responds with, "Hey, doll. We banging later, or what?"

Hurl chunks are getting ready to start coming up my throat, so me and my iPad go into the office one story above the dance floor where I can keep an eye on things without being subjected to vomit-inducing behavior.

The office is padded, insulated, or whatever they call the sound deadening, and I'm entirely grateful. I still hear the boom-boom of the bass a little, but otherwise, no shouted convos, no pawing, clingy coeds, or dumbass jocks with the worst pickup lines on four continents. I'm scrolling through my emails when noise blares at the bottom of the stairs, then I hear the door shut. I figure it's Randy, the guy who owns the space, coming to chill in his office.

I turn to say "hey," and there's Jonas standing with his mouth hanging open.

"Amy?" I stare, and I haveta admit, he's damn cute. "I can't believe it. I've been hoping to bump into you since the wedding."

Not the response I expected, but who knows with this guy. "Yeah? Well, here I am."

He walks over to where I'm sitting, pulls over a ladder-back chair, flips it around and sits straddling it, his long arms hanging over the back of the chair.

"Please," he's all earnest, "before I forget, what's your last name?"

I'm contemplating not telling him, but before I can get a word out of my mouth, the door opens and from the bottom of the steps in a high-volume whine comes the most obnoxious voice yelling, "Jo-nas. C'mon. We're supposed to…you know."

Jonas purses his lips and puts his forefinger over them in the universal *shhh* move. We sit quietly for a few beats and the door slams. Jonas's shoulders drop and he leans forward and says, "I thought I'd escaped her. I came in here to hide."

I'm beginning to think this dude is suffering from multiple personality disorder when the whiner starts clumping up the steps saying, "I knew you were in here. This where we're gonna do it?"

It's collarbone tits, and she stopped short at the doorway, punching her hands on her hips and cocking her head. "I'm not doing a threesome, Jonas. I'm not sharing you with anyone, especially this uppity bitch."

Now wait a damn minute.

"Bree, go back downstairs and wait like a good girl. I need a chill moment."

See. Now he's back to being the idiot with the 'tude.

She twitches and leans forward before spewing, "I don't fuckin' think so. You're not hanging alone with Miss My Shit Don't Stink."

Ya know, I'm done here. I get up, shove my iPad in my backpack, and push past Bree and jog down the stairs while Jonas is shouting, "Amy. Don't leave," at the same time Bree is screaming, "Let the bitch go. We got the place all to ourselves now."

The door slams behind me and I push my way across the dance floor to the DJ booth, where I squeeze in and plunk my ass down on the narrow bench behind the DJ, who's bopping and moving like a jack-in-the-box on coke. I see a pair of headphones tucked into a cubby, and put them on, cutting the noise level in half.

With nothing for it but to wait out the mania sitting here since Jonas is banging Bree in the office – ewww – I pull out my iPad to compose my return letter to my new Letter Club friend who calls himself David. I'm glad he's doing the premium overnight letters. I've never been known for my patience. I like the anonymity and actually writing letters, and I want to hear back fast.

I'm not looking for love or any shit like that, but my world is hectic and I deal with a lot of assholes. I thought it'd be nice, you know, normal to have a friend to talk to in a no-pressure, no-BS way.

I know two couples who met through The Letter Club and got married, Sofia's brother being one of them. I figured I'd aim to develop a good friendship with a dude, and prove to myself they're not all POS's, fuck-ups, or worse.

This David guy seems sweet. He loved hanging out with his grandparents, and his hippie grams sounds fantastic.

Since my only real family member is my grams, who I adore with all my heart, I'm thinking since David is close to his grams and values that relationship, he might be the guy friend I'm looking for.

David,

Hey. I love all that music too, though I found it on my own. My grams – my gramps died a few years back as did my other set of grandparents – means the world to me and I hang with her as much as I can. But she's more of a Mozart, Brahms, and Bach sort of person. It sort of runs in that side of the family.

She's cool, but I don't think the Jefferson Airplane's "White Rabbit" stuck with her through the years. Her thing is gardening, and I learned from the best. Her yard looks amazing. I didn't think I'd like getting my hands in the dirt and do the communing with nature thing, but for real, it has a calming effect, and I got invested in the plants thriving. I intend to keep up her gardens for as long as I live.

In other news, I'm contemplating buying my first car. I live in a city where parking is impossible and a pain in the ass, but I travel for work, and sometimes it's easier and faster to drive than rely on mass transit, especially when I go to remote areas. I've been looking at electric and hybrid cars. Not cheap. Plus, there's a thing about charging them when you go outside of major metropolitan areas. I don't want to buy an all-gas vehicle, but if the purpose of buying a car is the freedom it offers, then I have to get a car that I can re-charge easily in lots of places.

*Most of the electric cars don't have range past 250 miles per charge. That's not very far. *sigh* Being climate change conscious is important to me, so the research continues until I narrow the field. In the meantime, I'll continue to take public transit and the train as much as I can, and when needed, I'll rent a car when I head out to the countryside. I'll fly if I have to, but I admit to not being a fan of the whole experience.*

It's not only the TSA stuff – yeah, I know security and all that – but I was never too thrilled breathing recycled air with strangers. After the pandemic... I don't think so. I still go double-masked on public transit along with half of the other riders. Call me hypervigilant, but you know there's a ton of people walking around without masks who haven't been vaccinated.

And it's not only about me. My grams is in her eighties and I don't want to get her sick. *more sigh* As if life hadn't been complicated enough.

What are you plans for Thanksgiving? I'm going to hang with my grams. Every year we have a couple of her friends over, and they bring their kids and grandchildren. The house is overflowing with noisy, happy families. Shocker. They like each other and don't fight at the dinner table. My kind of crowd. Low stress.

TTYS –

Carly

Chapter Four

Near Miss

Jonas

Well shit. I had Amy sitting right next me, like inches away, and rancid Bree had to ruin a potentially excellent reunion. Three years ago, Bree wouldn't've even looked at me. The thought of not knowing her and all the people like her seems like a fantasy. But nine months from now it will become my reality when I've fulfilled the terms of my contract. Then I'm done, and I can't fuckin' wait.

Bree gave me one good thing during her rant. For real, she was stripping off and I'm standing up telling her it's not going to happen and she's all, yeah it is, unzip and I'll get that cock hard and ready to go. I mean, where's the joy in that?

I guess for some guys, it's a dream come true. They don't care what the person they're fucking is like as a human being, they only want hot, wet, and willing. I want Amy. And Bree, screeching like a zombie because I won't unzip and let her play with my dick, yells out as I'm heading downstairs, "Go ahead and see if Miss Up Her Own Ass Amy Stern will have anything to do with your tiny, shriveled, limp little cock."

I'm so thrilled I know Amy's last name I don't care what Bree's screaming. I'm barely down the stairs and out the door when three girls scream and pull me into their huddle to show me their IG feed. One of my underwear ads has a big red circle around my package. Yeah, you guessed it, Bree trolls, "That shit don't work" over the waistband, an arrow pointing to the circled package. She goes on to comment, "Can't even get hard, never mind getting it up."

What? Thirty seconds to get down the stairs and onto the dance floor and she's got over five thousand hits and about a hundred fifty comments. I shake my head and laugh.

One of the huddle girls grabs my arm and yells, "You've gotta handle this. It'll ruin you."

"Promise?" I ask, grin, pull out of her death grip, and leave the party.

While I'm totally bummed Amy bolted, it turns out to be a great fuckin' night. Bree did me a huge favor. I'm guessing by tomorrow no one will want anything to do with my dick. I can go back to being me, look for Amy, find her, tell her the whole story, and get my life back sooner than expected.

It didn't go that way. Don't shake your head. I'm not naïve. I'm hopeful. Optimistic. Goal oriented.

But people suck.

As I'd mentioned, my roommate, Collin, is a normal, decent guy. He doesn't spend hours on social media. In fact, I don't think he even goes on social media. So, when I get back to my room, we chill, I tell him the party sucked, he didn't miss anything, and I flop on my bed and fall asleep with a smile on my face.

The next morning, I wake to hundreds of notes stuffed under the door, and after I sweep them out of the way so Collin can get to class, I see about forty thousand sticky notes hanging on the door. I look up and down the hall, yank off as many as I can, and then slam the door shut. I can't help but read a few of the notes.

"She's such a bitch. Ignore her."

"Don't worry, honey. I know (three underlines) your dick works great."

"If I had that ho grabbing at my cock, I'd go limp too."

My head drops to my chest and I sigh. As I'm stuffing all the "correspondence" into a trash bag, my phone goes off. Sheree. Fuck.

Please tell me she's calling about anything else but Bree's social media shit.

I decide to play dumb. "Hey, Sheree. What's up?"

"Are you *trying* to be funny?" I wasn't, but I crack up because, hell, it's funny. "Really, Jonas. This is serious." I stop laughing because she sounds pissed the hell off, and Sheree doesn't get pissed off, she sends lawyers to get pissed off for her. "The clothing company wants to sue, and we sure as hell want to sue. So–"

"No," I shout. "Nobody's suing. Leave it be. It'll blow over by tomorrow, and someone else will become chum."

She heaves a huge sigh. "Oh honey. You're too sweet for this business." Don't I know it. "I'm taking your answer as an indication you haven't looked at social media, and haven't seen any of the morning shows yet."

Of course not. It's eight o'clock on a Thursday morning. I've got to shower, grab my backpack, and haul ass to my nine o'clock class. "No, I haven't. And I don't intend to." She starts to say something, but I jump in. "Listen, the clothing company doesn't have anything to complain about. Bree's anger was directed at my junk, not their underwear. You have nothing to complain about since I've stuffed into this trash bag I'm holding hundreds of notes all supporting me. Let it go. It's not a thing unless you make it a thing."

"Huh," she grunts. "Actually, our PR people and our marketing people said the same thing."

I can't believe they've been up all night dealing with this. "Sheree. It's five in the morning in LA. Call off the dogs and get some sleep." She chuckles. "Okay, don't sleep. I know you'll find a way to make this work to everyone's advantage."

"You're damn straight I will."

"Right. Listen, I'm not trying to be rude, but I gotta get to my nine o'clock class. I'll call you later and you can tell me what brilliant scheme all the suits have cooked up while I'm trying to graduate college."

"Okay, Jonas. Talk to you later."

Click. She's gone and I have ten minutes to SS&S, dress, and then get to class.

I should've skipped class.

There's a mob in the halls, and no one mobs the halls outside the Elements in the Theory of Computation class. I pull down my black BU cap as far as I can and try to navigate through the throng. I'm two feet from the classroom door and I bump shoulders with someone, and without thinking, I turn and say, "'Scuse me."

"It's him," someone shouts, and that's my cue. I dash into class and hope my professor tells everyone who's not supposed to be here to get the fuck out.

Eventually, she does, but she's glowering at me as if I'd orchestrated this disaster. After class I go up and apologize, but she shakes her head like I'm a lost cause. I drag myself into the hall, where, gratefully, the mob is half the size it had been. Now I have to decide whether I brave the next two classes or hide.

I want to hide. I want to disappear for the next few days and let this mess blow over. But I'm pissed off too, and I'm not going to let a shrill chick stop me from living my life.

I should've skipped my next two classes.

The mobs aren't as bad, but they're there, and it's fuckin' annoying. My Magic, Science, and Religion professor took pity on me and let me leave through the side door usually reserved for faculty.

I have work to do, and figure anywhere I'm expected to go would be where I'd find more hordes of people who, for reasons I'll never understand, want to be on the inside of this perceived drama. I have my laptop with me, and decide to go to the Mugar Memorial Library. Before I get in the door, my phone goes off. Dad.

"Hey, bud," he says right away. "This shit as stupid as I think it is?" My father's the Special Agent in Charge of some elite unit at the Boston office of the FBI. He doesn't suffer fools gladly, he's as serious as a heart attack, and he has zero tolerance for bullshit. He also loves me with everything he has.

"Yeah. Nuts, but it'll blow over."

"That's what I figured," he huffs. "You okay?"

"Totally. Laying low, letting the haters have their moment."

"Good man. Best not to feed the fire." I smile. My dad always has my back. "We doing dinner Monday night?"

"Yeah."

"Pick you up at seven. See you then, bud."

Annnd he's gone.

My mother had called around lunchtime and hardly said a word, she was laughing so hard. Being in the movie business, she knows not to take any of this shit seriously, and she's savvy about PR people and how they spin stories. "I love how this went from 'What did Jonas do?' to 'Another jilted coed with a bad 'tude.'"

When I hadn't heard from Sheree again, I figured her "people" had done their thing and she and the manufacturer were happy with the outcome.

I stuff my phone into my pocket and head into the library. I'm able to find a carrel in a corner, and I'm relieved to be alone in a quiet space.

I know I have hours of schoolwork to do, but I need to connect with someone normal who doesn't know me and the shitstorm swirling around me. I decide to write to Carly.

Hey Carly,

Cool you've been exposed to classical music. Can't say I've had much contact with it, but I have been to the opera once. I saw La Traviata, *and I have to say, I didn't expect to feel so much, especially at the end. For real, it seemed like everyone was crying, and I bet half those people had seen the opera before.*

Also, can't say I've done much gardening. When I was a kid, I mowed my grandparents' lawn with one of those old-fashioned push mowers. My gran didn't want to "foul" the environment with a ride-around mower. She said there were too many vehicles powered by "big corporate oil," and in her home she could at least control her environment.

Thankfully, they had grass only around the outer edges of the swimming pool, which took up most of the yard. Pushing that sucker was hard work. After I finished mowing, I raked up the cut grass, and put it in their big compost bin – no surprise with a hippie gran – and then I jumped in the pool to cool down. Gran always had homemade lemonade ready for me after I'd finished, and every time I must've downed three glasses while hanging over the edge of the pool.

I'll be spending Thanksgiving with my grandparents and my mom – it's her turn. My folks split up years ago, and I bounce between them for the holidays. This year Thanksgiving with Mom and her people, Hannukah and New Year's with Dad and his people.

My family on both sides are Dutch Jews who were able to flee the Netherlands before the Nazis invaded. According to my gran, most of the family emigrated to Holland in the 1600s because their government was more tolerant of other religions since they'd split from Spain to practice Protestantism.

My gramps was born in Amsterdam, but my gran was born in the US less than a year after her parents emigrated. My gran's family lived near my dad's parents, who were also born in Amsterdam. I don't remember them. They died when I was really little, but Gran keeps them alive by telling stories about them, which is how I know them. Stories and photographs.

Wow, sorry. I didn't mean to get maudlin. It seems around the holidays I miss having them around. I know my dad really misses them, but he doesn't talk about them much. I'm grateful my gran is the family's historian, and she's a wonderful storyteller.

So, where are you with the whole car situation? Maybe, for now, it'll be more cost effective to use rentals when you go out of town. I live in a city where we have pretty decent mass transit. I wouldn't keep a car here. The parking is too much of a headache.

Have a great Thanksgiving.

Talk soon –

David

Chapter Five

Go Figure

Amy

Without meaning to, Jonas got my attention. I would've bet a sizable chunk of money on him doing Bree on every surface in the office after I'd left. Since I'd been squirreled away behind the DJ writing to David, and then doing my rounds checking out everything to make sure the party was continuing to run smoothly, I didn't tap into social media until I got back to my room. By then, everything had blown up in a big way, and Bree did not come out of it smelling like a rose. As a matter of fact, she's been stinking like nasty baby shit for the past two days, and I have to say, it doesn't break my heart.

Sure, I'm a card-carrying member of the girls' club, and I support my sisters in their right to call out assholes, but in this case, Bree is the asshole. I mean, who'd want to fuck a person who treats you like you're dirt beneath their feet before you even take off your clothes. Can you imagine how bad she'd be after she thought she had her hooks in you? It gives me the shivers.

What I like best about how all this is shaking out is that Jonas hasn't said a word. I hear he's been swamped with people everywhere he goes, but he's keeping his head down, going to class, and acting like the whole thing's nothing but a nuisance. Commendable, really. I didn't think he had it in him.

It's five days after Bree debacle, and I'm heading to the Mugar Memorial Library to do some music research for my next big event set for mid-November. I'm doing a themed holiday party in two weeks at a mansion in Rhode Island not far from Taylor Swift's Harkness House estate. Yeah, super-fancy digs. Like I said, I found my calling.

I have an appointment at the library, if you can believe that, to learn more about music from the 1920s. I'm guessing they don't have enough staff, and visitors are required to schedule an appointment with a "guide."

While there's a ton of information on YouTube about the 1920s, and all of it is great, I don't know a lot about jazz, blues, swing, and ragtime. I have to get a bit more academic in upping my expertise. The party's theme is the 20s – the 1920s and the 2020s. I hired a specialist DJ, and he and I are going to go over the song list next week.

I've had to be really creative with this party – blending the musical styles with the decorations is forcing me to buckle down this weekend and dig in. I'm on target with my time line, and I have to be. I can't leave anything to chance. Especially not with the crowd that'll be at the party. If this event doesn't have wings, my business will suffer big time.

Friday afternoons in most campus libraries are quiet. Even the super studiers seem to take a break for a few hours. I don't think they go out and tear it up, but maybe they're doing pizza, beer, and Netflix with friends. I haven't done anything like that for years. It's not that I wouldn't love to, but I don't have the time, and I don't have anyone I really like to hang with except Sofia, who's a wife, mom, and full-time college student.

School is a time-suck when all I want to do is work, but it's not in my DNA to just slide by. So I go to classes – well, most of the time – and I study. When I take a night off, I'm either catching up on sleep, or I'm hanging at Sofia and Matt's place. Sometimes I babysit Alex, who, when not being a baby boy terrorist, has his father's demeanor – calm and sweet. He looks like his dad too. Long, lean, with olive skin and dark hair. The only thing he has of his mom's are his bright blue eyes. They really pop with his dark Mediterranean looks. Like all the men in Sofia's family, and probably Matt's, Alex is going to slay.

Don't tell anyone, but I like hanging with the kid. At nearly two and a half years old, he sees the world with wonder, and I don't remember experiencing anything like that. Everything for him is a new adventure, and even the small stuff is a joy. Right now, he's all about finger-painting. There's an old bedsheet on the floor of his room, and he has a painting shirt, but after one of his "sessions" he's wearing a rainbow of colors, and the walls have as much paint on them as the giant finger-paint pad clipped to his little-boy easel.

After painting, he always winds up in the bath where he giggles his head off at the colors swirling in the tub.

For real, I can't get enough of him.

Alex is a reflection of the love showered on him, and he's loved with a giant capital L. He has fantastic, involved parents. Grandparents who fall over each other to be with him, and a great-grandmother who would take bites out of him if she could. Every time *Nonna* sees Alex, she says, "I could eat you right up."

My parental units are poster children for people who should be neutered at birth. They have all the warmth and understanding of a glacier. If it wasn't for my grams, Sofia, and her family, I wouldn't know how it feels to be loved. I'd be like those kids in Russian orphanages who were never held and have Reactive Attachment Disorder.

Okay, yeah, maybe a bit over the top, but trust me, it's not far from the truth.

I climb the steps to the second floor of the library and meet my research guide, who's something of a hottie, but he's working hard at hiding it. Listen, I know a lot of students work at the library and other places on campus because it helps defray costs.

After I graduated high school, I fled my parents' house and have never looked back. Grams insisted on paying my way at BU, so I don't have money issues, but I understand the need to cut your own path.

With this guy, I'm not talking about him hiding behind his baggy clothes and ratty sneakers as much as how his hair needs to be washed, and if he wants to wear it that long, he should learn how to do a man-bun. All that hair falling in his face as he's walking and talking, it's like he's screaming, "Stay back. I'm hideous." I don't know. Maybe that's his shtick. How he attracts people into his orbit and gets them to take care of him.

Not my deal. The good news, he knows his stuff, and within fifteen minutes I'm set up and ready to hit it.

Research is where my nerdy inclinations lie. I love digging into a subject until I'm rolling around in it, absorbing the information into my skin. Three hours later – yep, I got totally lost in the 1920s – by the time I'm done, I'm totally working things over in my brain as I'm making my way to the staircase. I'm walking with my head down while humming the 1926 version of "Baby Face" when SMACK. I slam into the side of some tall guy at the top of the staircase.

I wobble, and he grabs my upper arm, saving me from tumbling down the flight of stairs. "Holy shit. I'm such a klutz," comes out of my mouth at the same time he says, clearly shaken, "Are you all right?"

At the sound of his voice, my head snaps up and I'm staring at Jonas Vandenberg, his really soulful moss green eyes wide and a little terrified. "Amy?"

"Hey, Jonas. Sorry about that. I wasn't watching where I was going."

He hasn't let go of me, and before I know what he's doing, he's steering me away from the staircase and around the corner into a quiet nook. "I'm so sorry," he says, staring at me like I'm an apparition.

"It wasn't your fault."

"No, not that," he tilts his head toward the stairs, "what happened with–"

"The bitch from hell."

He dips his chin and chuckles. "Yeah. Her." I'm getting ready to let him off the hook but he keeps going. "I ran after you, but by the time I got downstairs, you'd disappeared. Then all these people swarmed around me, showing me–"

"Her social media skills." That got me a smile. And I can't lie – I'm charmed.

"Yeah." He nods. "That's one way to put it."

In the lull between one sentence and another I look at where his hand is, realizing he's still holding on to my arm. I'm not complaining, and I'm not shaking him off.

I don't know which Jonas I have right now, the sweet nerd or the fuck-boy. Either way, he saved me from a serious fall. I feel him staring at me while I'm staring at his hand and when I look up, his gaze latches on to mine as he asks, "You want to get something to eat?"

A bit of a non-seq, but I'm rolling with it. "Sure." As if on cue, my stomach rumbles, and he grins.

"When was the last time you ate?"

"Ah…" Now that I'm thinking about it, not since my mid-morning breakfast.

"I'm taking that as too long ago. C'mon." He gives my arm a gentle tug, but he doesn't let go. "There must be somewhere decent to eat around here."

"Oh, tons of places. My friends, Sofia and Matt, you remember them, don't you? From the wedding?" He shakes his head. "The baby I was holding is their son, Alex."

"Okay. Yeah. I remember the kid."

Hard to've missed him. "They live a couple of miles away from here, and we've tried a lot of places in this area. You like Mexican food?"

His eyes light up. "Totally."

California. I remember his mom lives somewhere in California. "Duuude," I say, and he laughs, "let's go to *El Pelón Taqueria.* Prepare to fall in love."

For a moment, his face softens and he gets this dreamy look in his eyes, then bam, it disappears and he grins. "Dazzle me."

***

As always, the place is packed. It's tiny inside. Maybe there's seating for twelve people. Outside, there are four picnic tables, and even though it's mid-November, there isn't room to squeeze in anywhere.

"You vegan or vegetarian?" I ask him. He shakes his head. "You trust me?" He nods.

"Okay. You keep watch out here and if anyone gets up, you swoop in and save me a seat. I'll go inside and place our order." He gives me a thumbs-up, and I smile.

Only now, since he'd taken my arm to prevent me from falling down the stairs, he releases me. For a moment I still feel the warmth of his hand, and I shiver from the chill of its absence. Huh. That's never happened before. Not that I date all that much, but when I do, I'm clear from the outset: I'm there to have a good time, and there probably won't be a repeat of the evening. Sex is optional at my discretion, and frankly, most of the guys I've dated didn't interest me enough to take off my clothes. The ones who did weren't worth a second time around.

Between my classes and my business, I don't have a lot of time for socializing.

Actually, I've always had a small social circle. As in Sofia and her family, my grams and her friends, and the occasional girl in high school who joined me and Sofia at the movies or to go shopping. Most of those chickadees were trying to get into Sofia's good graces and they figured the best way was through me. Little did they know, Soph might appear tiny and shy, but of the two of us, she's the ferocious one. I'm not so much a coward as an avoider. If I think it's going to be a hassle, I don't bother, except when it comes to the people I love. Then, I'm all in. Soph always goes full bore, heading into the storm without a raincoat. She doesn't see obstacles: she takes on problems to be solved.

I don't want to solve problems outside my required math and science courses. I've had my fair share of issues dealing with my mother, who's used me as an emotional punching bag for pretty much all my life. She battered me because she couldn't rant at my father. Gone more than he was around, she lit into me to off-load her never-ending misery. When he was home, all they did was fight, and they didn't try to hide it, so I heard their dirty secrets.

Really. Kids are *not* supposed to know that shit about their parents.

The bottom line, the only reason they stay together is because it'd cost them too much money to split up. Division of assets is not a phrase either of them wants to hear or deal with. My father loves his money way more than people and he'd never let anyone disrupt his lifestyle.

They're married, but they're as apart as two people can be.

Me, I avoided being in that house as much as I could. Absolute truth, I spent so much time at the Di Caros' home, *Nonna* suggested I move in. I considered it but didn't relish the battle it would've caused between me and my mother.

She doesn't love me and never has, but she wouldn't have wanted to part with her possession, which is what I am to her.

I haven't been back to that house in years. Intentionally, I never see her or talk to her. She made attempts my freshman year, but after I ghosted her continuously, she gave up.

Best gift she ever gave me.

Finally, I'm at the counter and I order: salsa, chips, and guac, two *caramelos* tacos, a *calabacitas* burrito, a *pollo* burrito, and two *tamarindo Jarritos*. I pay, and then run out to see if Jonas was able to get us seats.

Yay. He scored. I go back inside, wait for our order, then make two trips to bring out the food.

"Hey," he says when I sit. "I could've gotten the stuff while you waited." I wave my hand at him. I'm totally into equality in all aspects. "You shouldn't've paid. I asked you out."

"Let's see how the night goes. If it looks like we'll do this again, you can pick up the next check."

"And the one after that."

"Confident, aren't you?"

He shakes his head. "Hopeful," he says. Seemingly engrossed in unwrapping his burrito, he doesn't look up, when he tells me, "When I returned to campus the September after the wedding, I looked for you everywhere. I didn't know your last name, and we never had another class together or lived in the same dorm."

Huh. At the wedding, I thought we'd made a connection, but I had no idea he was into me. Makes me wonder if he was always a fuck-boy, or if he changed when he started modeling.

He raises his head and seems a bit awkward when he says, "I was so happy to see you at the party and then–"

"The bitch from hell raised her pitchfork and took aim," I mumble around a fully loaded chip I'm chewing.

He laughs. "Right. She ruined us hanging out. The only good thing she gave me was your last name."

I wipe my mouth and ask, "How'd that come about?"

"I don't remember her exact words, but when she was cursing you out, she used your full name."

"Always good to be thorough and accurate when shitting all over a complete stranger." I load up another chip. "I don't remember ever meeting her anywhere. I wonder how she knows me."

"I'm guessing the private parties you put together. You're kinda famous for them." Well, that was nice to hear. "Her mission at BU is to land a rich guy. The education and diploma mean nothing. All her energy is spent on getting a rock on her finger."

"Well, after her social media *faux pas*, I'm thinking she's going to have to transfer to a different school or start studying."

He grins, and then bites into his burrito. "Damn." He chews and swallows. "This is really good."

I smile. "I love saying 'I told you so.'"

Chapter Six

Better Than I Imagined

Jonas

I'm sitting outside eating great Mexican food in near freezing weather, and I've never had a better time with a girl. I don't know if I'm supposed to say Amy is a woman, though we're both around twenty-one, so I guess she is – but we're not exactly worldly. As tough as Amy tries to come off, she's really sweet, which makes her seem younger. I've modeled with lots of women around our age and almost to a person they're fucked-up, neurotic, and, for the most part, cold as frozen fish.

Not Amy. She burns like a banked fire. I'm warm, but I won't get burned.

Throughout dinner, I keep stealing glances while she eats and talks. I'm thrilled she doesn't nibble like an anemic rabbit pretending she's not hungry. It's not only the models who do this, though they're the worst, a lot of girls on campus don't eat anything but salads, and they act like they're full after four bites. Not Amy. She's loading up chips after she demolished her burrito and taco. Her cheeks are a little flushed from eating, and she's telling me a story about her grams, and she's expressive and funny. Her golden-brown eyes flash when she's making a point, and her hands are always in motion. Her shiny auburn hair is sticking out from beneath her hot pink watch cap. I think it's called a pussy-hat, and I'm pretty sure I shouldn't say that out loud.

"Anyway," she's summing up the story, "Grams left me sitting outside in the mud, splitting orchids to re-pot."

"Not a 'don't mess up my furniture' kind of grandma, huh?"

She shakes her head, grinning. "Grams is not a fan of people who are so precious about their things they put pretension over comfort. She always says, 'Dirt washes off.'" She balls up all the trash on the table and gets up. "I need to walk." She pats the front of her coat over her belly. "That was sooo good."

"Totally." I take the trash from her and walk over to the near-overflowing bin. The restaurant is still packed, and two people swoop into our seats before I turn around.

Amy moves to the sidewalk, and when I'm alongside her, I look down and ask, "Where do you live?"

"StuVi-One."

"No shit?" She shakes her head. "I'm in StuVi-Two. How have we never run into each other?"

"Ah, thousands of students, entryways around the corner from each other, different schedules. More to the point, how do you not know about *El Pelón Taqueria*? It's like a mile from here.*"*

"What's the point of having a kitchen in what's more or less an apartment if I'm not going to cook?"

She slaps his bicep, and he feels it through his jacket. "Shut. Up." He rubs his arm like she hurt him, and she rolls her eyes. "You can cook?"

"Yeah. What's the big?"

"Dude. How many college guys, not counting the ones in culinary schools, can cook?"

"Based on the smells in the hallways, I'm guessing lots of them."

She snickers. "I'm not talking about heating stuff up or nuking it. I mean cook, as in prepare a meal."

"I can. Collin's not bad at simple stuff, but I prepare meals. Plural."

"Well, as my grams would say, knock me over with a feather."

I wrap my hand around her arm and steer us in the direction of the Student Village. "It was a necessity. The year after my folks split up, my mom got her job in LA, and we moved to Santa Monica. I'd just started the ninth grade in a famous high school in a new city. No friends, no family, and Mom worked long hours. If I didn't learn how to take care of myself, I would've subsisted on fast food, and that shit's okay once in a while, but not every day."

"Self-taught. I'm impressed."

I chuckle. "You do know we had YouTube back then, right?"

She stops and I hold on to her arm. I've waited three years to find her, and I have no intention of letting her go. "Yo. Don't sell yourself short. Even if, if–"

"Julia Child?"

"Yeah, she'll do. Even if Julia Child was in the kitchen with you, some people can't even make a cup of tea."

"Luckily, I'm not one of them."

"I'm coming over for Sunday brunch. Dazzle me."

Forty-seven thousand thoughts stream through my brain. *Holy shit. We're going to see each other again. She's into me. She'd decided tonight went well and she wants more. I've gotta get Collin to leave by eleven a.m. I can't believe this is happening. This is a BFD.*

Amy's coming over for brunch.

Before I give myself the chance to talk myself out of it, I dip down and capture her mouth, kissing her like I've wanted to do since freshman year the first day I saw her walking out of our dorm.

She puts her hand on my chest and I lift my head. A little. "Hey, fuck-boy." Uh-oh. She's pissed. "I don't remember saying yes."

"Whoa. Sorry. If you didn't want to kiss me–"

"I didn't say that. Good kiss. One of the top three. But anything to do with my body, you gotta ask. Especially since your body's been who knows where with who knows who."

I don't know where to start. Top three or fuck-boy. I go with fuck-boy. "You have to know the whole fuck-boy thing is an act."

She stares at me, her golden-brown eyes flashing. "How am I supposed to know that?"

"Ah, when we met at the wedding, did you think I was a fuck-boy then?"

"Pffft" comes out from between her teeth. "That was before you became Mister Boxer Briefs."

I hold back laughing. I have a feeling she doesn't think anything about this is funny, not even a little. "It's a job that pays stupid money. Like in stupid ridiculous. I'd be an idiot not to've taken the work. Next stop in my academic life is a PhD program, and I don't expect or want my parents carrying the freight. The modeling made sure I'd have more than enough money to pay for school, and then some. I'll be set up, and can follow my dream. How many people our age can say that from the work they do?"

She shrugs. "Okay. I'll concede like ten."

"Exactly." I lower my head until our lips are almost touching. I can feel her breath puffing out against my lips. "The fuck-boy thing is a way to keep the wolves away. I say what they want to hear and ghost ninety percent of them."

She sucks in a breath and I feel it. "I'm not a monk, but I *am* particular. I wouldn't've fucked Bree or any of the other chicks like her ever. As in never. And," I move close enough so our lips *are* touching so when I talk, it's against her mouth, "did you miss the part earlier tonight when I said I've been looking for you for years?"

She shakes her head and our lips brush, and damn that feels sexy as sin. "Since the library, have I looked at anyone else or given you any indication my attention was anywhere but on you?" Again with the head shake. Damn. I've never been so hot for a girl in my life. "Unless you tell me 'no' right now, I'm going to kiss you until we both can't breathe."

She doesn't say a word, and I take her silence as assent. I touch the seam of her lips with my tongue and she opens for me. I want to plunder – take her and taste every inch of her. But I'd bet my left nut she still doesn't believe I'm not a fuck-boy. So I take it slow, easing my tongue into her warm, tangy mouth. The residue of hot sauce tingles on my tongue. As if I needed help to amp up my desire for her. Not.

I wind my arms around her waist and pull her against me. Too bad we're in bulky clothes. I want to feel all of her, especially the press of her luscious tits against my chest. I remember back to the wedding and how full and heavy they looked in her simple dress. Way more than a mouthful.

Before I do something stupid, I lift my head and she gulps in air. Yeah, I want to grin, but smug wouldn't go over real well right now. "What time are you coming over on Sunday?" I whisper against her plumped red lips.

Yeah, I did that, and I want to do more. So much more.

"Um…" she hesitates as if she's a bit dazed. Yep. Smug. "Is eleven too early?"

Fuck no. Come by at six in the morning and climb into bed with me and let's work up an appetite.

"No. Eleven's perfect."

Chapter Seven

Too Good to Be True

Amy

Since I'd opened my mouth and invited myself to brunch tomorrow with the university's most eligible bachelor – stupid ridiculous money-making too cute for his own good *dude* – I wake up early, make a cup of tea, grab a banana, and lock myself in my bedroom. Technically, not necessary. My roommate, Sarah Goodman, is living with her boyfriend a few floors down. He has a single because he lost his left leg in a car accident when he was fifteen. Categorized as disabled, Jaime Marroquín is so far from being impaired it'd take two days for me to list how wonderful he is in every way you can and can't imagine.

Sarah, who always knew she wanted to be a physical therapist, was volunteering at a rehab center when Jaime was admitted. Don't cue the Hollywood music. He fought her like the angry bear he was, and did everything he could to push her away. But Sarah saw through him and didn't give up. Now you can cue the Hollywood music. Jaime's love for Sarah is a physical thing. Anyone within fifty feet of them can feel how much she means to him. There isn't a person alive who doesn't want someone to love them like that. And when she cheers him on at his meets as he tries to qualify for the Paralympics, no one yells louder than Jaime's Sarah.

In other words, I have the apartment to myself. Which is so necessary. I have to pull the last bits of the 20s party together, and make sure I have the playlist ready to go over with the DJ next week.

This immerse myself in all things party is part of my process. I work better with no distractions, which is why I'm in my room with the door closed. My bedroom is between the living room and Sarah's bedroom. Her room shares a wall with a quad apartment, as does the outer living room wall, specifically one of the other quad's bathrooms. The walls aren't paper thin, but the apartment isn't soundproof. In my room with the door closed is the closest I can come to being noise insulated. I hate headphones, and I don't listen to music when I'm working. Silence, or as close as I can come to it, is what I need.

Also, working in thick socks, flannel pajama bottoms, and a hoodie – no bra or shelf tank – is the physical comfort I require. My hair is in a topknot, and I'm wearing my glasses. I prefer them to the contacts, but I've lost so many pairs over the years, the contacts make sense for when I'm out in the world.

My phone is on vibrate, and the only reason I have it near me at all is in case Gran or Sofia needs me.

Aside from bathroom breaks, I don't resurface until after two in the afternoon. My stomach's rumbling and I know I better eat something or else I won't be able to concentrate enough to work through to dinner, which I eat around nine.

As I cut up apples to make a modified Waldorf salad – I use nonfat yoghurt instead of mayo or whipped cream – I can't help thinking about last night. Jonas was too good to be true, and that worries me. I'm cynical, and with good reasons. I'm wary, but what young woman wouldn't be, especially one with a best friend whose ex nearly shot and killed her, never mind the stellar relationship examples my parents provided. It's not that I think Jonas is leading me on. I have nothing to give him he doesn't already have: money, fame, attention from every female on the planet, including open invitations to a wide range of sexual favors. No, I think he's trying to convince himself he's not the fuck-boy he's become.

After the amazing kiss followed by the ground-shaking kiss – the first wasn't in my top three, it was the best kiss I ever had until the next kiss, which had to rate the absolute best for over half the world's population. The effects of that kiss shot right into the heavens it was so amazing. After he'd turned my bones to dust, we walked back to StuVi-One – good thing he never let go of my arm or I would've dropped into a heap – where he kissed me good night way too briefly. I would've been self-conscious if he hadn't turned around like five times to check if I was still standing in front of the building's door. The last time, when he was almost out of sight, he made a shooing motion for me to get inside.

Of course, I spent hours in bed recapping every moment of the night. He was looser and more comfortable in his skin than he'd been when we talked at the wedding. I'm guessing standing around for hours while people take pictures of him in nothing but boxer briefs would alleviate awkwardness.

Here's the thing: I want to believe he's the sweet nerd I met years ago. I want to believe he intends to get a PhD and follow his dreams. I want to believe he's pretending to be a fuck-boy, but really is a regular college guy who doesn't have threesomes with a couple of Brees, then heads out for another conquest before the night is over.

I want to believe, but I don't know if I can.

My reticence has more to do with me than Jonas. Though seeing his photo on a 100-foot-tall billboard in Times Square would shake even the most confident woman in the world.

As I'm eating my Waldorf salad – yum – I'm thinking about what I should bring tomorrow. I don't know how old he is, but I'm guessing around my age. I'll be twenty-one in less than three months, but I don't have to worry about buying alcohol. I have bottles of premium booze in my fridge, including great champagne, all leftovers from parties gone by. Maybe I'll bring a bottle of champagne and some peach purée for Bellinis. Cranberry juice and Cointreau for a poinsettia champagne cocktail might be a bit much, though they're delish. I could bring mango purée and limes for mango Bellinis. Or maybe…

Before I go down a two-hour rabbit hole, I get up, wash out the salad bowl, and fill my water glass. I have to get back to work. This little lunch and Jonas interlude has to be shelved. Damn, I'd hate it if he thought of shelving me, even if it was for work or studying.

See. This is why I've avoided dating. All these feelings... It's only a short ride to becoming a crazy person.

Okay. Work.

Then after dinner I'm calling Sofia.

I need a reality check.

***

"I'm losing it," I blurt out the moment Sofia answers the phone.

"Like I'm so busy I have no time to breathe losing it, or I'm so involved with work I forget the outside world exists losing it?"

This is one of the many reasons I love Sofia. She gets me and she doesn't care when I ignore social niceties. "Neither. Though both are true."

"Clearly, I'm not caught up on something. What's going on?"

I take a sip of water and dive in. "Remember the guy I told you about at Theresa and Ethan's wedding?"

"Um...not really."

Ugh. Why would she. "Sweet nerd who goes to BU." Silence. "He was in my English Lit class freshman year." More silence. "His dad is friends with Ethan."

"Sort of."

She doesn't remember. "Look up Jonas Vandenberg." I wait for it.

"Oh my god. He's...he's... Oh my god. He's gorgeous. He's famous. That's him? For real? Oooo. He's the guy who was trolled–"

"Yeah. That's him."

"Ah, okay. What about him?"

"I haven't seen him since the wedding, but since he started modeling, everyone at BU has been talking, obs, and word is this dude is president of the fuck-boy club."

"I can see that." She laughs. "I mean, if he's half as good at sex as he looks, people would definitely be taking numbers waiting for their turn." Shit. She's killing me and she doesn't even know it. "And you know this: lots of people would do him just to say they did him since he's famous and all."

So not helping.

"That trolling thing? Happened because of me."

"No," she shouts.

"He was at the private party I threw last week and I saw him with the witch who trolled him. He was all, 'We going to bang later?' and she was hanging off him. I went upstairs to the office, and he came up about fifteen minutes later and told me he was hiding from her. We'd barely got to say 'hey' when Bree, the troll, barged in, threw a shit fit when she saw me, and you know me, I was *so* not going to hang around for her brand of idiot, and bailed. I find out, he came after me, but never found me. When he left, she went live with her asswitchery."

"Damn, Ames."

"Yeah. So yesterday, I'm all in my head when I'm leaving the library, and I bump into him and nearly fall down the stairs, but he catches me, and well…"

"Well?" she asks really loud, drawing out the word.

"On the spot, he asks me out to dinner."

"Oh my god," she says all breathy, which means she's planning my wedding in her head.

"We went to *El Pelón Taqueria*. Great food, but not romantic. On purpose."

"Why?"

"Hello. Fuck-boy."

Silence, but I swear, I can hear her smile. "You like him."

"Now we're back to I'm losing it. He was great to talk to. Told me he'd been looking for me for years–"

"No."

"Yeah. He didn't know my last name."

"Wow." I'm getting the breathy thing again.

"And catch this. He lives in the dorm apartments next to mine."

"Wow." Shit. She's picking out floral arrangements and thinking about color schemes. "So what happened?"

At this point, I almost hesitate to tell her the rest. "He, um…kissed me."

"Please tell me it was all tongue and wet and bone melting."

"Well, I invited myself to brunch tomorrow morning."

"Yay," she screams.

"He cooks. Like for real. But I don't know, Soph. You of all people get I have major trust issues, and even though he told me the whole fuck-boy thing is an act—"

"He told you that?"

"Yeah."

"Wow."

"Shit, Soph. You've lost your objectivity. How are you going to give me advice I can rely on when you've become a puddle?"

She laughs and I can hear her slapping her leg. Though when she speaks, I get her mom voice. "Go to brunch. Have a good time. Kiss him a few times, but don't let it get anywhere past that. If he's as into you as he seems to be saying, he'll wait 'til you're sure of him. If he pushes too hard, or ghosts you after because you didn't fuck him, you have your answer. No great loss."

Okay. This is the kind of stuff I'd called her for.

"It's super early days, Ames. Everything feels like it's uber magnified and you're bound to question every move. Go slow. You set the pace. Sure, he's *really* gorgeous, and famous, but you're the prize. Aside from being pretty and having killer curves, you're an amazing person, the best friend anyone could have, and you're like candy that's hard on the outside but soft on the inside. Sweet, through and through."

Yeah. I love Sofia.

Chapter Eight

Impressed

Jonas

I got up at six, straightened up the apartment, and then walked over to Star Market to do a big shop. Even though it's only about a half mile from my place, I got a Lyft to take me home – too many bags to carry. I didn't want anything falling out or breaking. Yeah, I'm going for knock-out impressive. I mean, hey, it's Amy. I'm making *crème brûlée* Japanese *soufflé* pancakes with raspberry/blueberry *compôte* on the side. I don't have pastry rings, so I'm using BPA-free topless/bottomless cans so the pancakes are super tall. I'm also making tornado potatoes. Savory to balance out the sweet.

When I told Amy I can cook, I didn't tell her what started as a survival skill turned into an obsessive hobby. If the whole AI career doesn't work out, Plan B is being a chef. I love creating things – AI and cooking are alike that way – and building a meal is similar to being an architect and contractor combined. I have to design the meal first, balancing out flavors and presentation – you eat with your eyes first – and then I execute my plan. Making the idea come together is a rush. Collin says living with me is like having a Michelin-star chef for a roommate. Total exaggeration, but it's good to know my food is appreciated.

Since there's so much sitting around and waiting during modeling shoots, one of the things I do to entertain myself is watch all kinds of cooking shows and YouTube vids. There are so many recipes online, if

I cooked three meals a day, every day, for the rest of my life, I'd never get to them all.

The first time I had Japanese *soufflé* pancakes was at a little place in Pasadena call Motto Tea Café. Their ingredients come from Japan. Mine don't, but I try to make them taste as close as I can to what theirs taste like 'cause they're amazing.

By the time I get back to the apartment, Collin's up and when he sees all the grocery bags – yes, I use cloth bags, my mother would kill me if I didn't – he cracks up.

"She's special, huh?"

I nod. "Stay to meet her. You'll see."

"'Kay. But I'll head out right away. Don't want to ruin your," he motions toward the kitchen, "thing."

I smile. This is our second year of rooming together, and I know he's a really good guy. I really hope we stay friends after graduation. He's doing an internship at the Museum of Fine Arts in Boston this summer, and he's waiting to hear if he got into Columbia University's art history PhD program. Though he never talks about his grades, I'm sure he'll graduate with a 4.0 and stellar recommendations.

He makes himself toast, which he smears with peanut butter, gets a cup of coffee, and goes back into his room. As soon as he clears out of the kitchen, I put away the food. I shop for both of us. Collin leaves a list and money, and we share everything.

Before I set up the ingredients I need to prep. I put the bouquet of flowers I bought in a vase that came with a floral arrangement Sheree had sent after she landed me a contract with a famous activewear company. I don't know anything about flowers, but these caught my eye. They look like big, fat, golden daisies, and they're cheerful. I thought Amy would like them. I want her to be happy she's here.

I select my favorite cooking playlist, put my phone in the speaker dock, roll up my sleeves, pull out the pots and pans, and get busy. The whole time I'm cooking I'm smiling. A week ago, if someone had told me Amy would be coming over for brunch, I wouldn't've believed them.

***

Amy

I'm on my fourth outfit and I hate it. The jeans aren't flattering, the top is too tight across my chest – DNA from both sides of the family gave me a D cup, which is not the joy you think it is. Guys notice, most leer, and buying shirts is not an easy thing. More to the point, I'm only twenty, and I already have indents in my shoulders from my industrial-strength bras. Those sweet, sexy, lacy things don't do the job. Unleashing the girls when I come home is an enormous relief. But it's the only place they swing free. Me and braless in public is so not happening.

I shuck off outfit number four and start from scratch, standing in front of my closet wearing only my bra and boy shorts. Love them. They provide great lift for my tush. Yep, I have a matched set of ampleness. We're not going to discuss my thighs, and I'm not going to apologize for eating. Every day I clock way over ten thousand steps, and with my hectic schedule, I burn plenty of fuel. I'm healthy, and I'm active. End of story.

With a heavy sigh, I scan my wardrobe choices and I decide on a vintage turquoise scoop-neck crushed velvet top. The saleswoman told me it was a minidress, but even if I was skinny as a toothpick, no way would I wear it as dress. Never mind bending over to pick up something, I couldn't sneeze in it without giving everyone a show. As a top with a wide black belt I let ride a little above my hips, it rocks.

I select my favorite pair of faded wide-leg jeans and sit on the edge of my bed to yank on my kickass cowboy boots. In front of the full-length mirror on the back of my door, I turn to one side then the other. Yeah, this is much better. I'm comfortable, the top isn't too tight, the jeans are soft and make a balanced silhouette. After I double wrap a turquoise and black paisley scarf around my neck, I look again to see

I've got the boho chic thing going on, and I'm liking it. Okay, a little mascara, a swipe of barely there lip gloss, and I'm good to go.

I put on my peacoat, stuff my phone in the inside pocket, grab the bag with the champagne and peach purée out of the fridge, and get going. One bottle is in a separate bag inside the bigger bag 'cause duh – clunking.

Shit. I'm cutting it close.

It's ten fifty-five.

***

Jonas

At 11:09 the knock at the door makes my already racing heart skip a beat. I didn't want to believe Amy stood me up, and I remind myself some women fuss about what clothes they wear. Amazingly, many of the female models I've worked with looked like slobs when they came in for a shoot. Only a few were naturally elegant.

I open the door, and before I can get a word out, Amy lays one hand on my chest and says quickly, "I'm sorry I'm late. I don't like being late. I go out of my way to be early for almost everything. I feel bad for not getting here on time." She lifts a big black cloth bag and says, "I hope this makes up for my being rude."

While I heard every word, my entire focus is on the warmth in my chest from her hand laying over my heart. I don't even try to be cool about it. I'm so into her, I don't think I'd know how to be cool at this point. I frame her lovely, animated face with my hands, bend down and wait a moment for her to stop me. Silence. Then I kiss her. Deep, wet, and hungry. I force myself to go slow, to map her mouth with my tongue as I inhale her sweet, soft scent. No perfume, only Amy. Whatever's in the bag is leaning against my leg as her other hand slips under my shirt and caresses my back.

Every fantasy I have has coalesced in my dick, and it wants to act out all the scenarios I've imagined over the years. If I don't stop now, we're going to wind up on the floor half in the apartment and half in the hallway. As I lift my head, she sighs and takes a moment before opening her eyes.

"You're really good at that."

"Hmm. I'm thinking we're really good at that."

She smiles. "Sweet talk so soon?" She hands me the bag and steps into the apartment as I close the door. She looks around, then glances over her shoulder at me. "Something smells amazing." I put the bag on the floor between my feet and put my hands on her shoulders, helping her out of her coat. "And I'm getting the gentleman treatment." She turns, exaggeratedly bats her eyelids, then asks, "This part of the usual brunch treatment?"

I'm getting a clue – she pushes me away when she's nervous. Now that she's here, I'm not nervous, I'm grounded. Something about her makes me feel…I don't know how to describe it other than *whole*. I dip my head to her ear and say, "Aside from my roommate, you're the only person who's been here for brunch."

She moves her head to look at me with wide eyes. I can hear the wheels turning in her brain, and it takes her a moment before I feel her shoulders relax. "Oh. Okay. That's…that's pretty cool."

Sharp and driven as she is, getting one over on Amy is probably outside her experience. I'm not trying to one-up her, but I know it's going to take a while for her to believe I'm for real, so surprising her in good ways is a start. I'm sure she thinks I'm not the same guy she met at the wedding. If she did, she wouldn't be putting up her guard. I can't fuckin' wait 'til my modeling contract terms out.

I pick up the bag and carry it to the counter and look inside. "Whoa." I pull out the champagne and hold it up. "The good stuff."

She nods. "Yeah. I have all kinds of booze at my place left over from events. You'd be surprised how many people leave a venue and don't ask to have the overage shipped to them."

"Money to burn?"

"Nah. The richer they are, the tighter they are. They spend the money 'cause they want to put on a good show so they're not outdone.

But trust me, they scrutinize everything. They're always dickering with me to find ways to trim the bill." She shrugs. "I think they forget there's extra booze since they never go back into the kitchen or the storage areas." She lifts her nose with her forefinger and I chuckle. "Most likely, they're too tanked when they're leaving for it to cross their minds."

"A boon for you."

She smiles, and damn I love her smile. It's genuine, and it's sweet. "Yep." She walks over to the stove and leans against my side. I wonder if she knows her body's speaking for her when her expression and words are so cautious. "What's happening here?"

Before I have a chance to answer, Collin calls out, "Hey."

Amy and I turn and she stutter-steps. "Collin?" she whisper-shouts.

He tilts his head to the left and a wide smile breaks over his face. "Ames?"

"Holy shit." She runs to him, throws her arms around his waist, and says, "I can't believe you're...you're—"

"Jonas's roommate."

"Yeah." She breathes out the word. She turns, loops her arm through Collin's, and says to me, "Collin's grandparents were good friends with my grandparents." She turns her head to Collin. "I was sorry to hear about your grandpa."

He nods. "Yeah. I wasn't surprised though. Almost a year to the day after my grandma died. He was lost without her. They were together sixty-one years."

That's what I want, a long life with my wife. My grandparents have that, but not my parents. They didn't split up because they hated each other, or one of them found someone else. They decided to get a divorce since they didn't see the point in staying together when they were hardly together. Both of them are workaholics, and if they were married to anything, it's their jobs. Good people, loving parents, but they couldn't sustain their marriage.

I watch Amy nod then say, "I get it. My grams has hung on since Gramps died, but I worry how long she'll have it in her to go on."

Collin pats her shoulder and I can see she's uncomfortable thinking about losing her grandmother. She faces me again and changes the subject. "Did Collin tell you his grandfather was the famous portrait artist Julius Mackelbury?"

Typical of Collin, he never said anything about how famous and revered his grandfather was. He's the kind of guy who goes out of his way not to draw attention to himself. Kind of like me before I signed that damn modeling contract. I look at him and say, "Whoa. Good pedigree." He smiles sheepishly. "'Splains the whole art history thing." He dips his chin.

"I've gotta go," he mutters. "Got work to do."

"Aww." Amy draws out the word. "Can't you stay and have brunch with us?

Collin's eyes widen and his gaze latches onto mine. I'm pretty sure he wants to stay but is worried I'll think he's cockblocking me.

Sure, I want Amy all to myself, but I know he really has work to do, and he'll be gone in an hour.

As for Amy, I'll make sure she won't leave until tomorrow morning.

Chapter Nine

Inventive

Jonas

"Holy shit. What are these?" Amy holds up a forkful of pancake.

"*Crème brûlée* Japanese *soufflé* pancakes." I wiggle my brows. "You like?"

With a mouthful of pancake, she shakes her head, but her eyes are sparkling. It seems I'll never have to work to figure out what Amy's feeling. She's really expressive, except when her guard goes up. But then her verbal barbs let me know it's time to tread lightly and make her feel comfortable.

Since I default to shy, I appreciate not having to mine for her emotions, though I'd really like to find out what's made her so skittish. I don't think it's me. I think it's relationships. Since I plan to stick around, I'll find out what's up, but I'll go slow. Amy is not the type of person who responds well to being pushed, and as I've said, basically, I'm shy.

I wait until she swallows to hear, "I'm in love." And there goes my heart banging against my rib cage. I'd do almost anything for her say that about me. "I've never had anything like this before." She leans forward and bugs out her eyes to Collin. "Does he make these all the time?"

Collin chuckles. "I get incredible omelets and sometimes he makes waffles–"

"Wow. I adore waffles," she kind of shouts. Then she forks more pancake into her mouth.

"But," Collin continues, tilting his head at me, "he pulled out all the stops for you."

Her brows go up as I shrug. "No denials here. I wanted to make something special for you."

She takes a sip of her Bellini and then says, "You've succeeded." She moves her fork in a circle to encompass the food on the table. "Totally."

Her reaction to the potatoes is no less spectacular. She mmms and sighs and keeps shaking her head like she can't believe they taste so good. Yeah, I'm enjoying a good ego stroke, but most of all, I'm enjoying Amy.

Unlike most people, she doesn't waste time pretending. If she wants something, she gets it. If she likes something, you know it. When she's pissed off, she doesn't put up with shit. That night at the party when Bree went full-on bitch, Amy was definitely pissed off, and although I didn't want her to go, it was all kinds of classy she walked away. The whole stay and fight with a person who clearly feeds off drama made no sense, so Amy simply left.

Collin gets up and takes his plate to the sink, he rinses it and puts it, his fork, and his glass in the dishwasher. He didn't have a Bellini. I knew he'd blocked out a huge chunk of time to do some deep dive archival research, which requires a lot of concentration. He flat out told Amy he's a lightweight, and if he had a Bellini, he'd need a nap.

"I'm going to head out," he says, and I glance over at the microwave to see I was right. It's been a little more than an hour since Amy finally walked through my door. As she's finishing her pancakes, he goes into his room, and a couple of minutes later, I'm forking up some potatoes when he comes out wearing his jacket and shouldering his backpack. He bends down to brush a light kiss on Amy's cheek. "I'm so glad we got to spend time together."

She smiles up at him. "Me too. You have my number now. I expect daily texts."

"Count on it," he tells her. "Later," he says to me.

"Later," I call as he's walking out of the apartment.

"You know," she says, "it's pretty remarkable he's your roommate. I mean, we were friends since we were little kids. I never intended to lose touch with him, but he stopped visiting his grandparents, and we haven't seen each other since we were like eleven or twelve. Do you know why he stopped spending the summers with them?"

"Not really. I know his parents split up and he and his sister moved to Denver with his mother."

"Huh. I don't really remember his folks. Maybe I saw them when they dropped him off and picked him up. I don't know his sister at all. She didn't stay for the summers. I'm guessing they thought she was too young. I sorta remember her being in a car seat when they dropped him off."

"I think she's six years younger. She's a junior in high school."

She nods. "Sounds about right." She tops off my Bellini and pours herself another. "What about you? You have any sibs?"

"Nope. You?"

"No. It's bad enough I've had to suffer my parents. It would be horrible if there were more people involved in that shit show." Few words, but a big info dump. Seems her parents caused her a lot of pain. I don't like that for her, and now I have a place to start to find out the root of her having those thick shields.

"That bad?"

"Worse." She shudders. "So, tell me about being a famous model." Okay. She doesn't want to talk about it, and I'll give her that. I mimic her shudder, and she laughs. "That bad?"

"Worse."

Her eyes widen. "For real?"

"I'm not going to lie and say the money isn't great, but that's where the fun ends. I'm not cut out for that life, and I never sought it. I fell into it on a fluke. If I'd known what I was signing up for, I wouldn't've done it."

"How much longer you going to do it?"

"'Til my contract is up on August fifteenth next year."

"Then what?"

"If I'm lucky, I'll get into one of the robotics PhD programs I'm applying to."

"Ha." She graces me with her fantastic smile. "I knew you were a nerd at heart when we talked at the wedding."

Confirming what I'd believed for all these years feels great: she got me when we met. "Totally am. To my core."

"Well, that explains the square peg in the round hole problem."

Yeah. Absolutely gets me. "Exactly." I get up. "Wait right there." I go to my room and pull down two of my mini robots from a shelf. I'm holding one in each hand behind my back as I approach the kitchen table. "Close your eyes."

She takes a sip of her Bellini, puts down the glass, and complies. "Big trust going on here, Vandenberg."

I lean down and whisper in her ear, "Hundred percent, Stern. I'd never do anything to hurt you." I pull back and see her open one eye to give me a sidelong glance. "No cheating." She scrunches her nose, which is totally adorable, then closes her eye. I put down the robots and move the plates to the end of the table. Then I place one robot – that looks like a thin beer can wrapped in a dark blue coozie sleeve – in front of her, and I put the other bot on my chair. "Okay. Open your eyes."

She looks up at me, I smile and dip my chin at the table. When she sees the robot, she gasps out an "Oh." She leans forward and tilts her head as she examines it. "What's this?" I'm learning this is a favorite question of hers.

"Wrap one hand around the center of the robot. Keep your hand on the blue material."

As I'm finding is typical, she looks skeptical for a few moments before she lifts her left hand and wraps it around the robot. When it doesn't do anything immediately, she glares at me and I chuckle. A couple of seconds later it says, "Female. Twenty to twenty-five. Heart rate eighty-two. Hand slightly sweaty."

She pulls her hand off the robot and snaps, "Hey. My hand isn't sweaty."

I take her hand in mine and tell her, "Your hand feels perfect."

"Again with the sweet talk," she huffs, but she doesn't pull her hand away. "Is that all it does?"

"No. It also measures oxygen saturation like a pulse oximeter."

"It got all that from me wrapping my hand around it for like ten seconds?"

"Six to be exact, but yes. Its sensors are a cross between a version of paper skin and thermoplastic resin."

"You know I have no idea what either of those things are, show-off."

I don't let go of her hand as I lean over to grab the other robot. "This one," I say as I move the first bot out of the way, "is not me showing off." I put down an elliptical disc that looks like an old cloudy mirror balancing on a two-centimeter wedged platform. I pull a chair next to hers, sit, then say, "This one is me showing off."

I touch the base and within two seconds the robot says, "She's pretty, Jonas. I didn't know you like redheads." Amy leans back and stares at me. "Uh-oh, Jonas. She's getting angry. You better kiss her." I lean in and touch my lips to hers then pull back. She blinks rapidly and the robot says, "That's better. She seems to like the way you kiss."

"No fuckin' way." She squeezes my hand and opens her mouth, but before she can say another word, the robot speaks.

"That was fast. She's brought up fucking already."

She slaps me on the chest, and I can't help but laugh as I touch the base to turn off the robot. "You programmed it to say all that," she states in an accusatory tone.

"Yes and no."

Her lips thin and her eyes narrow. See she's defensive about something most people would laugh at. Someone really hurt her, and that pisses me off. I haven't hit anyone since the third grade, but right now I'd like to beat the shit out of whoever hurt Amy this badly.

"Hold up. Lemme explain."

She pulls her hand out of mine and crosses her arms over her chest. I know I shouldn't be thinking this right now, but Amy's got great tits.

From what I'd seen of her freshman year, and, of course, most recently, she doesn't wear tight clothes, and she's doesn't bare cleavage. But with the rack she has, it's obvious she has fantasy tits. The kind a guy could spend a lot of time on doing all sorts of things.

"I'm waiting," she snaps as her forefinger is tapping on her upper arm.

I hold back my smile and my chuckle. She's trying so hard to look pissed off, and all I can see is how sweet she is, and how vulnerable. Yeah, whoever did that to her deserves a beatdown.

"At its most basic level, AI is about providing an abundance of information and programming for the robot to select the correct response to stimuli. The 'thinking' part comes when the robot starts to understand there might be alternative 'correct' responses and it selects them. In a controlled environment, we can 'teach' it what responses are best, including humorous responses." She uncrosses her arms and leans forward, staring at the ellipse. "It doesn't know it's being funny, but it can register people's responses to what it elected to say. Repetition is key. If it gets the same or closely similar responses when it answers a certain way, it 'learns' how to use its programmed information and that's what makes it seem 'human.'"

"Oh." She blinks a few times and stops looking at the ellipse. "That's pretty cool."

"Totally cool."

"How much information is stored in something this small?"

"More than you think." I'm not going to explain silicon, the guts of computers, how it all works, and how much info is stored on a chip that's between thirty-two and forty-five nanometers wide. I don't want her to fall asleep while I nerd out. "Microprocessors contain massive amounts of information. Look at how much your phone can do."

She nods. "So what's the end game? For you I mean?"

"AI has all kinds of applications from smart fridges that can tell you when your tomatoes are about to go bad to spotting disease in MRIs and CT scans, or for diagnosing cancer from photos of skin lesions. My interest is in medical applications at a higher level like detecting cancer way before it starts harming the body. Super-early detection could lead to early eradication through early, less harmful treatments."

She maps my face with her intense gaze. "Hero stuff."

I smile. "If you want to think of it that way, sure."

"I thought you wanted to build a Data."

It's beyond cool she remembers our conversation from the wedding. "I do. But what we think of as a Data is a farther dream than some of the medical applications that are within reach. Anyway, what I think I want and what'll happen is fluid. The field changes almost every day with new discoveries. I have no way of knowing for certain, but I am certain about what I want to do with what I learn."

Slowly her lips turn up into one of her wonderful smiles. I could get lost in Amy's smile. "Good to know you're not just a pretty face."

I slide my hand down her arm and lace my fingers through hers, joining our hands on the table. "C'mon. Tell the truth. You've never thought I'm shallow."

She tilts her head to look at me and her expression softens. "No, Jonas. I never thought you were shallow. Which is why I can't figure out the fuck-boy thing."

Shit. We're back here again. One step forward, two steps back. I'm paying for the hurt someone else gave her. Damaged her. I really hate that motherfucker. I take a mental sigh, knowing I'm going to have to break it down for her.

"When I was a freshman, except for my roommate and my family, no one at BU knew I was alive. I went out, dated some girls, got lucky a couple of times," her eyes flashed, "but mostly I focused on school. And believe me when I say this 'cause I'm dead serious, I was fine with it. Preferred it."

"I believe you. But shit changed big time, and you changed with it."

I tighten my fingers and feel hers flex with mine. Again, her body is telling me something way different than her mouth. If I didn't think it would ruin what I'm trying to build with her, I'd take her to bed and let our bodies do the talking for both of us. It might prove me right, but I sure as shit know I'd lose her after we were done.

"I didn't, Ames. Swear it. What changed was how people saw me. I understand the phrase 'being treated like a piece of meat' all too well. When I pretend to be an asshole, it's like I'm slipping into someone else's skin. Same as when I'm modeling. I pose for the world, say what people want to hear, and I act like I don't give a shit. Which I don't. But not the way they think."

"Ha," she barks out. "How do I know you're not slipping into a different skin with me?"

I'm a patient guy. I don't stress over much, and I'm deliberate, which is why I'm suited to the kind of work I want to do. But in this moment, I'm about to lose my shit.

I lean into her, my face so close to hers I can see the individual gold spikes in her pretty brown eyes. "You don't," I ground out. "The same way I don't know what's going on in your head. The difference is, I'm taking you as you are. If I find out I'm wrong, it'll be disappointing, like major disappointing, but I can't change you being duplicitous if that's what you're doing."

Her eyes flash and she tries to pull her hand out from under mine. I don't let her.

"Doesn't feel nice, does it, when someone underestimates you, or thinks the worst of you?" For a long moment it looks like she's going to fight me, and I don't want to fight with Amy. I never want to fight with Amy. But I'll fight for her.

Her expression softens and I can feel the breath she's been holding leave her mouth and brush my cheek. "No, it doesn't." She looks down at our clasped hands. "I'm not good at this," she whispers as if she's admitting to killing someone.

"Can't speak for the rest of the world, but I'm not good at this either." Her gaze hits mine and she looks surprised. "But...I know what I want, and I want you. I wanted you when I saw you walking in and out of our dorm freshman year. It was worse when we were in a class together and you were unattainable, but I still wanted you.

"When I realized I didn't know your last name and couldn't find you on campus sophomore year, I didn't stop wanting you. But as time went by, you became more a dream than a reality." I shook our hands and leaned a little closer. Her lips were a hair's breadth away, and I wanted to kiss her until she couldn't think of anything else but me. "You're here and the reality is better than the dream. Do you really think after all this time of wanting you, I'd do anything to fuck this up?"

She closes her eyes and whispers, "I hope not."

"Believe, Ames."

I move and my lips touch hers. She throws her arm around my shoulders, opens her mouth, and the tip of her tongue touches the seam of my lips. The next thing I know, she's on her back on the sofa, her legs are locked around my hips, and our mouths are fused together in a kiss like nothing I've ever experienced.

Straight up mouth sex, and it's unfuckingbelievable.

Chapter Ten
Caution to the Wind

Amy

I've never been kissed like this in my life. No lie, his tongue is fucking my mouth, and I'm about to come. His arms are around my back, our crotches are touching, but he's not humping me, and his hands are in my hair, his fingers sifting through the strands.

I moan into his mouth, and I'm close. I'm absolutely going to come from a kiss.

He's relentless. The moan seems to have given him an extra gear, and he's mapping my mouth with his talented tongue then he starts thrusting again harder and faster than before.

That does it. My back arches, my legs tighten around him, and I grind my crotch into his. My head shoots back and I'm chanting, "Jonas, Jonas, Jonas" as every muscle in my body contracts from the force of my orgasm.

He frames my face with his large hands and begins kissing me again, deep, wet, and sweet. I'm coming down slowly, but I'm wired. I've never wanted someone inside me as much as I want to feel Jonas filling me.

He lifts his head a fraction of an inch away from mine and kisses my eyelids, my cheeks, and the tip of my nose. Then he rubs his cheek against mine and says, "Damn, Ames. You make me feel like Superman."

I smile and shove my face into his neck. He smells good. Sweaty and musky, and a bit like pancakes. A part of me wants to say something snarky about the Superman comment, but if I'm to believe him – and it seems like he laid himself bare when he told me in detail how he wanted me – snarky is not the way to go here. I don't want to crap all over his feelings, especially if they're genuine.

I know, I know. I should believe him. Take him at his word. But leaps of faith are not my thing. I'm the girl who burst my best friend's bubble like every day when she fell in love with her husband. Basically, I told her it wasn't going to work, and she should expect him to cheat on her since they lived so far apart. Then I kept at her with the honesty, but, to her credit, she didn't listen to a word I said. Or she listened but didn't pay me any mind. Good thing too. They're the most in love people I've ever known. And while it works for them, I can't see myself in that scenario.

I'm self-aware. I know I have major trust issues because my father is a shit husband, a worse dad, and my mother is a shrew. She might've started out okay, but I wouldn't know since my father has been an asshole for as long as I can remember. Which means she's been miserable for a long fuckin' time.

Yes, intellectually I know some people have happy marriages, and many people are content with their lives if not overtly happy, but I grew up in the middle of an unrelenting shitstorm of anger, resentment, and disappointment. It's hard to scrub that off when, having lived it for so long, it's seeped into my pores.

My grandparents had a super-happy marriage. They lived a good life together and they were in love. I saw kindness and caring in their home, and I know it was real. My grams would kick my tush to next Thursday if I didn't give Jonas a chance. She wants me to be happy, and she's gone out of her way to make sure I know what being loved feels like.

I might be making an irreversible mistake. The kind that'll stick in my soul and make me more bitter and distrusting than I am now. But Jonas is holding me tight and giving me my headspace. If he's half as good as he seems to be, I'll be one lucky ducky.

Here goes nothing.

I lift my head, lay my hand against his jaw, and say, "And you make me feel special." The smile he gives me is so bright and wide it's a beautiful thing to see. Okay. I've made him happy. Maybe I *could* do this.

"You are special." He lowers his head and touches his lips to mine. I'm reaching critical mass here. I can't take all the sweet. I'm not used to it, and I don't know what to do with it. As if he senses where I'm at, he asks, "How about we clean up the kitchen and then go over to the Museum of Science? I've been wanting to see *Superpower Dogs* at the Omni Theater."

Not what I expected, but it sounds like fun. "Don't you need tickets?"

He wiggles his brows, stands, pulls me up, and then reaches into his back pocket, yanks out his phone, and shows me the tickets for the four p.m. show. "We'll have time to walk around the museum before the movie. They have a Pixar exhibit I want to see."

There's the nerd I met. He looks like an eight-year-old getting ready to go to his first baseball game at Fenway Park.

I nod. "Sure. Cool." He gives me his megawatt Times Square billboard smile.

In other words, he nearly knocks me off my feet.

***

I don't know what I enjoyed more, the exhibits and the movie or Jonas's reaction to the exhibits and the movie. Actually, I know I enjoyed Jonas more. Talk about a kid in a candy store, this guy is so unabashedly nerdy, I'm drawn to his enthusiasm. I'm driven, and I like what I do, but I'm results oriented. I'm not a smell-the-roses kind of person. Though after spending the day with Jonas, I'm reconsidering my brusque approach to life.

Look, I know I can't blame everything on how shitty my parents are. I've spent enough time with my grandparents, not to mention Sofia and her family, to have basked in the warmth of love and acceptance. It's a me thing. I'm working on it.

"You hungry?" he asks as we're walking into his apartment.

Brunch was amazing, and I ate my fill, but it's been seven hours since then and my stomach is making its wishes known. "I could eat."

"You like soba noodles?" Again, I'm getting the gentleman treatment. He's helping me take off my coat and he's hanging it on one of the hooks by the front door.

I nod. "You're going full-on Japanese today, huh?"

He smiles, and no lie, it's makes me feel swoony. "I like theme cooking." He smacks his hands together and rubs them against each other. "Sesame soba noodles with ginger shrimp," he announces. "We'll start with sweet and spicy glazed edamame and finish with pistachio ice cream, which is store-bought, but I'll add some honey-roasted pistachios I made myself."

If any other dude was doing all this, I'd think he was trying to impress me. With Jonas, I'm beginning to believe this is him. "Sounds delish. What can I do?"

"Hang out. Tell me Amy stories."

There's not much to tell, but I say, "Okay. But I want to call my grams first. I talk to her every day. She's alone, and she's starting to feel her age. I like to check in." That got me his wide smile. Not the mega-watt one, but one filled with approval.

"You want privacy, use my room. If not," he motions to the kitchen table, "sit. I'll eavesdrop openly."

I plop down in the chair facing the kitchen and pull out my phone.

"Hi, sweetie. What'd you do today?"

"Hey, Grams. You'll be proud of me. I took a day off and had fun."

"Oh wonderful." I hear the rustle of newspapers. Old school. My grams reads the paper version of the Sunday *New York Times* cover to cover. In my mind's eye, I can see all the sections of the newspaper spread out over the couch in what she calls "the front room," which is the den, not the family room. "Tell me all about it."

Which I do in detail, spending more than a few minutes on the Japanese pancakes. She's thrilled to hear I've connected with Collin, and gives me the story of why years ago he disappeared. "Messy marriage. The only place they were compatible was in bed. Otherwise, they fought ugly, and his mother would walk out and disappear for a couple of days. Even after the kids were born. Since Simon worked in the city, when Fiona stormed out, he had to call his mother to come stay with the kids. One of the reasons Collin stayed out here in the summer was to keep him away from all the drama at home."

She sighs. "Fiona had a friend who moved to Denver and she got Fiona a job in the office where she worked. Poof, she disappeared. Simon came home one day from work, saw all the kids' and Fiona's clothes were gone, and there was an envelope taped to the fridge with the divorce papers in it. Marriage over. He fought for partial custody, and got the kids for a couple of weeks here and there. Fiona remarried about a year after the divorce was final. Simon never did. To the best of my knowledge, he's never lived with another woman."

There it is. Another sucky marriage where the kids got fucked. "Shitty story."

"Indeed." She clears her throat. "So I'm guessing this guy who's making you sesame soba noodles is more than a friend."

I shake my head. "Fishing much?" She laughs. "Let's call it a test drive." Jonas chuckles, turns, and grins.

"He's right there?" Grams sounds surprised.

"Yep. You know me. I'm not fond of secrets and deception."

"This is true. But if I had to guess, you're testing him. Any reason in particular?" This is one of the many reasons I love my grams. She's smart, intuitive, and she knows me like the back of her hand. "He has a fuck-boy rep." Now he puts down the knife, turns, and as he leans against the kitchen counter, he crosses his arms over his chest. "But he swears it's all an act."

"Amy, that's not nice putting him on the spot like this. You're not a callous person, and you know better. He made you brunch. Took you out for what sounds like a fun day, and he's cooking you dinner. If he'd wanted nothing more than a quick tumble, he would've made his move after Collin left. Now I'll wait while you apologize."

Well, shit. Another reason I love my grams. She makes me a better person.

I put the phone on the table, walk over to Jonas, who's watching me with narrowed eyes, and I lean against his rigid muscles. "I'm sorry. I shouldn't've–"

"No." He tilts his head down and glares. "You shouldn't've. Go back, finish your call, and then we're having one more conversation about this. One more."

I nod, go back to the table, and pick up the phone. "I heard," Grams says. "I'm going to let you go. Tomorrow, you'll tell me the outcome."

"Okay, Grams."

"And Amy."

"Hmm?"

"Remember he's a person with feelings, just…like…you." She hangs up and I know she's quantum disappointed in me.

Shit.

He's still glaring and looks impatient. I've never seen him wear an expression so forbidding. I don't know if I should go to him or have this conversation while I remain standing next to the table. I have the feeling if I stay here our "chat" isn't going to go well.

Suck it up, buttercup. You bought this.

I walk over to him, but this time I don't lean, I wrap my fingers over his tight forearms.

"I'm not him," he states. I blink a few times, not sure who he means. He reads the blinking and clarifies. "Whoever in your past screwed you over so bad, you can't see what's standing right in front of you."

He's cutting too close to the bone, and I'm not prepared to have that conversation with him maybe ever, and certainly not now. "I know that," I whisper.

"Do you?" His expression says he doesn't believe me. "How much plainer do I have to be?" He dips his head closer to mine. "I told you I've been looking for you for years. I've wanted you for years. I'm not a fuck-boy. I act like one to keep the leeches away. You've seen what that looks like up close and personal."

He's talking about Bree, and he's right. I've seen how those girls are around him.

"It's one thing if we didn't get along and went our separate ways, but," he leans even closer – so close his warm breath fans over my cheeks, "we work, and you know it. You're scared, we'll go slow. You want out, leave right the fuck now." I jerk my head back as a slimy feeling chills me from my scalp to my toes. "You stay, you give us an honest chance to see where this goes. I'm not doing this alone, Ames. We're in it together, or we're not going there." He leans back against the counter, his jaw tight, and his beautiful eyes are glazed over with a steeliness I didn't think he had in him.

First reaction: Dread. The thought of losing him knocks me off my pins. I hadn't realized I wanted him, as in *really* wanted him, until he told me to get my ass gone if I didn't pull my shit together.

Next reaction: Fuck you. I don't need you. I'm doing fine on my own. I've got Grams, Soph, Matt, Alex, and all the Di Caros. I'm busy. I've got a great business with lots of happy clients. I'm a semester away from getting my degree, and then I can devote all my time to growing my business. Maybe in ten years, I'll contemplate whether I have time in my life for a dude who's more than a night in the sack.

Last reaction: I'm an idiot if I walk away from Jonas. A frightened idiot, to be sure. But somewhere deep inside I feel the stirrings of trust, and as scary as that is, I want to follow the feeling. I know if I fall for him and it doesn't work out, I'll be a walking train wreck, but that'll be me and the gazillions of other people over time who've lived through heartbreak and come out the other side.

"I can do that," I whisper so low I'm pretty sure he didn't hear me since he's still leaning back and glaring.

He jerks up his chin. "Do what?"

Oh hell. He wants me to spell it out. "Um, be in it, you know, together."

"You don't sound like you're real sure about that."

Now he's pissing me off, and me being me, I snap. "I'm not sure, okay? I mean I'm sure about giving it a try, but I'm not sure how it's going to go. I haven't a fuckin' clue whether you're going to break my heart or become the reason I'm always smiling. You know the answer to that? Huh? Do you?"

I can feel his chest shaking through my fingers – which are still wrapped over his forearms – as I watch the light return to his amazing eyes. "There she is."

He leans down and his lips are on mine when he says, "I don't *know* the answer, but I have a pretty good idea what it'll be. How 'bout we see if I'm right?"

Briefly, he presses his mouth against mine, then he lifts his head and says, "I'm going to finish making dinner, and you're going to tell me Amy stories."

***

Awkward doesn't come close to how I felt after the mini-drama. Knowing I couldn't stay in the same room with him until I felt less wobbly, I went to the bathroom. I'd been here in after brunch, and it's cleaner than mine. For two guys sharing a bathroom, that's saying something. After I splashed water on my face a few times and gave myself a serious talking-to, I headed back to the kitchen and started telling him Amy stories.

"No shit?" he asks.

"No shit," I tell him. I'd started my Amy stories with what I call "The Polar Bear Club Saga." When Sofia and I were about ten years old, we'd seen on the news how people in The Polar Bear Club go swimming in winter in freezing water. "We figured since the pool cover was retractable, we'd jump in and come right out and that'd make us members of The Polar Bear Club."

"And that's when–"

"When one of us must've hit the lever by accident and the cover closed over our heads."

"You're lucky you're alive."

"Not the way you think. The pool's heated even in the winter. There's about a six-inch gap between the cover and water even at the deep end. When you're in the shallow end, there are steps you can sit on and there's a big gap. We had no problem breathing and we weren't cold. But once we were discovered, *Nonna* almost killed us."

"Sofia's grandmother?"

"Yeah. She's tiny, but she's mighty."

He chuckles and turns back to cooking. "Bet that cooled your jets for a while."

"You'd think," I mutter.

Now he's really laughing. "I can't wait to hear this."

"Sofia caught her brother, Gio, who's about two and a half years older than her, sneaking out his bedroom window and decided we could do that – not that we had anywhere to go like Gio who was thirteen and was already running with his buds – but Soph figured if Gio could do it, we could too. Thing is logistics escaped us. Their bedrooms are two stories up, and there's a drainpipe outside Gio's bedroom window. He climbed down the pipe, no issues. There was no pipe outside Sofia's window, but there were shrubs that came to halfway up the first-floor windows. Being it was January, they were covered with snow, and Sofia decided the snow was soft and the shrubs would break our fall."

"Don't tell me."

"Yeah, we jumped. And as you know, two inches of snow on top of shrubs is not a soft cushion. Plus, those particular shrubs have seriously thick stems, which don't have a lot of give."

He turns and stares at me with wide eyes. "What happened?"

I roll up my left pant leg and wave him over. He turns off the flame under the wok, and when he's right in front of me, he crouches to see where I'm pointing. I show him the two round scars above either side of my knee. "A stem went through—" Before I can finish, he bends and kisses each scar.

Holy fuck. Tingles zip up my leg and start playing with my thighs before becoming a small inferno inside my core. Apparently, the skin above my knee is an erogenous zone. Or it is when Jonas presses his lips there.

He rests his big warm hand over my knee. "How many stitches?"

My mouth is dry and I have to swallow to make myself speak. "Ten on the right side, twelve on the left. I got off lucky. Soph broke her arm in three places."

He shook his head. "Please tell me that cured you of your adventures."

"It did that year."

"Wild child," he mutters before he kisses my knee, stoking the fire swirling around my body, then he unrolls my pant leg and pats my ankle before he stands.

Somewhere in my lust-fogged brain I remember he was surfing in a couple of his modeling ads. "I bet you have more dings than me from surfing."

"You'd be right," he says as he returns to preparing dinner.

Although he didn't leave any words hanging, it seems he left out a sentence. Like: "I'm a guy and I can take it."

He doesn't throw off the macho vibe at all, but I swear, as he stood I caught him scowling.

Chapter Eleven

Sleepover

Amy

It's official. Jonas is my private chef. Damn, the guy can cook. Relatively simple food tastes so good I would've sworn it'd been made in a famous restaurant if I hadn't seen Jonas prepare it himself.

We're sitting on the couch eating pistachio ice cream that tastes a whole lot more amazing with the addition of Jonas's honey-roasted pistachios. Over dinner he'd agreed to share a few Jonas stories. We're still on the first one.

"Let me get this straight. You've been surfing since you were a little dude and you've never broken any bones?"

"Nope." He grins before he puts a spoonful of ice cream in his mouth.

"Either you surfed in the kiddie pool, or you're a statistical anomaly."

"Had a kiddie board when I was little. Graduated to a full-size foam longboard when I was eight. They don't knock you about as much as real boards."

"How old were you when you got a real board?"

"Twelve. My dad gave it to me on my birthday."

"And then you started getting knocked about."

He nods. "Yeah. But the usual. Nothing major."

"No scars?" *Does it sound like I'm begging to see them?*

He grins, and it's knowing. "Didn't say that."

He's figured out I'm playing I showed you mine, now you show me yours, though I didn't intend to do that. But...I wouldn't mind mapping his body to see where he got dinged so I could kiss it and make it better. *Holy hell. I'm turning into a swoony girl. Blech.*

I've got to change the subject. Immediately. I'm dangerously close to saying and doing things it's way too early to say and do.

"Were you always into science stuff?"

His spoon is an inch from his mouth and it remains suspended in mid-air as he smiles huge.

Shit. He's on to me, big time. He knows I'm changing the subject for the exact reason I'm changing the subject.

He puts the spoon in his mouth and audibly sucks off the ice cream. Now that's damn cruel.

As he's swallowing, he shrugs. "I guess. I can't say I noticed an inclination since I went with my interests and my parents seemed to be cool with whatever I liked. I had a low-pressure environment when it came to school. They expected me to try hard and do my best, but I wasn't brow beaten into getting As. When I brought home great report cards, they were pleased, but they didn't make a big deal about it."

The contrast between our upbringings is more war and peace than night and day. I can't remember a day in my parents' house when I wasn't stressed. Pressure was a constant companion. A rude sibling without a name or a face who made each step a walk through a mine field of hostility. The worst part of it was my parents didn't expect anything from me except to choose a side. The consequences of despising them equally had me in emotional triage every day I was in that house with one or both of them.

I can tell Jonas notices I've taken a bad acid trip down memory lane when he asks, "Where'd you go?"

"Nowhere pleasant."

"I can see that."

"Listen. I'm not hiding anything from you, but if I start talking about my childhood, we're both going to be so depressed, we'll need to go for counseling. For now, let's leave it at, I'm jealous you had such a low-stress upbringing. I mean, it must've been awful when your parents divorced, but from everything you've said, it's clear they love you and you've always known it."

"I have. They're good people who were living different lives, and decided to act on it by following their careers. My mother never remarried. My father did to a really nice woman named Sharon who's a sergeant in the Boston PD. This time seems easier for him since they understand each other's lifestyles and job commitments." He shrugs. "After my folks divorced, I wasn't subjected to a parade of boyfriends or girlfriends, so I've always felt, aside from their dedication to their jobs, their focus has always been on me."

"What does your dad think of you modeling?"

He laughs, reminds me his father is in the FBI, and then sits back and tells me a few of his father's favorite comments about his son, the model.

Just like that, Jonas goes with the flow. He doesn't push for me to say any more about my fucked-up childhood, and I'm guessing he trusts me to tell him about my selfish, insane parents when I feel ready.

Yeah, I'd be an idiot to let Jonas go.

After we clean up, and Jonas has "seasoned" the wok, I talk him into watching *The Hunt for Red October*. I can't believe he's never seen it, and he can't believe I'm addicted to every movie and iteration of Jack Ryan

"I'm going to indoctrinate you, and then we can argue about who's the best Jack Ryan and why."

He chuckles. "You want to argue with me?"

"Not fight argue. Take positions on an issue argue."

"Who knew Jack Ryan was a thing," he mutters.

"You'll see." I pat his knee, and he grabs my hand and brings it to his lips. One by one, he kisses each fingertip before placing my hand on his thigh, and then he rests his hand over mine and without a word, he clicks play and the movie begins.

Okay. No one has ever done anything remotely like that before. My pulse is jumping at the same time I feel cherished. My first real WOW with a guy and it's something small and tender.

The living room is dark except for the glow from the TV screen and a small lamp on a table on the far side of the sofa. It's cozy, and yeah, it's romantic. But not intentionally. Jonas didn't set things up to draw me in. I talked him into watching a movie.

The apartment is small, so it's easy for things to feel intimate, but it's not that either. This is hard to describe, but it's like there's a mellow aura around him. I'm always churning inside. Busy with work, busy with school, busy keeping up with Grams, Sofia, and the Di Caros. I don't slow down unless I'm sleeping, and even then, I toss and turn. I know this not because guys have spent the night and told me, but because my covers are in disarray every morning and I'm never in the same general area I'd been in when I went to sleep.

Jonas is like a calming stone, and he settles me somehow.

I give in to the vibe and lean against his arm. He gives my hand a light squeeze, and that's it. No big move to bring me in closer or lay me out on the couch. I relax into how easy this is, and I think, *how cool*. We're hanging out, watching a movie, and except when I nearly fucked things up, there's been no pressure all day.

I've never had this, and I'm pretty sure I can get used to it.

***

As the movie ends, Jonas says, "Great movie, but talk about suspending disbelief."

"I like to think of it as a ray of hope. Like *The West Wing*. Everyone knows it's not real, but they binge it because they'd like to believe it's possible."

He's grinning like a maniac.

"What?"

"You're an optimist."

I lift one shoulder. "I never thought about it like that."

"Underneath all the badass, *I don't give a shit, get out of my way I'm busy*, beats a heart full of hope." I don't know if I should be angry or take it as a compliment, which is the way I think he means it. "I like it."

I lower my brows and narrow my eyes. "Are you baiting me?"

He cracks up and in a move so slick I didn't see it coming, I'm on my back and he's over me, his arms outstretched so we're not really touching. He's on his knees between my legs and I can feel the outside of his knees against my thighs, but his torso is about three inches above mine, and all I can see is Jonas. Smiling.

"Yeah. It's fun."

"I'm thinking not."

His smile gets wider. "You make it fun without even knowing it. Trying to be all hard when you're a marshmallow."

"Humph," I grunt.

He lowers his torso so it's almost touching mine. His face is so close all I have to do is raise my chin and my lips would be on his.

"Stay the night."

Whoa. I blink rapidly, and I'm rendered speechless, which never happens.

"Clothes on if you want. We can sleep on top of the covers. I want to wake up to you."

Well, shit. Now I'm ten seconds away from freaking out or giving in. I don't have the luxury of taking a few minutes to mull this over, which was surely his intention with the slick move. Fully clothed on top of the covers sleeping next to Jonas sounds safe, but I know better. I can get used to this. Like addictive used to it, and I'm not a fan of losing control in any way. But maybe this could work. Maybe we can take this real slow and I can find a way to feel safe with him.

He's staring at me with a soft expression. Jonas might really be the *he gets me* guy I didn't think was out there. He's not pushing for an answer, which is why I say, "Yeah."

He lowers his lips to mine and says against them, "Excellent."

***

I'm learning all sorts of things about Jonas. First is that bright smile is no accident. He has a dentist's supply of toothbrushes, dental implements, whitening toothpaste, and whitening gel.

He's leaning against the bathroom doorjamb watching me examine his toothbrush stash. "Please tell me there's a non-OCD reason for all this," I wave my hand at the drawer, "tooth stuff."

"There is." I nod, waiting for him to go on. "When I started modeling, they sent me to get my teeth bleached. My teeth and gums hurt for over two weeks after the procedure and I told them 'Never again.' But part of my contract requires I 'maintain' my appearance. The bleaching wears off after a year or two, unless you're extreme about upkeep. I've become extreme about upkeep to avoid another bleaching so I don't violate my agreement." He shrugs. "It's a small thing I won't have to do much longer."

"Were your teeth bad?"

"Nope. Normal teeth. But not," he gives me the sexy Times Square billboard smile then points at his mouth as he grits out, "this." I'm laughing and shaking my head at the same time. "I know. It's all bullshit. But, Ames, I've got bank I wouldn't've had. I can't complain even if it is a ridiculous way to make a living."

Did I mention how I love him calling me Ames?

"Even though I've ragged on you, I don't think it's a ridiculous way to make a living. For some people, their physical attributes are all they have to trade on. What's ridiculous, obscene, and nuts is how people react to what you do." He looks like he's bracing for a rant, and I laugh. "I'm not going on a lecture bender, I'm just saying..." I bat my lashes. "I don't need to tell you. You live it."

"Yeah. And I'm glad it's coming to an end."

I make a shooing motion and say, "I'll meet you in your bedroom."

He grins. "I'd hoped, I mean I really hoped, but I never thought I'd hear you say that."

Me neither. But I find I'm excited about where this seems to be going. And while it surprises me, and on various levels scares the shit out of me, I'm willing to take a leap. "Go away so I can get done in here." He saunters away, and the view is *fine*.

Ten minutes later I'm standing at the foot of his California King – which takes up most of the room – watching him sitting cross-legged in the middle of the bed fiddling with a little robot he hasn't shown me. There are tiny tools all around him, and he's wearing a thick band around his head with a lighted magnifying glass that's positioned in front of his face exaggerating his near perfect features.

Without looking up he says, "Come sit next to me. I'll show you what I'm doing."

I'm so far from being a man expert it's sad, but I know most guys don't invite their non-geek or non-mechanically inclined friends (I'm calling myself that for now so I don't become presumptuous) to sidle up to them while they're geeking out. I toe off my boots and climb on the bed and position myself next to him.

"This little guy's application is to take the place of an insulin pump. Some people hate having it embedded in their body, and some bodies reject the pump. This bot is an alternative. Working in tandem with other glucose-sensing technology, instead of an implanted sensor, this bot will take a pinprick of blood, determine what the patient's body needs, then respond by administering the appropriate insulin dose. All the patient needs to do daily is load the insulin capsule into the bot for daily service delivery."

I'm so impressed, I don't know what to say, and before I can tell him I'm dumbfounded by what he's doing, he goes on to tell me, "The best part is the bot is preprogrammed to the patient's base – what they usually need – and when something's really out of whack, the bot contacts the patient's doctor. If it's after hours, the second contact is nine-one-one." I look at this tiny machine that's smaller than a pepper mill, and I'm amazed. "It'll have a small display screen that'll interface with the patient's phone. IOS or Android."

I never thought I'd say this, but Jonas's brain is sexy as fuck. "Did you think this up on your own?"

He flips the magnifying glass up and looks at me. "Yeah. Nearly nine and a half percent of the global population has diabetes. That's about four hundred sixty-five million people. This bot can have real impact and implications for a lot of people's health."

I can't help myself. He's too wonderful, and for reasons I won't examine right now, I'm completely enamored with a geek with a lighted magnifying glass resting on his forehead. I lean in and press my lips to his and my tongue sweeps out and licks his delicious bottom lip.

I'm getting ready to pull back, but Jonas has other ideas. He knocks off the headpiece, pushes the tools and bot aside, turns, and lays me down on the bed, his torso across mine, and he kisses me full tongue: deep, wet, and intense.

He's kissing me like he's communicating, and what he's saying is profound: he wants me, and not in a drill her tonight and good-bye tomorrow kind of way. He's telling me with his mouth and tongue he's into me in a way he means to keep me, and I swear, I don't have one single objection to that.

When he breaks the kiss and raises his head, he says in a breathy whisper, "In my whole life I've never wanted anything more than I want you. But not tonight, Ames. You don't trust me enough yet."

I open my mouth to protest, but he puts two fingers against my lips. "I'm fucking thrilled out of my mind you want me too. But I'm right, and in the morning you'll thank me for knowing this about you."

He removes his fingers and touches his lips to mine. Then he lifts his head and I stare into his amazing eyes.

"When I'm sure you're sure, we're going to a swank hotel with deluxe room service and we're going to do everything we want to do with each other." He rests on his elbows, his hands bracketing my jaw. "Then you're mine. Always and forever, and I'm never letting you go."

Gulp.

Chapter Twelve
The Sorcerer

Jonas

I'm in the shower chuckling at the black and blue mark on my shin. Amy, who's still in dreamland, near beat me up last night with her active sleeping. After being kicked twice, and slapped once, I tangled our legs together and threw my arm around her waist. That shut her down. She slept like a log for the rest of the night, which meant so did I.

Spending the night wrapped around Amy had featured in some of the many fantasies I'd had about her being in my bed. Reality, though, turned out to be a whole lot better than my imagination. And I'm pretty damn creative.

My first class is at eight, so I'm up early. Luckily, I'm one of those people who has a great internal clock. If I know I have to be up at six-thirty, I'm up at six twenty-eight. Amy never said whether she needed an alarm, but to be on the safe side, I put the volume all the way up on her phone, which she'd plugged in and put beside her on the nightstand. I intend to call her just before I go into class to wake her so she can get back to her place with enough time to get ready for her first class at ten. I know she has a busy day. She's totally wrapped up in the party she's planning.

Collin is walking toward the bathroom as I'm coming out. I tilt my head at my bedroom door and tell him, "Amy's still sleeping."

He grins, nods, and whispers, "I'm heading back to the library. I'll be outta here in about a half hour."

"You don't have to rush out."

"I'm rushing because I've got to get to the library before anyone finds the pile of books I hid under one of the upstairs carrels."

I laugh. It's always the quiet ones. "'Kay. Good luck, and I'll see you later." Then I walk into my bedroom with only a towel around my waist and close the door as silently as I can. When I turn, I see Amy up on her elbows wearing a smirk while she's eying me up and down.

"Mmm. No deception in advertising with you, huh? No need to air brush or photo sculpt." Her voice is husky with sleep and she has really sexy bed hair.

I'm glad we slept in our clothes, it relaxed her, which was last night's endgame. But that does little to keep my dick from getting ideas right now. I open the closet, but it's too late, she's laughing.

I crane my neck around the door and scowl. "Not funny."

"One hundred percent funny, and really flattering, so thanks for that. Great way to start the day."

I'm watching her as I pull on my boxer briefs and jeans. She throws her legs over the side of the bed and I have just enough time to adjust myself before I feel her arms wrap around me. She leans in and her wonderful breasts press against my back.

I swear, I have to bite my tongue, hard, to keep from coming.

"I'm embarrassed to ask. Did I hit you or anything like that last night? I know I move around a lot."

I turn in her arms and kiss her forehead. "A few love taps. Nothing requiring casts or surgery."

"Now who has all the jokes?"

I smile. Yeah, I could get used to mornings like this. "How about a smoothie before we head out. Give us a boost for the day."

"Will it be green and taste like leaves?"

I tug gently on a hank of her beautiful auburn hair. "No, brat. I'm thinking protein powder, pomegranate juice, blueberries, and mango."

"Oh. Okay. I can do that." She gives me a squeeze then takes a step back. "I'm going to brush my teeth and pull myself together. Meet you in the kitchen?"

I nod, and then put on a tee and a V-neck sweater. Ten minutes later we're leaning against the kitchen counter finishing our smoothies. "Can you do dinner tonight?"

She dabs her mouth with a paper towel as she's shaking her head. "I've gotta finish this twenties playlist. I'm meeting with the DJ tomorrow. He needs as much jump time as he can get to make sure he can access all the music. We have to be totally ready in ten days. How about tomorrow?"

"I have Sensory Neurobiology until five-thirty, then I have lab time scheduled to work on my bots. I won't be back 'til late. Midnight, maybe."

She screws up her lips until they're halfway between a pout and an exaggerated kiss. "Wednesday is my standing weekly girls' dinner with Sofia, but I can do lunch. I have twelve-thirty to three open."

"Yeah. I can do that. One o'clock here?"

She nods, then rinses her glass and puts it in the dishwasher. I follow suit. We gather up our stuff, and I grab our coats. I hold hers, and as she puts in her arm she looks up and says, "You're gonna make me get used to this."

"That's the plan."

She turns and grabs onto my shoulders, pulling herself up to give me a sweet, soft kiss.

Totally could start every day exactly like this.

***

When I'm in class, I put my phone on vibrate, and at eight forty-five a.m. my ass is getting a mini massage.

A: Did I thank you for the great smoothie?
J: No, but I figured the kiss kinda covered it.
A: Kisses are multifunctional.
J: Since I'm in class, I'm going to take that answer as academic.
A: You can take it however you want it.

J: Ames.
A: Oh, all right. Academic it is.
J: Appreciate it.
A: TTYL

***

At two p.m. I text:

J: How's your day going?
A: I met my roommate, Sarah, who I hardly ever see cuz she actually lives with her
former BF, now fiancé as of Saturday night, in his single a few floors below our
place. She and I had a minor celebratory lunch.
J: I'm taking that to mean alcohol was involved.
A: We can accurately say it was more a liquid than solid lunch.
J: Where are you now?
A: I'm in class and I'm suffering with a bad case of senior doldrums.
J: What's the class?
A: Corporate Public Relations. Sort of redundant wouldn't you say?
J: For you, probably. For most of your classmates, I'm guessing no. But there might
be nugget or two you can take away from today's lecture.
A: My geek guru.

I'm not sure how I know this, but I'm pretty sure that while Amy is happy for her friend, the whole getting engaged thing smacked her in the face a bit.

At nine p.m., I text:

J: I'm outside your building. Come downstairs. I have something for you.
A: Why am I coming downstairs? You come up.
J: You're working.
A: And coming downstairs will interrupt working more than you coming up.
J: Okay, buzz me up.

Amy's standing in her doorway wearing an oversize slouchy orange sweater, loose black sweats, and huge bright blue fuzzy socks. Her hair is pulled back into a low tail, and she has on large, square-lens tortoiseshell glasses. She looks utterly adorable.

"What's in the bag, GG?"

"GG?"

"Geek guru."

I put my hand flat against her upper chest and gently push her into her tiny vestibule as I shut the door. "Soup and sandwiches."

"Takeout from where?"

I shake my head. "Please."

Her eyes go wide. "You made these?"

"Was that you at brunch and dinner yesterday?"

"Again with the jokes."

I walk past her into a small living room area and put the food bag on the oval wooden coffee table. I take off my messenger bag and lean it alongside the sofa. "Sit," I tell her as I point to the couch.

"Are you expecting me to say 'woof'?"

"I'm guessing you haven't had any real food all day, so I'm expecting you to sit down and eat your sandwich and drink your soup."

She looks in the bag, and then up at me. "There's enough in there for two people."

"Handy, since I'm a person." I lift a brow and hers drops as she stomps around the table to the sofa then plops down and sticks her hand in the bag.

"Didn't you have dinner with your dad tonight?"

"I did. We met at six and went to his favorite sushi place."

"Is that your way of saying you're hungry again?"

I shrug. "I could eat."

"Are you going to stand there and continue to scrutinize, or are you going to sit the fuck down and eat with me?"

I don't smirk, though I want to. I take off my coat and toss it on a side chair, then I sit next to her and wait as she doles out the wrapped sandwiches and the capped giant mugs of soup.

"You even put spoons and napkins in here." Before I can confirm my thoroughness, she asks, "Are they the same or is this mix and match?"

"Same. A lot of vegetables in vegetable bouillon with pastina, and grilled eggplant and zucchini sandwiches with melted mozzarella on toasted kalamata olive bread."

She stares at me with her mouth partially open. Then she snaps it shut before saying in an accusatory tone, "You're going to spoil me for anyone else's food, aren't you?"

"That's the plan."

"Hmmm. Seems you have a lot of plans, GG."

I chuckle as I take the lid off my soup. "Eat, Ames. It'll give you energy to finish your project."

She takes a sip of the soup and hums. "This is sooo good." After a couple more sips and a spoonful of veggies, she asks, "What's in the messenger bag?"

"Some work."

"You're going to do work here?"

Typical Amy reaction. I'm prepared with an effective counter. "If you don't want the company, I'll go back to my place."

She narrows her eyes as she takes a bite of the sandwich, and then she moans long and loud. "Holy shit. You're a sorcerer and you're seducing me with your food."

"Yet another plan."

She points her spoon at me. "I'm not easily fooled."

"I have no intention of fooling you."

"So says the seductive sorcerer."

"What happened to GG?"

"He was a decoy so I wouldn't see the sorcerer at work."

At least the whole fuck-boy thing's been laid to rest. I can work with GG and the seductive sorcerer.

I lean over and kiss her soft cheek, then I move my lips down to kiss the corner of her delicious mouth. "Seems only fair since you ensorcelled me at a wedding while holding a baby, and it took me nearly two and a half years to find you again."

"You can't say things like that, especially when I'm eating your food."

"I can and I will. Until you believe. And then I'll keep saying them to ensure you never stop believing."

Chapter Thirteen

A Slow and Steady Rush

Amy

I'm totally wrapped up in Jonas. This isn't a metaphorical statement, though it could be. It's a physical reality. After enduring one night of tossing and turning, he's found an effective way to keep me from flailing about in my sleep. His long legs with their yummy muscled thighs are tangled in mine, and his surprisingly weighty arm is wrapped entirely around my waist. I'm not going anywhere. And, though it freaks me out to admit it, I don't want to.

His soup was tasty and filling. The sandwich was magic disguised as food.

For some people, cooking for their friends and families is a declaration of love. Jonas is one of those people. And that sandwich was nothing short of the best seduction a girl could ask for.

More than yumalicious, it tasted like care was layered in between the grilled – with lines and everything, I checked – eggplant and zucchini.

For some women, dinner at a fancy restaurant, then heading to a box seat at the ballet, followed by a nightcap at a ritzy bar, would say *he cares enough to seduce me.* Jonas would do all that if I asked, but somehow, and doing it breaking land speed records, he'd figured out I pay attention to the little things. The everyday stuff that can be taken for granted. Like helping me into my coat, which, over the course of time, says I care enough to notice what you like and what you need, and I'll be the one to give it to you always.

So, obviously, I didn't send him away after we finished eating. I went back to my room, closed the door, and continued to work on the twenties playlist while he stayed in the common room – that's what the dorm brochures call it – doing whatever he brought over to work on. Somewhere around midnight I surfaced and announced, "I'm getting ready for bed." I didn't tell him to go home, and he didn't act like it was a big deal he was staying over. He closed his laptop, stuck it in his messenger bag, and asked if I had an extra toothbrush.

Now, I'm in my favorite long-sleeve sleep shirt snuggled up against Jonas, who is wearing his tee and boxer briefs.

With my eyes closed and my face smushed into the pillow, I ask him, "What time's your first class?"

"Ten," he says in a soft, sleepy voice against the top of my head. "You?"

"Same. I'm meeting the DJ for lunch at twelve-thirty. Then I have a three o'clock class, and after that, I'm heading to the library to do more research on nineteen-twenties decor and decorations. I've exhausted my online searches and need more nitty-gritty."

"Stop using such clinical terms. You'll confuse me."

I smile as I tell him, "Smartass."

"Shut down the brain, Ames. We both have full days tomorrow and need our sleep."

He sounds like he's ten seconds away from drifting off, so I relent, though it's tough. "'Night, GG."

He kisses my neck. "'Night, Ames."

Most nights, it takes me a while to fall asleep, but with his big, warm body blanketing mine, I'm feeling all sorts of comfy, so it might not take as long for me to drop into slumber.

In what seems like ten minutes later, I'm half awake and facing Jonas as he kisses my eyelids, cheeks, and then softly places his lips against mine where he says, "'Morning, Ames."

Huh. Apparently, I fell asleep and didn't know it. And now I'm waking up to a sexy man with a sleep-soaked voice whose soft beard is tickling my face. Niiiice.

"Hey." I kiss his exceptionally talented mouth then pull back and mutter, "Morning breath."

His "I don't care" comes through loud and clear when he lays his hand against my lower back, presses me into his serious morning wood, and kisses me like he's going to war and this has to hold him for two years.

What's a girl to do? I wind my arms around his shoulders and give as good as I'm getting. And holy shit, I'm revved. I'm thinking he's going to do it again: make me come just by kissing me.

Sadly, he pulls back, and I complain with a noisy, "Nooo."

He fists my hair and holds me still. "I want to, really want to. But it's gotta be more than only getting off."

"Ah, right now, I'm not feeling sensible and considerate."

He chuckles. "In reflection, you will in a couple of hours." He smacks my tush, then rolls out of bed. "I'm heading back to my place. Get ready and come over. I'll have breakfast waiting."

I pick up my phone and check the time to keep from staring at his monster hard-on. It's seven forty-five. Plenty of time to shower, put myself together, and have breakfast with Jonas. Absent having what I know will be the best sex of my life – actually, I'm sure it'll be the best sex of anyone's life – I can't think of a better way to start my day.

***

I'm sitting next to Collin who's scarfing down his omelet. I can't blame him. Spinach, sautéed mushrooms, and feta cheese. It tastes unbelievable. And we have biscuits and fig jam. A quick throw-together is what Jonas said. I'm calling it divine.

"How's the research going?" I ask Collin.

"Slow, but I'm enjoying the deep dive. Even the extraneous information is fascinating."

"I know what you mean." We all stand and take our dishes to the sink. "I didn't think the nineteen twenties would hold so much allure, but I find I'm really into it. I slide into side trips I don't need to take, but it's interesting and a lot of fun."

Without any discussion, I rinse and Collin puts the dishes in the dishwasher while Jonas cleans the counter and table, and puts away the last of the cooking supplies. We all gather up our stuff and head out to face the day.

Collin peels off in one direction and Jonas and I head in another. Here's another little thing he does I'd never thought about before since I'd never had a guy in my life who mattered. But now I do, and it's wild and foreign at the same time it's easy: Jonas is fine with PDA.

Nothing that should remain private, but, like now, when he's gotta walk a couple of blocks to get on a bus, he's stopped us at the corner where I'm getting on the subway.

He wraps his hand around the back of my neck and pulls me to him so he can kiss me good-bye. Sweet, short, and soulful, his kiss lingers as I pull out my CharlieCard as I head down the stairway to the green line. Usually, I walk it, but it's bitter cold this morning, and I'm a wuss.

Ten minutes later, when I'm topside again, I feel my phone vibrating in my coat pocket. Collin.

C: Hey. I didn't think of this until I got inside class and my brain began to defrost. I know Jonas is going to be in the lab tonight and I wondered if you wanted to get dinner. Give us time to catch up.
A: When he's not around to cook, do you feel like you're foraging in the forest for something edible?
C: Funny, but sorta true. Usually, I make myself a sandwich. Sustenance, but far from Jonas level. Even his sandwiches are gourmet.
A: Tell me about it.
C: You like Alfredo's in Allston?
A: Who doesn't?
C: No one I know. See you there at six thirty?
A: Yeah. Now I'll spend the day totally craving homemade pasta.
C: Me too.

I endured class, met with Carlo the DJ, and we hammered out the final playlist, a mix of songs from the 1920s and the 2020s. I've heard more than a few of his mixes, and I know he's going to have everyone on the dance floor for hours.

I skidded into my three o'clock class, which didn't put me to sleep, then I made tracks to the library, got lost in my research, and had to jam to catch the subway.

Sitting on a packed car, I took out my phone and saw I'd missed a few texts from Jonas.

J: How's your day going?

J: Ames?

J: Okay, I guess you're swamped. We'll catch up later.

A: Hey. Sorry I missed you. I put my phone on silent when I met with the DJ and forgot to turn it back on. And, yeah, totally swamped all day, but it's all good. I'm meeting Collin for dinner at Alfredo's. Looking forward to catching up with him.

The phone vibrated the moment I stepped onto the staircase.

J: Great restaurant choice. I'll call later and you can tell me all about your day.

A: Have fun playing with your robots.

J: <g>

Alfredo's is a really small neighborhood joint, and it's busy mostly with takeout orders. Collin's huddled near the door waiting for a table.

"Hey," I say as I hug him.

"Shouldn't be more than five minutes," he tells me, tilting his head to a couple at the two-seater against the wall. "They're getting ready to pay the check."

"'Kay. As long as we're inside, I'm good. It's freezing out. Does it smell like snow to you? They didn't say it was going to snow, but I swear, it smelled like it on the way over."

He pointed to the scarf dangling around his neck. "Didn't smell much of anything with this over my face, but it's bone cold for sure."

I grew up in Connecticut twenty minutes away from the Massachusetts border. Nor'easters and ten-foot snow drifts have been a way of life for as long as I have memory. I can't say being used to brutal winters means I like them, but I'm no fan of the tropics and their giant bugs and intolerable humidity. I've never been to California, but I've heard they have seasons in NorCal. Their version of winter is what we call early fall here. Maybe I could get used to it if I had to. I don't think I'd ever get used to the near endless summer life of SoCal. I need *some* weather, and there's nothing like New England in autumn.

Technically, we're in autumn now, but we're only nine days away from Thanksgiving, so it's holiday season, which means it's winter.

Collin nudges me forward. The couple is leaving and we're moving in to sit down at the same time the busboy is clearing the table.

As we're shedding our outerwear, I ask Collin, "What are you doing for Thanksgiving?"

He lets out a hefty sigh. "Did your gran tell you anything about what happened with my folks?"

"A little."

"Gasoline meet flame."

Already, from those three words, I know his childhood was as awful as mine. Maybe not the same, but shitty nonetheless.

"My dad was and is a pretty steady person," he says as he rubs his hands together. "Gasoline isn't inert, but without a lit match always around it's relatively harmless. My mother is a torch whose flame is always on high. The only time they weren't fighting was when she left him for a few days. Sometimes she dragged me and my sister, Aileen, along, and that wasn't fun on any level. The three of us in a hotel room with our mother who's ranting and drinking, and sobbing and cursing. When she left us with our dad, home felt almost normal."

The busboy returns with two clean setups and two glasses of water, then tells us the waitress will be over soon.

Collin waits until the busboy leaves before continuing. "Then, one day, she packs up all Aileen's and my stuff and the next thing we know, we're living in an apartment in Denver. Sometimes I heard her yelling at Dad on the phone. Whatever fighting went on with the divorce, all we knew was our dad got us every other Christmas and for four weeks in the summer. He came to Denver about three times a year to spend long weekends with us staying with him in a nice hotel, like President's Day weekend, and we talked to him on the phone almost every day."

He takes a few sips of water before going on. "The guy my mother married is all right. He was never mean to us, but it was clear he was fine letting her be the only parent in the house. His house. They didn't fight the way she and my dad went at each other." He shrugs. "They seem as happy as she can be with anyone."

I reach across the table, grab his hand, and squeeze. "Sucks out loud."

He nods. "That sums it up. It got better though."

"Yeah?"

"Yeah. After I turned fourteen, I told my mother Aileen and I wanted to spend the whole summer with Dad. I don't know why she agreed, but we were beyond grateful. The day after school ended, we were on a plane to New York City, and we didn't go back to Denver until two days before the new school term started.

"When I was filling out my college applications – I applied only to East Coast schools – I talked to Aileen, who was twelve at the time, about living with our dad full time. Of course, she said yes.

"I told Dad, who talked to his attorney, who contacted our mother's attorney. Apparently, a judge considers the preference of which parent the child lives with if the child is old enough to form an intelligent opinion. For whatever the reason, twelve is the magic number for a kid to be old enough. I don't know if my mother didn't want to spend the money on more court proceedings, or if her husband talked her into it because he wanted both of her kids out of his house. Really, I don't care why. The result was all that mattered. After I graduated high school, Aileen and I moved in with Dad."

"Whoa."

"Yeah. And after we moved in, he made us go to therapy."

"Together?"

"Sometimes. Sometimes it was me and Aileen, sometimes we each saw the therapist alone. We went twice a week all summer. Best thing for all of us. Aileen kept seeing the therapist for about a year." He gripped my hand that was still in his. "We healed, Ames."

"I'm so glad, Collin. For real."

"I'm so glad I got you back. For real."

"Totally."

The waitress came and took our order.

"Do you ever go back to Denver?"

"Me, never. Aileen goes back for two weeks in the summer."

"That's it?"

"That's all she can stand, and our mother doesn't seem to care it's not longer, or that she doesn't see us for the holidays."

"Whoa some more."

He laughs. "Yeah."

"So I guess the answer to what you're doing for Thanksgiving is you're going home to New York City."

"Looking forward to it."

"I bet."

The food arrives and we dig in like we haven't eaten in weeks. As always, it's great.

The best part of tonight is knowing Collin isn't walking around with the weight of his fucked-up childhood.

It's an unexpected and most welcome gift.

***

At eleven-thirty p.m. I hear the front door close and about a minute later Jonas is standing in the doorway to his bedroom with a huge smile.

After dinner, Collin and I went to his place and kept talking. By the time he was ready to go to bed, it was ten thirty, and I figured I'd stay and wait for Jonas to come home.

Now, I'm sitting cross-legged on his bed with my open laptop on a pillow in front of me, and I'm wearing one of his Henleys and my grass green satin boy shorts.

"Another fantasy fulfilled."

His smile is wicked and knowing.

"Really? How's that?"

"Trolling for compliments?"

"Totally."

He sits on the bed and puts his hand on my thigh. "I come home to find I've got a hot chick wearing my shirt, cute underwear, and nothing else waiting up for me in my bed. In general, any guy would find that a living fantasy. Me? You're the only person I want here."

Um, WOW.

He's so good at the gushy stuff, and I don't think it's an act. He always treats me like I'm special. A girl could get used to that sort of thing really quick.

"Well, I wouldn't do this for anyone else."

I'm treated to another of his Times Square billboard smiles, then in a couple of swift moves, he shuts my laptop, places it on the nightstand, and tackles me.

His hands are on my tush yanking me up against him, and his tongue is sliding along mine, drinking me in like I'm the elixir of life.

He's such a great kisser, I'm gone in like two seconds. I don't have one coherent thought left in my brain. My body's doing all the talking, and it's saying I need him inside me. Now.

His lips leave mine to latch on to the skin beneath my ear. His tongue is teasing while his teeth are nipping, and I'm squirming, trying to rub up against his jeans. I *need* the friction.

His mouth lifts from my neck at the same time his hands yank down my boy shorts.

Yesss.

He kneels between my spread legs as he raises me up with both hands and then bends to place his talented mouth against my clit.

I explode.

I'm biting the inside of my mouth to muffle my moaning, and does he stop and give me a chance to catch my breath? Hell no. He's going at me like he's looking for the world record to make a woman come.

I can't take it at the same time I pray he doesn't stop.

My hands are fisting the sheets and I'm soaring. Honestly, I don't know if I'm having a series of orgasms or if it's one continuous orgasm making me shake like an 8.0 earthquake.

When he lifts his head and nips the inside of my thigh, I grab on to his hair to keep him where he is. I can't take anymore. I never thought I'd feel this way, but if he goes for it one more time, I swear, I'm going to pass out.

I feel him smiling against my thigh, and if I had the strength, I'd smack the smug out of him.

He lowers me to the bed and I let go of his hair as he lays most of his body on top of mine, balancing the rest of him on his elbows on either side of my torso.

His gaze locks with mine, and gently he brushes my hair off my face. "You taste like sunshine and Montmorency cherries."

"You're such a sweet talker."

"Is this a bad thing?"

"Not if you mean it."

He lays his heavy body all the way on mine, wraps his arms around me, and tells me in a really serious tone, "I mean everything I say to you. No bullshit. Ever. So mark this, Ames." He looks down my body then returns his intense gaze to mine. "I've tasted you. Had my mouth on you. My tongue inside you. That's mine now. You understand me?"

I nod because really, I wasn't going to argue with him. I mean, I don't want anyone else, and holy shit, he's not only a good guy who cooks like a four-star Michelin chef, he has the ability to turn my bones to dust with one kiss.

"Just one thing."

His brow wings up. "Hmmm?"

"What are Montmorency cherries?"

He hugs me to him as he laughs deep and long. "You're such a smartass."

"Who tastes like sunshine and some kind of cherry."

"Oh yeah."

I kiss his cheek. "For real, what are Montmorency cherries?"

"They're tart cherries with a hint of sweet used mostly in pies and jams. My opinion, the best kind."

 I smile. "Niiice."

He grins then lifts off me, but I grab him by his shirt before he can leave the bed. "What about you?"

"What about me?"

I rest my hand on the impressive bulge behind his jean's zipper.

"When I'm sure you're sure."

I want to tell him I'm sure right now, but that's our chemistry talking.

Truthfully, I'm almost sure.

But he's right.

I need more time to be absolutely certain because I know, once I'm all in, there'll be no turning back.

I arch up and kiss him. "You'll be the first to know."

Chapter Fourteen

Reality Check

Jonas

Without discussing it, and kind of organically, Amy and I have slept together every night since our first brunch. Most nights we sleep at Amy's since her roommate is never there. After the first time I gave her an Aussie kiss, I knew there's no way she could be quiet. And I didn't want her to be. Of all the guards she'd erected to protect her fragile heart, almost from the beginning, physically, she let loose. No way am I going to put a clamp on that.

We've established a rhythm to our days and nights. We get up together, Amy showers and gets ready at her place, me at mine, then she comes over and we have breakfast together, often with Collin. During the day we text to keep up with each other's schedules, and most nights we have dinner together at my place, often with Collin. When we can't, Amy brings me takeout, or I make something to bring over to her place.

Today mid-morning, we're leaving for Long Island to have Thanksgiving with Amy's grandmother. My dad and Sharon were supposed to join us, but Sharon got tied up with a big case, and my dad had to go to DC early this morning for some last-minute hush-hush FBI meeting. He won't be home until tomorrow, and he'd rather be there for Sharon even if she's able to get away only for a little while on Thanksgiving.

Collin's taking the train with us a to NYC, where he'll go home and we'll have to head crosstown from Penn Station to catch the bus to

Bridgehampton. Then we'll take a taxi to Amy's grandmother's house in Sagaponack. Long fuckin' day. But the good news is we all like each other, we all have laptops, and we all have a lot of work to do.

The bad news, which I'll talk to Amy about on the bus to Long Island, is I got my shooting schedule for the winter break, and I'm not going to have more than five days with her over the whole break. Sucks big time.

My phone dings. It's Amy.

A: I'm all packed. Are you coming to me, or am I going to you?
J: We'll be there in ten.
A: Please tell me you're bringing food. I totally forgot to say something.
J: That you ask is insulting.
A: Well beg my fucking pardon.

I'm laughing so hard Collin wants to know what's so funny. I show him my phone.

"Yeah," he shakes his head, "that's Amy all over."

***

Amy's giving Collin one last hug before we head off to catch a cab to Lexington Avenue. We have thirty-five minutes before the bus leaves, and we're cutting it close. Driving in NYC is always nuts, but the day before Thanksgiving is totally whack.

Thankfully, we get a cabbie who believes in perpetual forward motion and we get to the bus stop with fifteen minutes to spare. We get in line, and almost immediately, the line is longer behind us than in front of us, which means we'll probably get seats together without having to beg someone to move.

Of course, the bus is late, but once we're on and sitting together, we look at each other and let out long sighs.

"That's an ordeal," she says as she unwinds the scarf around her neck.

"Yeah, it is. But we'd figured it'd take the same amount of time to fly, and agreed the airports are insane around Thanksgiving and probably more aggravating."

"I know. I'm sorry we didn't ditch and drive down. I would've left on Sunday."

"Yeah well, Collin absolutely couldn't leave 'til today, I couldn't leave until late yesterday." I took her hand and laced our finger together. "One more semester, Ames."

"For me. You've got five to six years of classes ahead of you."

"Different kind of programs. Some classes, but mostly seminars, independent study, and tele-meetings with the profs. Most of my time will be spent in the lab, on research, and writing my thesis."

The bus is moving through NYC in fits and starts. I have a feeling this ride is going to take about an hour longer than billed.

"You never told me. Where did you apply?"

I smile. Seventeen days ago, I'd seen Amy in a club for the first time since I'd talked to her at that wedding after our freshman year. What she calls "the Bree debacle" happened that night in the club, and five days later, again by serendipity, we bumped into each other in the library, which led to dinner.

If I was a betting man, on the night of the Bree debacle, I wouldn't've put down a dime on Amy seeing us having a future together. But in the days between eating Mexican food outside in the freezing cold and today, we're together in a way that more than hints at the rest of our lives.

Fast?

Maybe for her.

But not for me.

"I've applied to three schools offering PhD programs covering the work I want to do. Carnegie Mellon, Stony Brook, and WPI – Worcester Polytechnic Institute."

"Stony Brook?" Her face lights up. "Here?" Her voice has gone up an octave. "On Long Island?"

"Yeah. The big university on the north shore side of the island."

She's pulling at the fringe on her scarf, knotting it between her fingers. "Do you, ah, have a favorite?"

If she only knew how transparent she is. It's sweet, and it makes me want to kiss her until we can't breathe. She wants me to go to school near where she's going to live: with her grandmother in Sagaponack.

"Each has their strong points. Really, I couldn't go wrong with any of them."

"When do you think you'll hear if you've been accepted?"

"Anywhere from four to ten weeks from now."

"Pins and needles time, huh?"

"Since it's out of my hands, I try not to dwell."

"I'd be a nervous wreck."

"Were you nervous when you applied to college?"

"Nah. I had the grades, the recommendations, and the requisite extracurriculars."

I grin. "There you go."

She grips my arm and squeezes. "I hope you get into all of them so you can pick your fave."

I lean down and kiss her luscious lips. "Give me your party lineup for the holidays." Her twenties affair was such a hit the couple who'd hired her booked their Valentine's party right after the last guest left the twenties' bash.

"Ugh." She scrunches her nose. "The holidays are crunch time and always falls around finals. This year shouldn't be too bad, though." She digs out her phone from her messenger bag and pulls up her calendar. "Since Hanukkah starts a little before Christmas, I'm back-to-backing it." She starts reading. "The Siegels, who 'summer' in Southhampton, which is how I got to know them, have to be the first and best at everything. Their Hanukkah party is on Saturday, December tenth. This year's theme is Ancient Italian Jews. I'm having the best Italian Jewish restaurant in the city, Lattanzi, cater. The Siegels have decided on fancy dress, so there'll be togas, tunics, the whole *gedilla*."

She surprised me. "You speak Yiddish?"

"Not really. I know words and phrases. My grandparents used to speak Yiddish when they didn't want me to know what they were saying. Since I didn't like being left out, I learned enough to follow the gist."

"Huh. My grandparents spoke a little Yiddish, but it wasn't used much by Dutch Jews. I know a few words, most of them are what's been assimilated into English."

"Like *schmutz*?"

I nod. "And *schlep*."

She laughs. "You know a word's totally assimilated when a burly delivery guy with a cigar hanging from his lips, who's standing on the sidewalk in New York, yells at his crew, 'Be careful going in and outta the elevator. You scratch anything, we're gonna havta *schlep* all this furniture up the stairs.'" She says it in a heavy New York accent.

"You have hidden talents, Ames."

She purses her lips into an exaggerated kiss and bats her lashes. "Just you wait, Henry Higgins. Just you wait."

Hardly a day goes by that Amy doesn't delight me.

She goes through the rest of her calendar, five more parties right through to January first. At least she'll be busy when I'm gone.

As I get ready to tell her, *Sounds like you'll need a real vacation after all that,* an idea sparks. "So I got my shoot schedule, also back-to-back jobs. December twenty-second I fly down to Miami for three days, then it's off to SoCal for six days. New Year's Day, I fly to Costa Rica for five days. We're working at a swank place near Playa Negra. Wanna meet me there, and on the sixth head back to SoCal with me for a week?" She looks skeptical. "There'll be plenty for you to do in both places while I'm working, and we'll have time to be together where it's warm."

"You sure? I mean, how long does a shoot last?"

"These are all location shoots for summer wear. They can go as long as ten hours, but most, about seven. That'll leave lots of time for us."

I've seen her narrow her eyes the way she's doing now. She's mulling over the pros and cons. "Promise me my being there won't mess with your job."

"You plan on sulking around the photo shoots all day?

She gave a grunt-laugh. "Ah, that'd be a hell no."

"Then, no worries, so I promise."

We spend the next half hour working out the Costa Rica logistics, then book her a flight from JFK to San José, Costa Rica, and another in-country connecting flight to Tamarindo Airport, which is close to Playa Negra.

"You'll have to hang out in the San José airport for about two and a half hours before the connecting flight."

"It won't be that long. You gotta figure, even if the flight's on time, by the time I get through customs, and then get my bags, I'll be ready to get some food and chill before the connecting flight."

"Yeah."

"I can't wait to drink fresh tamarind juice and eat tamarind candies. You ever try Pulparindo?"

"Can't say I know what it is."

"Oh. Really? You've gotta try it. It's Mexican candy made with tamarind and chili pepper. It's sweet and spicy and makes your mouth pucker."

"A ringing endorsement."

She bumps my shoulder. "Don't be a food snob."

"I'm not. I'm serious."

"Your expression does not say serious. It says *let me fuck with Amy*."

I grin. "No truer words spoken."

"Well, shit. I walked right into that one."

Chapter Fifteen

Home

Amy

By the time we got off the bus in Bridgehampton, I'd called Grams twice to give her updated ETAs, and Jonas had made sure my flight to LA was the same as his. With little effort, he talked me into staying another couple of days in SoCal so we could hang with his mother. Unlike my own, I'm good with other people's parents. I'm chatty and curious, and they seem to enjoy my company.

Also, Jonas changed his flight from LA to Boston to the flight I booked from LAX to JFK. We'd agreed to spend the last few days of our winter break with Grams.

I'm scooched up to the edge of the seat so I can direct the taxi driver where to turn since most people just zoom by, especially at night.

"There, on the left," I tell him, and he swings the car onto the driveway, goes up toward the garage, and turns around in the wide courtyard before he parks. We all get out at the same time, and he meets Jonas at the trunk to get our bags. I've opened the side gate and I'm standing on the walkway to the house when I see Grams coming out through the far set of the dining room's French doors.

I run up the path so she doesn't have walk to us.

"Amy, honey," she sighs as I wrap my arms around her. Recently, every time I do, I can't help but think she's shrunk. She's always been a small woman, and her short wavy hair had started to go silver when I was about ten. But since Gramps died, she seems to've diminished, and the sparkle has gone out of her light blue eyes.

I hear the cab take off at the same time I feel Jonas at my back.

"Grams, this is Jonas Vandenberg." He puts down the bags, then leans down to kiss Grams on the cheek. "Oh my. He's a tall one." She pats his arm, then says, "And so handsome."

"She's a terrible flirt," I tell Jonas.

"Who wouldn't want to be flirted with by such a gracious woman?"

"Ooo. And a charmer to boot."

Grams is wearing one of her indoor cardigans over a blouse and loose pants. The night air is cold, and I don't want her to get a chill. "Why don't we go inside?" I suggest.

As I put one arm through Grams's, Jonas pushes my messenger bag onto my other shoulder and follows us to the deck and into the house.

***

Jonas

We walk inside and I let out a long whistle. The heavenly aroma of home-cooked food hits me. The long white-washed farmhouse table with its mismatched chairs are in front of us, and the colorful ensemble totally fits the feel of the space, which flows into a family room with its sage green slouchy couches filled with different patterned pillows. Between two big windows draped with bright aquamarine floor-length curtains stands a large dark navy distressed hutch.

As beautiful as all this is, it's the open-space kitchen to the left that has me drooling.

A restaurant-quality eight-burner stove with a pot-filler and double ovens is in the middle of a long counter that runs the length of the back wall. In the middle of the U-shaped kitchen is a huge island, and over it hangs two half-moon drop lights focused on the vegetable sink.

To the left is a long counter broken up only by the farmhouse sink, and to the right is another long counter with a wine fridge below. From what I know of Amy's grandparents, they entertained often, and the multitude of cabinets, a few glass-fronted, lay testament to their need for lots of dinnerware.

The slatted wood ceiling, the countertops, the walls, the cabinets, the fridge, the dishwashers – two – and the subway tile backsplash are all white. But far from antiseptic, the kitchen is alive with color. Bowls in bright red and burnt orange are scattered over the counters. Some hold fruit, others have seashells, and the one on the island is filled with multicolored glass balls. There are two large aquamarine vases filled with assorted flowers, each standing tall near the end of the long counters.

The tied-back shirred curtains – there are five kitchen windows – are ruby red and the material is shot through with silver veins. The same material covers the windows in the French doors, but these are cinched in the middle.

Amy, who is standing between me and her grandmother, says, "Give him a moment, Grams. He's suffering from kitchen envy."

Her grandmother smiles. "Amy's told me you're a wonderful cook." She waves an arm at the kitchen. "*Mi casa es su casa.*"

"Thank you, Mrs. Stern. I'm going to take you up on the offer."

"Lilli. Or Grams. I'll answer to both, but not to Mrs. Stern." I dip my head as I smile. "You two go upstairs and get settled." Lilli points her forefinger at Amy. "Take whatever you have in your old room and starting now, use the master bedroom."

Then she focuses on me. "Since Sam died, I moved downstairs to what the contractor called 'the first level junior primary en-suite.'" She laughs. "Sounds fancy, huh?" I nod. "It's a nice-size bedroom with a big closet and an attached bathroom. It has a private patio, which I love. I'll show it to you tomorrow." She pulls out a dining room chair and sits. "But most of all, I don't have to walk up and down that long staircase anymore, which at my age is a boon."

"Okay, Grams." Amy bends down to kiss her grandmother's cheek. "Give us a half hour and we'll be down for dinner."

"Take your time." Lilli looks at me. "I made Amy's favorite. My artichoke lasagna."

"Sounds fantastic." And it does. I've never had artichoke lasagna and now I'm dying to taste it. Actually, I could eat a shoe, I'm that hungry.

"Go." She flaps her hands toward the front of the house. "I'm going to toss the dressing into the salad, then put the garlic bread in the oven."

I gather our bags and follow Amy through the family room, with its brick fireplace and walls crammed with art, to the staircase, where that wall is crammed with art too. I'm up close to three of the works, but can see the artist's signatures on only one piece: Frankenthaler.

Sotheby's much?

***

While Amy is finishing transferring her clothes, knickknacks, and photos into our bedroom – I love saying that – I'm standing on the huge deck that runs almost the length of the master and the private den beside it. Amy told me it's called the sitting room.

The sound and smell of the ocean are all around me, and although Long Island looks nothing like anywhere on the West Coast, being this close to the ocean gives me the same feel: peace and tranquility.

Amy comes up behind me and wraps her arms around my waist. I can feel bunched padding between us and figure it's the throw that was draped on the end of the bed.

"This place is amazing."

"Wait 'til you see the view of the eighty-three acres of preserved farmland across the way."

"The land your grandparents sold off."

"Yeah. Years later, the land was designated preserved."

"So this will always be the view."

"It will." She hugs me tight. "Tomorrow, I'll take you through the gardens. Even though a lot of them are winterized, you'll still be able to see how fabulous Grams has made the yard look."

I cross my arms over hers. "You love it here."

"This is home. Every good family memory I've ever had has been made in and around this house."

I sense she's ready to tell me about her past, so I take her hand and lead her to the double chaise lounge angled in the corner of the deck.

As we cuddle up, Amy tosses the throw over us. I wait, knowing she'll speak when she's ready.

"My grandparents had two kids. My aunt Rebecca was five years older than my father, and she died from breast cancer at thirty-one. She'd been married but didn't have any kids."

I squeeze her arm. Already this is heartbreaking, and vaguely familiar.

"I never knew her. My grandparents told me lots of stories about her though. They said she loved life, especially her work. She was associate concertmaster, second violin, for the New York Philharmonic. Music was her world. She was seriously pretty and had Grams's light blue eyes. I'll show you. There are photos of her all over the house. She played a Stradivarius. Grams had it sealed in a shadow box, and it hangs on the wall in her bedroom."

Ames snuggles closer, her cheek resting on my chest over my heart.

"About nine years after Rebecca died, my parents met at some fancy charity thing. I'm sure my father was there for business. Money's the only thing he cares about. Back then, after he'd made a killing as Wall Street analyst, he'd started his own private equity firm and was probably in hustle mode. My mother, who was gorgeous, was there with a date. Which makes perfect sense since my father covets. If he wants something, anything, no one can have more or better than him."

She looks up at me, shaking her head. "Knowing my grandparents, and hearing stories about how Rebecca was so much like them, I have no idea where my father came from. If he didn't look so much like Gramps, I would think he'd been switched at birth.

"There's not a word bad enough to describe him. In my head, I call him 'The Supreme Asshole of the Universe.'"

"That about covers it." She smiles, and I can see by her expression, she knows that's what I was going for.

"It took him a year to get her down the aisle. I doubt affection had anything to do with it. I'm sure he thought he needed her to be his and no one else's and that was the only way to guarantee it. All he was after was a declaration that no one else could have her. He married her to lock down the possession."

Her phone beeps. "Time for dinner."

***

Lilli has set the table and put the salad in the middle of where the three of us are sitting. Amy waves her grandmother into the chair at the head of the table. "Take a load off. I'll get everything else."

"Don't bother searching for the trivets," Lilli calls out. "I put them down already."

I help Lilli into her chair.

"Such good manners. You're going to have to tell me about your people."

When I see the size of the lasagna's casserole dish, I jump up to take it from Ames.

"Please tell me Gloria put the lasagna in the oven," Amy scolds as she places the basket full of garlic bread on the table.

"Honey, I'm old, not stupid," Lilli chides. "Gloria helped me assemble the lasagna, and put it in the oven before she left. And before you ask, yes, I sat here at the table and chopped up everything for the salad."

"Okay. Good. And, yeah, I admit it. I nag." Amy uses fork and spoon tongs to plate the salad.

Lilli pats my arm and holds my gaze. "She does nag something awful, but I don't much mind. Don't you think it's good to know you're loved?"

As Amy hands her grandmother a small portion of salad, she says, "Sneaky."

I laugh. "A trait you apparently inherited."

Lilli grins and Amy narrows her eyes.

These two are a comedy act that doesn't abate throughout dinner.

As we eat, I tell Lilli about my parents, modeling, and what I plan to do with my life. As I get up to help clear the dishes, I say, "You have to give me the recipe for the lasagna. It's fantastic."

"She doesn't write anything down," Amy says with bite. "It's an actual crime. Nothing for her brisket, her matzo ball soup, her noodle *kugel*, her stuffed cabbage, her *mun kikhl*, her *platzel*...not one word."

"Pffft. I've showed you how to make everything every time you asked."

"But you didn't tell me how many cups of flour, how much salt, or how long I'm supposed to cook any of it. You cup your hands, or holds your fingers apart as measurement, or say 'You'll know when it's done.'"

Before I lose my chance to keep all these treasures from slipping through the sands of time, I suggest, "How about we record Lilli talking us through the recipes. Whatever is inexact, I can guess, and it's fun to experiment. Since you know how everything's supposed to taste, you'll tell me when I get it right."

Lilli smacks the table and lets out a loud, "Ha."

I don't speak Stern fluently, but from her expression, Amy knows exactly what that "Ha" means.

"Don't start," Amy warns.

"I don't have to anymore. You've found him."

Ahh. The "Ha" means Amy's met her match. Well, I'm not going to argue the point since Lilli's one hundred percent correct. But I'm not going to crow about it either. Amy's walls have been crumbling, and I'm not going to do anything to disrupt their demise.

After Ames and I clean up, Lilli directs us to peel and slice some pears, and drizzle balsamic vinegar over them. Lilli really knows food. Tomorrow I'm going to start recording her recipes.

We go into the family room and I ask Lilli to tell me about all the art. It's like we're at a gallery showing. We're standing in the middle of the room, bowls and napkins in our hands, and as we eat dessert, Lilli shares about each piece, when they'd acquired it and where. She's knowledgeable about all the artists.

I like art, but don't know much about it. But some of the names, like Helen Frankenthaler, I know. Lilli has what my mother would call a well-curated collection.

After my journey through the Sagaponack wing of a number of museums, we go into the study where Lilli tells me with pride, this is where one of the two TVs are in the whole house. The other is the upstairs sitting room. Given the floor-to-ceiling bookshelves both here and in the den, I'm guessing she finds TV a lower form of entertainment.

Lilli lowers herself into a cushy floral chair that turns out to be an elegant recliner. After she's situated, Amy brings over one of the throws from the so-comfy-you're-enveloped-in-it sofa.

"Thanks, honey."

"What do you want to watch, Grams?"

"Find that Tom Papa comedian on Netflix. He makes me laugh."

Again, as with the art, I enjoy comedy, and I've watched a few comedians, but I don't know who Tom Papa is.

Amy finds the special, which is from before the pandemic, hits play, and within three minutes, we're all laughing out loud, and pretty much don't let up.

Lilli has a way of guiding an evening. I'm sure when she and her husband did all that entertaining, her guests left happy, having had a wonderful time.

Amy helps Lilli out of her chair, and we walk her to her bedroom and give and get kisses good night.

Even though I've met Lilli only this evening, it's like Ames and I have done this a hundred times.

It's comfortable.

It's effortless.

It's family.

***

Amy is standing at the foot of the bed wearing flannel dancing panda PJ bottoms and a hot pink long-sleeve sleep tee. On anyone else it would look ridiculous. On Ames, it's adorable.

"You've fallen in love with her."

"Is there anyone you know who hasn't?"

She crawls onto the bed then sits in front of me cross-legged. "Nope."

"She loves you something fierce, Ames."

"The feeling is mutual."

"She knows."

Amy crawls up the rest of the bed, then arranges herself so she's lying down beside me, her head on her pillow facing me, her hands tucked under her cheek.

"The last time my mother was here was for the high school graduation party Grams threw for me. That was about three and a half years ago. Guess how long it's been since my father was here to visit his parents, his widowed mother, the house he grew up in."

"Longer than three and half years."

"Try nearly eight years ago, when I was bat mitzvahed. My grandparents were the ones who helped me learn my Haftorah. They were the ones who spent time with me and the rabbi. They were the ones who gave me a big bat mitzvah party. As a matter of fact, my grandfather planned the whole house upgrade around my bat mitzvah. He made sure everything was completed before that weekend.

"You wanna know who's been here every year for my birthday parties? The Di Caros. They came to my bat mitzvah. They come to the annual Memorial Day weekend party. They came to the funeral to sit shiva when Gramps died. Sofia and *Nonna* stayed here in the house with me and Grams the whole week. My mother came to the funeral. My father was a no-show for all of it."

If I thought finding her father and beating the shit out of him would make her feel better, I'd do it. But the wounds her callous parents inflicted couldn't be mended by a good beatdown. Amy needs to know

I'll always be there for her, and the only way to prove that is to do it, and keep doing it until we're old as dirt.

I pull her into my arms and hold her head against my shoulder. "I'm sure you've heard this a thousand times, but it bears repeating. Their behavior had and has nothing to do with you. This is who *they* are. They're incapable of love, decency, and kindness. That sucks large in general, and was especially shitty to've grown up with but, Ames, you were and are loved. Huge. By people who have and will stand by you."

I stroke her hair and hold her tight. "Your parents missed out on the greatest gift and joy in the world: loving you. They'll never get the opportunity to be and do all the things they should've. But right downstairs you have the best role model anyone could ask for, and that woman loves you with every fiber of her being. Never doubt it."

I feel her shoulders shaking as her tears seep through my tee.

I want to take away her pain.

I want her to realize how special she is. How much she's overcome.

I want to tell her when she meets my family, she'll be gaining more people who'll love her.

My mom will go nuts over Amy. I have no doubt they'll become fast friends. My dad already adores her. He appreciates intelligence and wit, and she makes him laugh. I bet Sharon and Amy will hit it off. Sharon's reserved, but Amy's warmth is infectious.

Slowly, the crying subsides and her breathing evens out. I wait a few more minutes to make sure she's fully asleep before I turn out the lights and pull the sheets and comforter from under us to over us.

I kiss her forehead, tangle our legs and hold her tight, hoping she can feel I've got her.

And I aways will.

Chapter Sixteen

T-Day

Jonas

First things first. No one's getting out of this bed until we get our morning frisky on. Amy had been pushing for mutual gratification, and two days ago she stopped talking about it and ambushed me. While I was still sleeping, she'd pulled down my boxer briefs. When her mouth surrounded my dick, I woke with a groan. For a moment I'd thought I was dreaming, but it was too good to be another of my fantasies. I had to watch, and the sight of her thoroughly enjoying what was making me harder than steel had me closing my eyes to keep from losing it within the first minute.

Of all of Amy's talents, that one is mine and mine alone, now and forever.

I turn her to me and push my hands under her PJs to grab on to her fantastic ass.

"Mmmn," she moans, and presses her soft lips against mine.

What starts out slow and sweet turns into deep, wet, and wild. Tongues gliding, teeth nibbling, drinking deep of each other, we don't stop until we have to take a breath.

"Hey," she whispers.

I answer by moving one of my hands to her belly and slide it down until my fingers are coated with her wet warmth. I take her mouth again, and when I curl up to stroke her sweet spot, she starts trembling and grips my shoulders.

"You're so good at this," she pants into my neck.

I love getting her off. Yeah, it strokes my ego to no end, but more than that, I revel in her enjoyment.

"Look at me, Ames. I want to see your face when you fly."

Her eyes are glazed over and her cheeks are flush with color, and when it hits her, she gasps as if she's surprised. I swallow her gasp and kiss her as the rush subsides.

"Damn," she mutters against my lips. "You're turning me into an addict."

I grin. "That goes both ways."

***

Lilli is sitting in the family room wearing black framed glasses with large oval lens. She's reading one section of *The New York Times*, and the finished sections are rumpled and spread out on the sofa. An empty mug and a plate with a jam smear and crumbs are on the large square dark wood coffee table.

"Good morning, my darlings. Did you sleep well?"

Amy bends down and kisses her grandmother on the cheek. "Like I was in a coma."

I follow suit with the cheek kiss then say, "Terrific mattress. Super comfortable."

"Good, good. Now go get some breakfast. I'll join you in the dining room in a few minutes and we'll talk about today's menu and who's coming."

Staring into the huge, fully stocked fridge, I smack my hands together and rub. "What do you want to eat?"

"Surprise me." Amy leans on the island. "And I'm leaving you to do your own search of everything kitchen."

I smile and I'm comforted. *She knows me.*

***

As I'd guessed, Lilli's organizational skills are masterful. She'd already taken into account I'd be doing most of the cooking. She has three signature dishes she wants to prepare – the stuffing, a sweet potato soufflé, and apple cranberry pie – otherwise the menu is all mine with only two must-haves: the turkey and cranberry sauce. We agree I'll start on the turkey immediately, then yield the kitchen to her and Amy, her helper, before taking over.

The table seats fourteen and we're going to have a full house. Two of Lilli's closest friends are widows, and each has one married child who lives close by. They're coming with their children, who have kids. The guests are Ruth, her daughter Deborah, Deb's husband Stewart, and their children, Claudia, age sixteen, and Quentin, age thirteen. Sarah, her son Evan and his wife Bethany, and their children Wyatt, age seventeen, and Gwyneth, age fifteen. They all know each other and have been having Thanksgiving with Lilli and Amy for years.

Everyone is expected to arrive at three p.m. and it's nine a.m. now.

"I'm putting on Bach, Grams."

"Good choice, honey."

And the organized chaos begins.

After surveying the fridge and the pantry, I decide on assorted mini-tacos for pre-dinner finger food, and in addition to Lilli's dishes, the turkey, and cranberry sauce, we'll have carrot soup, rosemary rolls, a beet salad with walnuts and goat cheese, two spinach and artichoke quiches, garlic sautéed green beans with red potatoes and brussel sprouts, and a berry trifle.

I'm in kitchen heaven, and the hours fly by.

When I have a few minutes, I call Dad. Sharon isn't home yet, and I'm sorry Amy and Lilli won't have a chance to meet her today. Dad and I FaceTime and he meets Lilli, to whom he apologizes for missing Thanksgiving with her. He'd met Amy on Monday at our standing weekly dinner. We tell him all about our upcoming feast, and Lilli says, "The door's always open for you and Sharon to come to visit."

A little while later, Amy is touring the kitchen with her tablet, which looks like a food explosion happened here, and is explaining what we're having to eat to *Nonna*.

Lilli walks in and *Nonna* calls out, "*Amica mia*. It's been too long since we've seen each other."

Amy props up the tablet and lets Lilli and *Nonna* have a visit. Then Sofia and Matt come on, and I'm introduced to the rest of the Di Caro family. I'd met Sofia and Matt last Wednesday at the weekly girls' night out, and got reacquainted with Alex, who's a walking, talking bundle of energy.

Sofia tours us through her parents' house, and I'm treated to the dining room where they're hosting Thanksgiving. I never seen a table that big, outside photos of state dinners. It has to seat forty, maybe fifty people.

Mr. Di Caro comes on alone and asks Amy, "This is the boy I met at Theresa's wedding?" She explains we've been seeing each other, and he nods then looks me in the eye when he says, "I hope he knows he better treat you with love and respect."

Yeah, a really scary dude.

When I'm almost finished with my meal prep, I take a minute to survey the dining room. Lilli and Amy have laid a magnificent table with a centerpiece filled with orange and gold flowers, matching napkins in orange and gold paisley, and delicate, old dinnerware with muted roses, blue flowers, greenery, and brown leaves and branches. I'd be nervous someone would break a dish.

"Really pretty china, Lilli."

She smiles. "It was my mother's. She gave it to me when Sam and I married."

"It looks antique."

"It's not quite a hundred years old, so it's almost antique." She points to the dinnerware's matching gravy boat on the island. "Don't forget to put the gravy in there."

"Yes, ma'am."

A little before three, I FaceTime my mom. Today and tomorrow are two of the few days during the year where she goes nowhere and sees no one, except me when it's her year. She says she gives thanks she has a couple of days she can stay home in her sweats, nap at will, catch up on some movies, and drink Bellinis all day and all night. She meets Amy and Lilli, who gives her the same open-door welcome she'd given Dad and Sharon.

At three-fifteen Amy calls out, "The cars are pulling up into the driveway," and goes out to meet everyone.

I turn as I'm folding my apron when I hear the French doors open, and the girls, Claudia and Gwyneth, take one look at me and start screeching.

"Oh. My. God."

"I can't believe it."

"It's him."

"I knooow."

"It's really him."

"I knooow."

One of the mothers shushes the girls. "What are you two carrying on about?"

"Look," a tall pretty girl with big eyes and long dark brown hair points at me while the shorter blonde with a pixie haircut stares frozen in place.

"I see, Claudia. Now put your hand down. You know it's not polite to point or scream. That's Jonas, Amy's–"

"Man," I finish for, I'm guessing, Deb.

"I knooow," Gwyneth reanimates and swoons.

"Mom," Claudia snaps. "He's like the world's most famous supermodel. We saw him on the huge Times Square billboard." Deb looks unimpressed. "You remember. Board shorts. *No* shirt." She makes a face I interpret as *Mom, you're so lame.*

Amy's laughing, Lilli winks at me, and Wyatt and Quentin roll their eyes.

Deb sighs. "Hello, Jonas. I'm Deb Weinstein. This is my husband, Stu, and our children Claudia and Quentin."

I walk over, say hello, and hold out my hand. Stu, Deb, and Quentin shake and make their way into the family room. Claudia seems to be rooted to the spot.

"Shake the man's hand, Claude, and stop gawking," her father tells her.

She barely touches my hand before moving away to make room for Gwyneth, who squeaks when we shake.

The two girls take off and disappear.

**

We're in bed and Amy's wearing hot pink Hello Kitty PJ bottoms and a white long-sleeve sleep tee. She's straddling my thighs.

"Oh Jonas." She exaggerates breathing heavily, and shudders her shoulders. "You cooked all this food?"

She pushes her hands into her hair and musses it as she makes her eyes go wide.

"Oh Jonas." She bats her lashes super fast. "You really surf? Like for real, real?"

I tackle her onto her back and kiss her until all I hear are the little moans she makes in the back of her throat when she's turned on.

"Oh...Jonas."

Chapter Seventeen
All Too Soon

Amy

I hated leaving Grams. I hate thinking of her alone in that big house. I know she has friends, and they visit each other regularly, and she has Gloria, but it's not the same as having people around all the time who love and care for her. She was thrilled to have me and Jonas at the house, and we were equally happy to be there. *My darlings.* She called us that all the time, and I know she meant it. She and Jonas are completely in love with each other, and I think his heart broke even more than mine when we had to go. The good news, I'll be home on December 22nd.

Jonas and I are back in Boston and we returned to our routine of sleeping at my place and eating at his until classes end. On top of everything school, I've had to spend time getting my parties organized. The Siegels' bash was a knockout hit. They immediately booked for a Purim party. A first for me.

Now we're two days away from finals week, and we're pretty much living at my place. While in heavy-duty study mode, it makes sense to hunker down in one place. I lock myself in my room, and he has the common room. I have a little fridge and a hot plate, and it's amazing what Jonas can whip up with such basic tools. It's not typical Jonas gourmet, but it's tasty, filling, and healthy.

I have two parties in the middle of finals week, another on the day of my last test on December 20th, another on the twenty-third, and another on the twenty-fourth.

Jonas's last exam is on December 21st, and the next day he leaves for Miami for work. I'm going with him to Logan Airport to see him off, then I'm flying to JFK, where I have a rental car booked to drive to home to Sagaponack. I'll need the vehicle to get back and forth to all the parties I have in NYC, and I'll return it when I fly out to Costa Rica.

I'm bummed about Jonas leaving. I don't say anything 'cause what's the point. He's under contract and can't wait until he's free from all of it. Me getting all maudlin will make him feel worse than he does already, and I wouldn't do that to him. For him it'll be the same ten days until we're together again as it'll be for me. It sucks, but I've dealt with so much worse it isn't funny.

At least we'll start off the new year right. We'll be together.

When I think about it, it shocks me that it's only five weeks since we ran into each other at that douche's party, and then one week later we spent the night together. More surprising, but not, we've never been apart since.

Four weeks of Jonas and I'm already missing him and he hasn't even left yet.

Talk about an unscheduled detour.

My life was on track. My plans were in place, and no guy factored into my grand scheme of things.

At Thanksgiving, he accused me of being sneaky, when in truth, he's the one who's been slowly knocking me off my feet. He thinks I haven't cottoned on to what he's doing, but I see him. Kissing me until all I can feel and think about is him. Doing the almost-having-sex tease. Easing me into wanting him and only him.

Yeah. I see him.

And he's good. I mean really good. Patient and kind. He's made sure he's the last thing I see before I go to sleep and the first thing I see when I wake up.

And even though his plan of attack is stealth, he's not playing a game. I can see it when he looks at me. Feel it when he holds me. He wants this to be forever, and since I can't envision being without him, it seems that's exactly where we're headed.

"Ames," he calls out. "I'm starving."

This guy has a metabolism most women would kill for. I come out of my room and pull the elastic out of my topknot. My scalp hurts from my hair being up too long.

"I'm taking the bellow to mean you're hungry *and* you have cabin fever."

He grins.

Why does he always have to look so lovable?

"Where do you want to eat?"

"How about Punjab Palace?"

"Done." I wave my hand up and down the length of my body. "Give me five to put on some serious outdoor clothing." I look at my phone. "It's twenty-nine degrees."

"It's a mile. We'll walk fast. We need the fresh air and exercise."

I come out of my room wearing my boots, cords, a heavy sweater, a hoodie, my parka, a watch cap, and a scarf. I hand him my dark navy scarf, and as I pull on my gloves I tell him, "Don't argue, just put it on."

His right eyebrow goes up. "You must be starving too."

"And you say that because…?"

"You get extra bossy when you're hungry."

"Extra bossy?"

"More bossy than your usual bossy."

"Are you complaining?"

"I'm observing."

"You're bullshitting."

"That too."

He kisses me, then pulls me by the hand to the door.

***

We're in a cab on our way to Logan. He's quiet and I'm a little nauseous. To give me something to do, for the ten millionth time, I check his flight then mine. It's not snowing, but it's threatening. I want us to be in the air before that happens. I'm scheduled to leave forty-five minutes after him, which shouldn't be a logistical problem. My gate is only ten away from his.

"Both flights are on time."

"Is it snowing in New York?"

I check the weather. "No. It's too warm. A balmy thirty-four degrees."

He chuckles. "So it's raining."

"Not right now, but they say it might be by the time I land."

He takes my hand and squeezes. "Be careful driving."

"I will. It's a straight shot on the Southern State Parkway."

I go back to the weather app. "Ugh. It's sunny and seventy-six in Miami."

He gives me his Times Square smile.

"Ya know, it's not polite to gloat."

The cab pulls up to the curb and we go inside the terminal, check in on the machines that remind me of little ATMs, and then suffer through TSA. I swear, people don't listen and become more stupid when they're in airports. The agents are yelling a litany of instructions, including to put your all your electronics in a tray. Everyone hears them yelling. The guy in front of us has to hear them yelling, but what does he do? He leaves his laptop in his shoulder bag. Now we're all jammed up waiting for the TSA agent to hand his bag back to him, have him take the laptop out of the bag and put it in the fucking tray.

Jonas looks down at me grinning. "You should see your face right now. It's classic."

"Classic like Grace Kelly or Gene Tierney?"

"More like Cookie Monster when he doesn't get a cookie."

"Cookie Monster? You're bringing out the jokes right now?"

"If it'll keep you from biting off that man's head, yeah."

"Stop. I can't take all the flowery compliments."

We make it to his gate just as they start boarding. I step into his body and push my cheek against his sweater.

He wraps me in his arms and puts his mouth against my ear. "I'll call you when I land. You'll probably be home by then."

I nod against his chest.

"Text me all the time and tell me everything."

More nodding.

He puts his fingers beneath my chin and lifts my head as his is descending. Such a soft, sweet kiss, I'm in danger of becoming soppy.

"See you in Costa Rica, Ames."

I don't watch him walk away.

I turn and head toward my gate, the terminal a great deal fuzzier than usual.

***

December 23rd

A: The alcohol distributor screwed up the order. I got bourbon instead of vodka, and Prosecco instead of Champagne. I just got off the phone with the owner, and he promised everything would be straightened out and I'd get the correct order by five p.m. He better come through. And yeah. I have a back-up place, but it's the holidays. I can't be sure I'll get enough of everything. What a clusterfuck.

J: Less than an hour ago, one of the female models projectile vomited on my legs and feet.

A: Ewww. Is she sick?

J: Not the way you mean. The ambulance came and took her to the hospital. Word is she OD'd on something.

A: Do you know her?

J: Never saw her before today. It's a long shot I'll ever see her again.

A: You topped out on the disgusting meter. I win the aggravation prize.

J: Nine more days.

***

December 24th

A: These people, my clients, who have more money than the federal reserve, are crazy, as in complete lunatics. They have a Christmas fetish to beat all Christmas fetishes. All their guests have to wear red and white striped knee-high socks that curl up at the toe and have bells at the tip of the curl. Their decoration order was nuts. Wreaths on every door in the house, including the bathrooms. Cone and berry garlands to wind around every banister and baluster, and cinnamon stick bundles wrapped in gold ribbons are to be placed on almost every flat surface. Fairy lights are to be strung from every corner of every room, and there are fourteen fully decorated Christmas trees in the house, each with a different motif.

J: I'm guessing their regular decor isn't understated.

A: Imagine gold fixtures everywhere, tassels on everything, and red and purple as the house color scheme throughout.

J: I don't want to imagine that.

A: Well you have to. Misery loves company, and I'm stuck looking at this nightmare for too many more hours than my brain can bear.

J: In my world, today we had a thunderstorm roll in during the middle of the shoot. A bunch of us ran to stand under the craft services tents, but lightning struck one of the generators nearly frying everyone working to cover them.

A: OMG. Are you all right?

J: Yeah. I was on the other side of the shoot.

A: Was anyone hurt?

J: One of the crew got singed by a flying spark, but he's okay. The EMTs came and put some burn ointment on him, bandaged him up, and said he was able to return to work.

A: Two ambulances in two days.

J: I was never particularly fond of Florida, and after these past couple of days, I don't see any reason to come back.

A: Eight more days.

***

December 25th

J: In the brilliant planning column, whoever is in charge of craft services neglected to confirm today with their supplier. There's been no food until a half hour ago when someone found an open supermarket and bought whatever they could find to make sandwiches and other stuff. We have fruit, and in an ironic twist, given how most of the models obsess about their weight, we have more than twenty boxes of Cap'n Crunch cereal and huge jugs of whole milk.

A: Classy.

J: Ames, help me out. I need some perspective. I'm standing here wearing $600 shorts that are substantially the same as the ones I buy at Target for around $15.

A: In about an hour, Grams and I are leaving to go to a shelter in Southhampton to help feed anyone who wants a meal on Christmas Day. Gramps and Grams have always donated food and money to the local food pantry, and they got involved with this shelter a dozen years ago. I've been going since I was ten or eleven.

J: Give Lilli an extra hug and kiss from me and tell her how glad I am she knows what's important and that she taught it to you.

A: I will.

J: One week.

***

December 26ᵗʰ

David,

It's been a minute. I'm guessing you've been as busy as I've been. The holidays will do that to a person. I hope yours have been great.

So, I'm going to dump on you to get your opinion of what's been going on with me.

I met someone who I kind of knew. He goes to the same university I go to. Anyway, we reconnected and within a week, I was falling for him. Now, I'm crazy stupid about him, and I think this is it. He's the one. We haven't spent a day apart in the past four weeks.

I'm going to be twenty-one in March, and I can't help but wonder if I'm too young to be in the kind of love that'll last a lifetime. It doesn't feel like it, but obviously, I'm not objective here.

My grams adores him, and in her mind, we're together forever. She's a practical person who knows me inside and out, so I don't think this is wishful thinking on her part.

And before you ask, he's totally gone for me. I know I'm not in this alone. He's into me and he has no trouble letting me know. Truly, he's a really great guy. An example: He has to work over the holidays, but he doesn't want us to be apart, so I'm flying to Costa Rica on New Year's Day to be with him until his work is done.

Two months ago, I would've thought something like this is too intense and sappy. Now, I'm counting down time until I see him again.

Tell me what you think. The truth and nothing but the truth.

Happy New Year.

Carly

***

December 27ᵗʰ

J: *It's good to be back in SoCal. I can't say I think of it as home, for me that's Portland, but I'm staying with my mom and that makes it feel like home. My agent kind of freaked I'm not staying at the hotel with the rest of the models, but I reminded her I've lived here and I know my way around. Actually, my car stays in my mom's garage, so I'm back in my wheels. We're shooting on the beach in Malibu. Not Zuma this time, farther up the coast at El Matador. Lots of emo shots with all the cool rock formations. The whole atmosphere at this shoot is more laid-back, and the food is amazing. Mom can't wait to see you. She pumps me for info about you like three times a day.*

A: *Is that supposed to make me feel less self-conscious when I meet her?*

J: *You've met her already on FaceTime. And, Ames, I've never seen you less than totally comfortable no matter who you're around. I promise, you two will be best friends in like five minutes.*

A: *I'll be happy with affably friendly.*

J: *That'll be the first two minutes.*

A: *So, guess who's coming to the house tomorrow?*

J: *Collin.*

A: *Damn. Did he tell you?*

J: *No. But he's the only person we have in common who used to spend summers with you when you were kids.*

A: *Well, okay. I'll give you that. He's coming with his dad, Simon, who I don't remember at all, but Grams knows him, and his sister, Aileen, who I don't know, but Grams did when she was a baby.*

J: *I expect there'll be lots of good reminiscing, and I bet Collin will be happy to be back in Sagaponack.*

A: *He's really looking forward to the visit.*

J: *Has he seen the house since it's been upgraded?*

A: *I don't think so.*

J: *Then they'll all get a real treat.*

A: Grams has me on kitchen duty. I'm her sous chef, and I'm on cleanup.

J: When we get back, I have to get her to record more recipes. If she's making something we haven't recorded yet, video it and have her talk you through it. Don't forget to get all the ingredients.

A: Yet another job. I'm the assistant director of your movie.

J: Now who has all the jokes?

A: Five days.

***

December 29th

A: It's two p.m. and I'm sitting in parking lot traffic. The Southern State wasn't too bad, but the minute I hit the Long Island Expressway – which, btw, is called the L.I.E. for short, but the "lie" is it's an expressway – I don't think I've gone over 20 mph. I've checked all the driving apps, and I've found a clearer, although circuitous route. Next exit, I'm cutting across Long Island to eventually get on the Grand Central Parkway. I knew traffic was going to be murder so I left myself plenty of cush. But I need to be at the Rutherfords' by three-thirty mostly to contain Bonita Rutherford. She's a little high-strung. That's what Grams calls a nut-job.

J: So I won't tell you it's sixty-eight degrees and I'm lying on a surfboard taking in some sun while they set up for the next shot.

A: Waaaay cold-blooded.

J: Ah, come on. Tell me you don't wish it was sixty-eight degrees in NYC instead of… Shit. Damn. It's twelve degrees?

A: This from a guy who's lived in Boston for the past 3.5 years?

J: You lose the pain of it after a few days in Cali.

A: So I've heard. Gotta go. Almost at the exit.

J: Three days.

***

December 31st

J: I know you're knee-deep in your event, but I wanted to say Happy New Year, Ames. See you tomorrow.

Chapter Eighteen

New

Amy

I don't know why I didn't associate Costa Rica with humidity, but here I am, sticking to myself even though I'm inside the air-conditioned airport in San José. I'm sitting at the gate waiting for the flight attendant to call boarding for my connecting flight, and my stomach is b-girling at the same time my knees are jiggling to an entirely different beat.

This is stupid. It's Jonas. We've texted like five times a day every day for ten days. He's looking forward to seeing me as much as I'm looking forward to seeing him. *What's with the nerves?*

I refuse to examine this too closely, and thank the universe and all the stars that we're finally boarding. I begin to change my mind when I have to go down a flight of stairs and cross the tarmac in the blazing sun and thick air.

And that's when I see the plane.

Holy, holy, holy shit. It's a dinky little thing with a *propeller*. There are seven people behind me, and I have no idea where they're going to sit because it looks like this plane has room for me and two other people, max.

I walk up rickety metal stairs and step into a clean, narrow plane that has – I count them – nine seats. The smiling male flight attendant takes my rolly and carries it to the back of the plane where there's a cutout and huge straps, apparently for the luggage.

In a plane this size, I don't think sitting in one row is safer than another, so I choose the first single seat – I don't want to hurl on anyone – and fasten my harness/seatbelt combo. I'm thinking the harness probably comforts some people, but I'm not taking it as a good sign.

Let's just say taking off and landing were the least bumpy parts of the flight. No matter what I have to do, Jonas and I are not taking one of these planes back to San José. There has to be another way to get to LA.

The terminal is super small, metal, and rounded. It looks like a plane hangar. I figure I have to walk through it and out the front doors to find the car Jonas arranged to take me to the hotel.

I'm about halfway through the building when I see a tall, clean-shaven man in a ridiculous Hawaiian shirt, huge dark glasses, and a wide-brimmed straw hat holding a sign that says "Amy Stern."

It appears my ride has arrived.

As I get closer, I notice his board shorts, then his legs.

Hey. I know those legs.

Intimately.

I drop my rolly and run at the same time Jonas breaks into his Times Square smile.

My legs are around his hips, my mouth is seared to his, and his hands are under my tush holding me up.

Damn, he tastes good. Better than I remember, if that's even possible, and we're going at it as if we weren't in a public place, until we have to come up for air.

"Missed you, Ames," he whispers against my lips. "Missed you every day and every night."

"Me too." I take off his glasses and place my hand on his cheek. "They made you clean up, huh?"

"Yeah." He puts me down, takes off his hat, and runs his hand through his hair. "They prettied me up too."

Whoa. The cut is totally Hollywood movie star gorgeous. "Wow. They put in tons of streaks."

As he takes my hand and walks us back to my rolly, he says, "The shoots are for summer wear, so I'm supposed to look all beach-ified." He grabs the handle and turns us to the front doors. "The car's waiting for us."

Standing beside a medium-size sedan is our driver, Alberto. He tells us it's about a half hour to the hotel and puts my rolly in the trunk, where I see Jonas's rolly.

"You waited here for me the whole time?"

"I want to claim martyrdom, but we got in about an hour before you."

As we pull away from a loose collection of small buildings that make up the airport, I grab his arm and say, "Before we do anything else, please, please, please, we have to find another way to get to LA."

He laughs. "Already done. I changed out our flight to LA. We're leaving from Liberia, which is about a half hour away from this airport, and we're taking a nonstop flight on a real commercial airline."

"A jet?"

He grins. "Yeah."

I pepper his face with a hundred kisses. On the last one, he holds me tight and kisses me hard. "We have a lot of catching up to do."

I smile. "Totally. Do you have to work today?"

"We're doing a night shoot on the beach. It shouldn't take more than three hours."

"So I have you to myself all day?"

"Oh yeah."

The hotel is lovely, decorated in a colorful tropical theme, and it's on the beach. Our room is a freestanding round hut with a thatch roof I think is made from palm fronds. We have two hammocks hung from the ceiling outside the front door, and a table and chairs are also on the semicircular porch. Our nearest neighboring hut is about two hundred feet away.

Inside, the bed with its gold blanket and white, white sheets sticks out from a curved wall into the middle of the room. I head straight to the bathroom behind the curved wall, dragging my rolly behind me.

Ten minutes later, I walk out in a pleated, light pink baby doll teddy with a big white bow snugged beneath the plunging neckline. Jonas, who's already in bed, sits up, swings his long legs over the side of the bed, reaches out, and pulls me between those fantastic legs.

"Do you know how much the fates want us together?" He's looking up, his gaze holding mine. "How inescapable our destiny has always been?"

I shake my head, enthralled by the intensity of his words and the brilliance in his eyes.

"I had my mail forwarded to my mother's house."

"Um. Okay."

"And I had time to review prior correspondence I received from The Letter Club since so much of it seemed familiar."

I lean back, shocked right down to the tips of my toes.

"David got Carly's letter on December twenty-eighth."

Ho-lee shit.

"You're not too young to be in the kind of love that lasts a lifetime. I'm right there with you, Ames. In deep, and I plan to stay there."

My mouth is dry and I'm having trouble speaking. "You…you love me."

"Like crazy, baby."

Gently, he tugs me to him and places a soft kiss between my breasts.

"And now I'm going to show you just how much."

***

I'm lying across Jonas's chest replaying the last three hours in my head. Three glorious, unbelievable hours where Jonas worshipped my body. He took his time, slow, deliberate, and tantalizing, making sure I knew everything he was doing was a mark. A brand. That I am and always will be his.

My lips throb with the memory of his deep, soul-altering kisses, how he trailed his mouth over my body not missing one spot. His focus unbreakable, he gave his full attention to my breasts. Licking the undersides and kissing his way around them until I thought I would scream with want until finally…finally, he took one nipple in his mouth while his fingers worked the other. And once there, he was beyond thorough, and I was out of control.

I begged. Me. Begged and begged for the release chasing around my body.

He inflicted sweet torment, going down on me over and over, giving me what I begged for with his talented mouth and clever fingers.

He flipped me over, brought me up to my knees and he went at me from behind, his mouth traveling over my tush as his fingers probed my tight hole, making me pant out *please, please, please* until he squeezed my clit and I mewled, whimpered, and collapsed from the intensity of my release.

Before I could get my wits about me, he was on his back and I was straddling him. "Take me, baby," he ordered, and for the first time I lowered myself onto him, and was stretched and filled by *my* Jonas.

Weeks ago, when we'd started to fool around, we'd gotten tested, and boy am I glad we did. I wouldn't've wanted anything between us, especially the first time our bodies joined.

I know this sounds unbelievably sappy, but I swear, I'm different now. When he grabbed my hips and coaxed me to move, the slip and slide, the groan and grind of us felt elemental in a way I've never experienced. Yeah, incredible sex can be transformative, but this had been so much more.

He'd felt when I was close, sat up, wrapped his arms around me and said, "Give me all of you because you definitely have all of me." And the words, the movement, and the love shining in his eyes made me have an orgasm that rocked my body and didn't let up for what felt like hours.

We'd barely had time to catch our breath before he started again. This time from the bottom up, rubbing my feet while nibbling my toes. Who knew ankles could be so sexy? And backs of knees.

When he bent between my legs, I pushed him back and tortured him the way he'd tortured me. When I finally dropped my head and took him in my mouth, his cry of relief made me feel like I have a superpower. And maybe I do. But no more than he has over me.

We coupled. We fucked. We mated.

And I mean that.

We are bound together.

We belong to each other.

His hand is trailing up and down my spine. "I can feel your smile against my chest. What are you thinking?"

"I'm doing slo-mo instant replays."

He sits up, grins, and takes me with him as he untangles us from the sheets. We're on our feet and in the shower, our bodies slick from the warm water cascading over us.

Already sensitized, when he lifts me and presses my back against the wall, my inner thighs start to quiver, my heart bangs against my chest, and I wrap my legs around him tight as he slides into my drenched core.

"I love you," he says against my ear. "I'll never get enough of you." His thrusts increase in depth and pace, and I'm gone, spasming around him, lost in the heady sensation. His head falls back as he roars his release, my inner muscles quaking, gripping him to me.

I'm limp and my legs slip down from his hips. He holds me until I'm steady on my feet, which may be a transitory thing.

He turns me, squirts liquid in my hair, and his talented fingers massage my scalp. I lean against him to keep from crumbling into a heap on the tiled floor. When he's finished with my hair, he soaps my body and is thorough, making sure every nook and cranny gets his attention.

I want to return the favor, and try to soap up his chest, but my fingers don't seem to be working.

I'm woozy.

For the first time in my life, I understand the actuality of overindulging.

He grins, holding me to him with one arm while he washes his hair using the hand of the other. "I'm clean enough," he says as he turns off the water.

He wraps me in a beach towel and carries me to bed, then disappears for a moment and returns with a towel around his waist.

How it's possible I find this sight so sexy and I want him again, I can't explain.

"Don't give me that look or we won't have time to get something to eat before I head down the beach to the shoot."

"I'm thinking I need you more than food right now."

He chuckles. "I'm thinking you could barely stand in the shower. When was the last time you ate something?"

I widen my eyes and stare at his lower body.

"As in food, Ames. Ingesting calories."

"I've heard—"

"Don't even go there." He reaches down, rubs the towel over my body, then lightly smacks my stomach. "Get ready, we're going to eat." He eyes me staring at him. "Food."

***

Three things: Four weeks of semi-sex and sex tease built up a hella reserve in both of us. Morning sex is a two-part deal – tearing up the sheets, and being inventive in the shower. Directly-after-his-shoot sex is energetic and works up our dinner appetite. Before-we-sleep sex is slow, languid, and full of emo. After, there's lots of cuddling and pillow talk, which can lead to round two. I'm loose, I'm happy, and I've never smiled so much in my life.

Which leads me to the second thing: The world's a small place. Sitting under a giant umbrella, reading for pleasure – I never get time to read for pleasure – I'm laughing at the antics of the book's heroine when a woman calls out, "Amy?" I look up and there's Bonita Rutherford's sister-in-law, Carmela Rutherford. *What are you doing here?* leads to a long story about how they just *had* to get away from the cold weather, and since they've sworn off Palm Beach for obvious reasons, they need to find where they're going to buy their new place.

Next thing I know, Carmela's husband, Winston, pulls up two chairs, and we become a threesome under the umbrella. Win jumps up and runs across the beach and into the ocean when Carmela asks me if it's too late to book a Valentine's party. A casual run-into-an-acquaintance-in-the-tropics becomes a party scheduling sesh that turns into an elaborate lunch on the beach. The staff must be used to the exceedingly rich and pampered because a table with a thick white tablecloth appears, along with a full setup for a formal lunch. Win orders *for the table*, not bothering to ask for a menu or to enquire if they have what he wants. He spouts a litany of culinary requests, including expensive champagne, expecting them to produce all of it. There were only a few items missing, but they filled them in with excellent substitutes.

After lunch, Carmela announces she needs to retire to their bungalow – they have one of the giant huts that typically sleeps eight – which seems like code for a nap followed by some afternoon delight. I run off into the ocean to work off lunch.

Which brings me to the third thing: I've turned into a fish. Actually, a sea mammal. While the humidity sucks, the breezes are gentle wafts of warm air, and the ocean's temperature averages eighty-two degrees. I've always loved swimming, and I've been lucky enough to live by the ocean for a good part of my life.

In the summer off Sagaponack, the Atlantic's temperature averages seventy-four degrees. In early January, it's about thirty-eight degrees. Clearly, in the Northeast, ocean swimming is curtailed to the warmer months.

Here, only days after New Year's, I'm swimming in the Pacific whenever the spirit moves me. After Jonas leaves for work, I've been moved to morning swims, swims to break up my pleasure reading, and after-lunch swims. At night, I swim with Jonas. There's enough light on the beach for me to feel comfortable walking into an endless pitch-black ocean, and we don't go out far.

Knowing the havoc the ocean's salt water plays with my hair – in this weather, I don't even bother to try to tame down the day frizz – I packed, and distributed into Jonas's rolly, fifteen mini bottles of heavy-duty conditioner.

Now, sun-kissed – Jonas told me they'll use a computer program to darken his skin tone to make it look like he has a perpetual tan – and more relaxed than I've ever been, we're on a normal plane heading for LA.

***

It's a little before five p.m. when our Uber pulls into Elaine Alpert's driveway. Before our first FaceTime, I'd gotten a primer on Jonas's mom. She didn't take the name Vandenberg when she got married, which confused Jonas's elementary school's secretary, and that was about all the hubbub the different names caused. Elaine has always worked in post-production. First at a Portland news station, then in a post-production company that contracted with local TV and film studios. After his parents divorced, she moved to SoCal and carried her experience to a major post-production company, where she still works.

And because of her important job, she's not home right now. I'm not being bitchy, but I'd really like to clean up and make a good impression. I mean, it's his mom, and from everything he's told me, they're tight. Sure, we've FaceTimed, and we have a general idea of what each other looks like, but it's not the same.

The house is stucco and painted white with a sage green door. One window sits on each side of the door and has sage green shutters. It's cute and looks small. Not an indictment. I know California property prices are outrageous. I bet a house the size of a Porta Potty goes for a mil.

When we step inside the entryway, I know I've been deceived. Even from here, I can see even though the house is narrow, it's long. Jonas said the house was built in 1934, and it truly has the feel of the era. All the archways are wide and rounded, the floors are a beautiful polished cherry wood, and the living room ceiling is not quite curved, but more like vaulted with a flat middle.

The oatmeal-colored sofas look slouchy and super comfy, and are draped with deep maroon throws that match the colors in the floor-length curtains and area rug. As we make our way through the house the vibe is *sit down, relax, be comfortable, enjoy yourself.*

I get the tour, and he shows me our room. "Mom made it into a guest bedroom after I left for BU." He points to the loft above a wide built-in closet, where I can see plaques on the short walls, and trophies fronting the railing. "My awards. Mom didn't want to stuff them away, so she put 'em somewhere she could see them without interfering with the room's aesthetic. Her word, not mine."

"Well, it's a lovely room," I climb halfway up the loft ladder, "and science and math trophies don't exactly go with the lemon walls and floral comforter."

He shrugs. "Whatever."

I laugh. That's the first California-ism I've ever heard him say. Being home must bring it out of him.

We go back to the kitchen and out the back door to the yard, which is a revelation. Huge magenta bougainvillea cover the half-walls and the fencing on top of them, and the garage wall is a covered with hot pink climbing roses. A sweet little citrus garden is planted in front of the roses: dwarf lemons, interspersed with small, rounded shrubs of blue hydrangea. There's a multicolored painted wooden table with six wooden chairs in the middle of the yard that sit on a round patio, and a wide lounge chair is strategically placed under an umbrella in the far left corner abutting the bougainvillea.

"Your mom do all this?"

"Most of it. The roses were here, but were a mess. She brought them back and babies them." He points at the bougainvillea. "They thrive on neglect. A couple of times a year a gardener comes and trims them."

"It's so pretty. Grams would love it."

"When we call her, we'll give her the tour."

He shows me the laundry room, a little bathroom, and a small gym all attached to the back of the garage.

I elbow him in the ribs. "You pump iron when you were in high school?"

"Nope. This is Mom's. I surfed." He grins and I know what he's thinking.

Jonas told me Playa Negra is known for world-class surfing. Every morning, at high tide, after bedroom sex but before breakfast, he surfed and I watched. And went squishy girly. No matter how much sex we had, watching him surf made me want to rip off his shorts and fuck him until we collapsed. Good thing we had shower sex after he surfed. It contributed to our inventiveness and leveled me out.

"I need a shower."

He gives me the Times Square smile, lifts me so I'm forced to wrap my legs around his hips, and walks us into the hall bathroom with its little white octagonal tiles.

I smack his shoulder. "What if your mother comes home?"

"I doubt it. We're meeting her at a restaurant that's nearer to her office than here."

I get what he's saying, but I narrow my eyes. "You sure?"

"Ninety percent."

"Okay." I relent, but I'm skeptical.

The shower is old school. Sliding glass doors sit on the tub's rim, and the tub is not wide. Jonas seems unconcerned and has us out of our clothes in record time. The water is warm and strong. Good water pressure. My back is to his front and I can feel just how happy he is to have me naked. He squirts the liquid soap from the inset cylinder, and slides his hands down where he makes lots of froth and teases before his hands move up and he starts massaging my breasts.

He bites my earlobe and whispers, "Have I told you how much I love your body?"

"Mmmm."

Does he really think I can speak right now? It's been like nine hours since we had morning sex, and I'm past needing my fix.

He pinches my nipples and pulls on them, making me wriggle my tush against his super-hard cock. He reaches around my body and in, working my clit in tandem with my nipple.

I'm moaning and he's relentless.

"Jonas."

"Yeah, baby. Let go."

"Jonas."

I grip his arms as my head flies back and knocks against his shoulder.

"Jonas."

That's it, I'm gone. My knees turn liquid and the world is reduced to what his hands are doing.

I'm panting, and he's not letting up.

"I can't."

"Oh yeah, you can."

He's so right. I'm so primed, I go over again, and I'm gasping for air.

I've barely come down when he turns me, and I slap my hands on the tiling. He grabs my hips, tilts up my tush, then drives into me over and over and over.

He lays his torso over my back, and with his teeth, he latches on to the muscle between my neck and shoulder. He's thrusting so fast, I can't breathe. And with my cheek pressed against the tile, I pant out a series of cries at the same time he groans his release into my skin.

We're trembling, but somehow he manages to say, "I love you, Ames. Absolutely love you."

We take an actual shower, and when we step out, he towels my body, wraps me in the towel, then slings one around his hips. I do a towel turban over my hair, then get up on my toes and kiss him.

"I love you. Absolutely love you."

He grins and looks smug.

I gotta say, it's a good look on him. But I keep that to myself.

As we're walking down the hall to our room, a little brown dog barrels past us, stops, turns, and barks at Jonas. Shit. I'd forgotten about the dog and was so focused on cleaning up it didn't dawn on me the dog wasn't here.

"Bosco." He bends down and picks up the scruffy little brown dog. "Buddy. How've you been?"

I dread what I know is true but force myself to deal. I turn, and sure enough, there's Elaine leaning against the kitchen archway wearing a wicked smile.

In a total guy move, Jonas turns, grins, puts his arm around my shoulder, and says, "Hey, Mom." I want to kick him.

I don't embarrass easily, but I'm sure as fuck blushing now. I can feel the heat rising up my neck into my cheeks, and onward to my scalp.

"Hello, Ms. Alpert," I croak out, clear my throat then try again. "I wondered where the dog was."

"Elaine," she tells me. Then she tilts her head toward Jonas and says, "I can't believe you didn't tell her about Bosco coming to work with me." He shrugs. "Not cool, Jonas. Bosco's a member of the family. You need to keep people updated."

As awkward as this situation is, I can't help but like his mom already.

As if he knows he's the topic of conversation, and he doesn't like what he's hearing, Bosco squirms in Jonas's arm.

Jonas squats, Bosco jumps down, and races to Elaine.

"Get dressed," she says and waves her hand in the direction of our room. Then she walks into the kitchen and I hear the back door open.

"Ninety percent, huh?"

He grins, turns me, puts his hand between my shoulder blades, and scoots me down the hall to our room.

***

We're riding back to the house in Elaine's electric SUV. She's totally a SoCal person, and so opposite Skip, Jonas's dad, I can't imagine how they got together in the first place. I'm guessing lust. She's a looker.

Tall, maybe five-ten, dark blonde hair she wears in a chin-length bob with long sweepy bangs, and she's built. Super curvy and proud of it. Jonas has her moss green eyes, and her smile. Wide and mischievous.

In all other ways, Jonas favors Skip. Tall, lanky, quiet, intense, and nerdy. Skip's a looker too, but in a low-key way. His sandy hair is cut FBI short, and his dark blue eyes are serious, even when he's laughing. Jonas has his father's strong nose and lush lips.

Between them, his parents made a knockout kid who's the sweetest man I've ever met. After spending a little time with Elaine, I'd say Jonas has Skip's temperament, and Elaine's joy for life. But more toned down. Elaine lives out loud and is unapologetic. Jonas is more subdued, but he has her sense of humor.

On the way to the super excellent Thai restaurant, we heard why Elaine came home. Bosco. Part of her routine at work is to take an hour lunch so she can walk him. Then they hang out in the park and play. Today, she didn't have a chance to do that and thought it would've been cruel to make him wait in the car while we ate and gabbed. So she brought him home to his yard to give him some outside time. If he wants to be inside, he has a doggie door that goes into her little gym.

Now, we're on our way home and I'm feeling full and mellow.

"So, Amy, what are your plans for tomorrow?"

"I'm going to the library that has the local history museum, then I'm going to walk around Santa Monica and probably spend too much money on things I don't need."

"Excellent. I recommend you try Fritto Misto for lunch. They make their own pasta, which is hard to find anymore."

I take out my phone and put the restaurant in Notes.

Since the garage is behind the house, Elaine had heavy wooden gates put in alongside the front of the house for safety, and to give her more outside space. When we pull into the driveway, Jonas gets out to unlock the gates. He hadn't toured me on this side of the house, so it's only now I see all the colorful pots filled with a variety of succulents lining the wall.

He meets us in the yard where he turns on café lights crisscrossing the space.

"How pretty."

"Thanks," Elaine says. "I spend most evenings out here decompressing."

"I can see why."

"I know Señor Gorgeous is going to say no, but drinks?"

I nod.

"Any preferences?"

"Surprise me."

That's how Elaine and I got plowed drinking lavender margaritas. Jonas had to escort us into the house one at a time.

Lying on the bed watching Jonas undress, I lick my lips and say, "I think I'm too drunk for drunk sex."

He grins, then proves me wrong.

***

Today is our day. Jonas finished working yesterday, and now he's driving us up the Pacific Coast Highway to Leo Carrillo Beach where we'll explore for a while. Then we'll head down to Malibu Village where we'll wander.

I love his car. A vintage 1971 Camaro in electric blue. Elaine and Skip split the cost and bought it for him for his sixteenth birthday.

When I saw it in the garage, I said, "I didn't know you're a car buff."

"I'm not. Not really. There was a guy who lived in our neighborhood in Portland, and he owned a vintage Camaro. I fell in love with it. Me and my dad would go to the guy's house to look at the car and talk to him about it. I started saving up my money to buy one for myself."

"What were you, ten?"

"Yeah, about that."

"Where did you get money to save up?"

"Cut lawns, trimmed hedges, washed cars."

"This was all neighborhood stuff."

"Yeah. The people where we lived were nice. Friendly."

"What did you do with the money when you found out your parents paid for the car?"

"You know how much car insurance costs for a sixteen-year-old boy?"

"With a hot rod."

"Yeah. I got a job in a restaurant in Santa Monica as a busboy to keep up the insurance payments past the first year."

"So she's your baby."

He smiled. "She's my ego gratification toy."

"Are you going to bring her back east?"

His eyes sparkled when he grinned. There was something knowing in his expression, but I couldn't put a finger on it.

"I'm going to have to, but I must have a garage. No way am I leaving the car to the elements."

So here we are cruising up the PCH, windows down, and I'm singing "Born to Be Wild," which is what Jonas has cranked up on his phone.

It's a perfect day.

*****

It's the next day, and it's Elaine's day. We're leaving for NY tomorrow, and we want to hang with her before we leave. She's taken the day off work. According to Jonas, that's a miracle.

So what's her wish? To go to the Hollywood Bowl and watch an artist practice. Since she's in the business, or, as she says, business adjacent, she learned one of her favorite jazz singers is going to be practicing today. So she called someone who called someone who made arrangements for us to be there when the artist rehearsed.

We're going full bore with the Bowl experience. We're bringing Bosco, who I adore and want one of my own, and a giant picnic basket with all kinds of food. We agree to save the drinking for when we get home.

***

We decide to say good-bye at Elaine's house where we can be mushy. Jonas was right again. Elaine and I are besties. I adore her. She's warm, witty, wise, and she loves her son with an intensity that's beyond the beyond. Grams is going to flip when she meets Elaine in person. They're totally different, but they're cut from the same cloth. Loyal and loving.

Jonas gets into the Uber while I stand on the driveway hugging Elaine, tears rolling down my face.

"I'm so happy it's you," she whispers. "He's so into you, he's walking two feet off the ground." She hugs me tighter. "And you, you love him the way he deserves to be loved. I'm so happy for all of us."

I kiss her cheek and say, "I'll see you in May. I love you."

Then I run to the Uber, slide in next to Jonas and cry into his neck.

For the first time in my life, I have someone I can call mom and mean it.

Chapter Nineteen

The Question

Jonas

We took the red-eye to New York so we could have the entire day with Mom. Amy is sleeping, her head tucked into my neck. I'm glad she's able to rest. We packed in a lot in a short period of time. I'm about ready to conk out myself.

Leaving Mom is always difficult, but for Amy, this departure was wrenching.

As expected, Mom and Amy fell in love with each other over Thai food. But more than that, Amy now has a mother who loves and cares for her, and leaving that behind had to tear her up.

My sweet Ames. She's not only everything I thought she'd be, she's so much more. I don't think she realizes how warm and loving she is. I don't know one person who doesn't bask in her glow. I'm not counting Bree. She's only half human. But everyone else? When they walk away from Amy, they look like they've just gotten a huge dose of vitamin D.

Sofia, who's known Amy almost all her life, calls it "the treatment." *Ten minutes with Amy and you feel better.*

With that thought, I close my eyes and drift into sleep.

I'm half dozing when the captain announces we're forty minutes away from JFK.

"Ames." I kiss her mouth. "Baby. It's time to wake up."

"Do I have to?" she mumbles.

I chuckle. "Yeah." I stand and take her hand. "C'mon. Go to the bathroom before we land. It'll help wake you up."

Unlike California, where people start their day early, at five forty-five a.m. almost no one is on the road heading into NYC, and less than no one is on the road in the opposite direction heading out to Sagaponack. We rent a car since Amy wants to drive back to Boston. We told Collin, and he'd rather drive with us than endure the train, so we'll go into NYC to get him before heading north.

Amy's found a classic oldies station and she's singing along with Jim Morrison to "Hello, I Love You."

"Hey," she shouts. "Join in. With your background, you should know the words to all these songs."

"I do, but I can't sing."

"You think what I'm doing is singing?"

"I value my life too much to answer."

She laughs. "Well, we'll both be off-key, but we'll be doing it together."

And there it is. Amy, making everything all right.

I start singing and I'm awful. Amy laughs and joins right in. For the next half hour we crack each other up with how much we're mutilating iconic songs.

"You know," I say, "if you play any of this music around Helen, she's going to start singing with you."

My gran, who Amy FaceTimes once a week to exchange dirty jokes, doesn't warm up to most people at all, and when she does, it takes forever. With Amy, it took one FaceTime call.

"I can't wait." Amy claps her hands. "She *can* sing. I'll do backup doo-wops."

I shake my head. Those two are kindred spirits. "Did I tell you? Gran says she and Gramp's names are switched. She has hell in her name, yet he's the one who's 'the man' and his name is Arthur, but she's the one with all the art in her soul."

"When you're with them, is it like watching a comedy act?"

"Yeah. He's the straight man in every way that can be connoted, and she plays off him and entertains herself."

"Okay, so I know this has ick factor attached to it, but he can't be as rigid as he appears. She loves him, and has for a long time. I'd lay good money on them being an inferno in bed."

"Thank you for putting that thought and its related image in my head. I'm going to need therapy for the rest of my life."

She smiles. "Happy to oblige."

"Baby, I'm going to have to stop to stretch my legs. I've been sitting too long."

"Okay." She picks up her phone and a minute later tells me which exit to take. "There's a Dunkin' right there and I need a donut bad."

"You know Lilli's going to feed us ten minutes after we walk through the door."

"That's healthy stuff. I need fried dough and copious amounts of sugar, stat."

"Stat?"

"Well, yeah. All that singing, I worked up an appetite."

***

As foretold, Lilli feeds us healthy stuff ten minutes after we walk in the door. But not before she makes a fuss over my clean-shaven face and shorter hair. I understand grandmother speak. I'll be shaving for the next few days.

Stuffed, and lounging in the family room, I'm listening to Amy regale Lilli with stories from our trip. Somehow, none of them are repeats. We FaceTimed with Lilli every day, and gave her tours of the hut, the hotel, the beach, me surfing, Mom's house and yard, Bosco, and she even spent time with us at the Hollywood Bowl. Yet, Amy has a lot more to say, and, as always, Lilli hangs on every word.

She laughs, nods, and interjects as she moves her hand up and down the cashmere cardigan Amy got for her in Santa Monica. When Amy put it on her, I caught the tears in Lilli's eyes. She saw me watching, and in that moment something heavy and intense passed between us.

Don't ask me how, but in that silent exchange, I felt her love and care for Amy pass to me.

So later in the day, when Lilli and I are in the den reading and she asks, "Where's Amy, honey?" I know it's time.

"She's stuck on a call with one of her more demanding clients."

"They're all demanding,"

I can't disagree so I grin. "While we're alone, I want to ask you something."

She's a wily one, Lilli is, and from her expression, I'd lay good money on her knowing what I'm going to say.

"Go ahead. Ask."

"I want to marry Amy, and I'd like your consent."

"I said it when I met you. Such good manners." She leans over and puts both hands over mine. "Jonas, my darling, you have my consent and my blessing. I couldn't have found a better man for our Amy."

I let out a relieved breath.

"But before you go out and spend a fortune on a ring, could I ask a favor?"

"Sure."

She stands. "Come with me."

I follow her to her room, and she disappears into her closet. I hear a large door creak, rummaging, then the door thudding shut. She comes out holding an old small black jewelry box and presses it into my hand.

"Sam gave this to me the day he asked me to marry him. It was his mother's. After he died, I took it off and wear only my wedding band." She looks down at the diamond band on her thin hand. "Would you give this ring to Amy as her engagement ring?"

My heart is in my throat, and my stomach flips. Wow. This is really happening.

I nod before I even open the box. It doesn't matter what the ring looks like, Amy will love and treasure it.

"Go on, open it."

I look down and carefully lift the lid to find a beautiful, large, round center diamond set in what I'm guessing is a platinum band, that has an intricate design down the sides with small diamonds set into the decoration. Inside the band is Tiffany's imprint. The ring is flawless, tasteful, and too generous. I don't know anything about expensive jewelry, but even I can tell this ring is worth a fortune.

"It's exquisite."

"It is, isn't it? I always loved that ring. Both because it was Sam's mother's – she died when he was fourteen and as he was the oldest, it came to him – and because it's pure Art Deco."

"You've told Amy the story of the ring."

"Oh yes. Starting many years ago, and many times. Amy loves to hear stories about her family."

I bet, I thought. Especially since her family doesn't include her fuckin' mother and father.

"Would it be too presumptuous of me to ask you when you plan to pop the question?"

I shake my head. "I thought it would take me a while to find a ring, but I planned to ask her after I did." I shrug. "Now that I have a ring, I guess I can ask her… right away."

She claps her hands together. "Can you do it here? In our home?"

I smile. "I don't think anywhere else would be as perfect."

"Tomorrow, I'll ask Gloria to bring up a couple of magnums of champagne from the wine cellar."

I put the ring back in the box and shove the box into my front pocket. Then I put Lilli's hand in the crook of my arm and I walk us back to the den so Amy doesn't wander in here looking for us. She'd ask a million questions, and we'd look guilty.

Being back in cold weather has me yearning for a hearty dinner, so tonight I'm preparing one of my favorite Dutch meals with a bit of a twist: chicken satay *kroket* and *stammpot* with a cheese board and rye bread. Traditionally, the *kroket* are made with a meat ragout, but I prefer the light savory flavor of the satay. It offsets the heaviness of the *stammpot*, which is basically a mashed potato casserole flavored with carrots, onions, garlic, and something green. I like it with chard.

But first I have to go shopping for rye bread, and gouda and edam cheese. Gran makes rye bread from scratch. It's a project, and it takes a day to rise. Since I have a hankering now, I can live with store-bought.

I go upstairs to find Amy in the sitting room hunched over her laptop.

"Hey. What are you doing?"

She looks up and seems confused for a moment. Like I pulled her out of a reverie. "I'm working on my winter/spring party spreadsheet."

"It looks like it's working you."

She closes her eyes, lifts up her face, and smiles. "Well, yeah. Sort of, I guess. I'm having a hard time getting out of vacation mode."

"Then don't. At least for the next few days."

"Easy for you to say."

"Not usually. But we're going to hit the ground running the minute we get back to Boston. Let's enjoy a little more of don't worry, be happy."

"I can do that."

Downstairs, we look for Lilli to ask if she needs anything from the market. We find her napping in her recliner. Amy takes the throw off the sofa and covers her grandmother, then we slip out quietly.

In the car she tells me, "The past year or so, she's been doing that more often. Napping for a couple of hours in the afternoons."

"My gran and gramps nap. She says it's one of the benefits of being older. You can drift off whenever you want."

"Huh. I always thought of it as a sort of wearing down."

"I'm sure it's that too, but Lilli's a vital woman. She's sharp and really present. It's a cold day. Why not have a nap?"

Everything I'm saying is the truth, I'm not sugarcoating it, but I can tell she's still worried. I pull into the parking lot of one of the six million gourmet markets in the Hamptons, shut off the car, and turn to her.

"Ames. I've never lied to you, and I never will." I take her hand and lace our fingers. "She's going to be eighty-two in a couple of months.

That's not ancient, but she's had a long, full life. You know you're the light in her soul. She'll stay with you as long as she's able."

I lean in so all she sees is me. "Baby, you're not alone. I'm yours forever. Mom is yours forever. Dad is yours forever. Gran and Gramps are yours forever. You have all the Di Caros forever. When Lilli leaves us, it'll break our hearts. We'll be sad, and it'll be hard. But I swear, you'll be all right. Everyone who loves you," I kiss her forehead, "me especially, will make sure of it."

Tears threaten, but she takes a couple of deep breaths to steady herself before kissing me sweetly. "I'm so lucky to have you."

"I'm the lucky one."

She smiles. "Such a charmer."

I squeeze her hand and ask, "Ready?"

She nods, and we go shopping.

***

Gloria is all smiles as she tucks the champagne in the back of the fridge. Amy and Lilli are out getting their nails done. A ploy Lilli initiated to give Gloria the all-clear for subterfuge. Celebratory champagne has turned into champagne and a nosh. Canapés made with leftover ingredients from last night are toasting in the oven. Melted cheese over anything usually does the trick, but Gloria added flourish. She chopped up the leftover chard and mixed it with spinach, roasted garlic, shaved edam and gouda, and put the mixture on cut-up squares from the remaining rye bread. She's holding back the halved cherry tomatoes to put on the canapés at the last minute.

To add a little sweet, she mashed up Oreo cookies, Lilli's favorite, with vanilla ice cream, dolloped the mixture on graham crackers, and put them in the freezer.

Every five minutes, she races over to the French doors and sticks her head out to peek at the driveway. This, the thirty-fifth time – an approximation – produces a stuttered, "The, The... They're here."

I'm not nervous. I was when I talked to Lilli. But asking Amy to marry me isn't scary; it's the best thing I'm going to do before actually marrying her. I can't imagine my future without her by my side.

I pull on my jacket and walk to the driveway to help them bring in packages filled with who knows what.

"I thought you were getting your nails done." Amy wiggles her fingers at me. Cotton candy pink shines in the thin afternoon sun. "Pretty. But what's with the bags?"

"Grams wanted to get a jump on her seeds, so we stopped at her usual garden center. But they had only some of what she wanted, so we went to her backup garden center for the rest. Then she decided we needed a huge puzzle to work on. One puzzle turned into three."

I nod. Wily Lilli was stalling to give Gloria time to get the food together. I take everything into the house and put the bags on the kitchen island. Then, before Amy can smell the canapés or notice the setup in the family room, I grab her hand and guide her outside to the long stone bench in front of a covered flower bed that faces the pool.

"Let's sit."

"My tush is going to get cold."

"We won't be here that long."

She gives me squinty eyes. "You look, I don't know, like you're plotting something."

I grin. "Good guess."

"Huh. What are you plotting?"

"It's more like planning than plotting."

She sighs. Huge. "Okay, Mr. Exactitude, what are you *planning*?

"The rest of our lives."

I didn't intend to get on one knee, but it seems my body made up my mind for me.

She's watching me with wide eyes and her mouth forms an "O" as I reach into my jacket pocket and pull out the little black box.

"Amy, my love, will you marry me?"

I open the box, take out the ring, and push it on her finger. It doesn't go past her knuckle. I knew it wouldn't. Lilli's hands are small and thin. No worries. I've already made an appointment at Tiffany's in Boston to get the ring sized.

Tears are rolling down her face. "This is Grams's ring."

"No, baby. It's your ring now."

"It's too small."

"I figured. So when we're back in Boston, we'll go into Tiffany's and have it sized."

"You made an appointment already, didn't you?"

"Yeah, I did."

"Confident I'd say yes."

"Hoped with all my heart."

She's mapping my face like she's looking for a chink in the armor. I wait.

I know my Ames. She always takes another minute to make sure she's making the right choice. Since *I know* I'm the right choice, I'm good with waiting the minute.

"I can't picture my life without you, so… Yes."

She throws her arms around my neck and kisses me with her sweet mouth that has a hint of salty tears. And I can't help but think, that's life. Some salt makes the sweet sweeter.

I hand her the box.

"No. I'm not putting *my ring* back in that box."

She takes off the necklace she always wears that has a peace sign pendant, and a Jewish chai, and slides the ring on. She turns so I can re-clasp it.

The moment we're inside Amy and Lilli do the swaying hug, both of them laughing and crying at the same time. Gloria is standing in front of the counter with a bright smile and a tissue balled in the fist over her heart.

I pull out my phone and call my mom.

***

We drink champagne and munch on excellent canapés at the same time we're talking to everyone we know. We caught Mom with Bosco in the park. Perfect timing there, especially since Mom is yelling "Hooray" repeatedly at the top of her lungs. Dad's in his office, gets up, closes the door, and lets out a loud whoop. Sofia is home with Alex, and she's laughing and crying along with Amy and Lilli. Gran and Gramps are both home, and Gran starts dancing at the same time Gramps tells me it's important to make good investments and I should start by buying a house as soon as I can. Collin is walking somewhere in NYC and ducks into a deli to hear what we're telling him, then hollers, "Fuck yeah." *Nonna* is home and is crying and mumbling in Italian, then switches to English when she and Lilli start planning Amy's bridal shower.

The last FaceTime call Amy makes is to Mr. Di Caro. She's never told me why, but I sense they have a special connection that goes beyond the general family love Amy has from the Di Caros.

Years ago, after seeing Amy at that wedding and how Mr. Di Caro seemed so protective of her, I looked him up. While no article said directly, *Don Di Caro*, it was implied. I wasn't surprised. The guy looked like a rich Wall Street banker, but, no doubt, he's one scary dude.

"Amy." Mr. Di Caro's voice is rich and deep and full of affection. "And Jonas."

From the little contact we've had, I know I have to be formal with him. "Hello, sir."

"I wanted to tell you myself, Jonas and I are engaged."

"Well, congratulations. What does Lilli have to say about this?"

Before Lilli can answer, I say, "I asked for her permission first."

Mr. Di Caro nods. "As well you should."

Lilli grabs the phone and walks off toward her bedroom. All I hear is, "Alessandro…"

I lift a brow.

"They're good friends. They talk all the time."

***

If leaving Mom hurt like surgery, leaving Lilli is ten forms of torture. I have to endure leaving an old woman I love alone. And, if that's not bad enough on its own, the light of her life is leaving and won't be back for a couple of months.

Totally sucks having to watch Amy force herself to walk away from the person she loves most on this earth.

The ride to NYC is quiet. But thankfully, Collin is full of a million holiday and engagement questions, so the ride back to Boston turns out to be fun and filled with lots of laughter.

Chapter Twenty

The Homestretch

Amy

I'm in the homestretch to graduation. On January 19th, when I started the counter on my phone to May 21st, graduation day, I thought the days would move at a snail's pace. But Jonas and I have been so busy, time has flown.

School: If I was suffering from senior malaise in the fall, I'm in full-blown *I barely give a shit* now. All my classes are electives, and while a couple of them are interesting, I'm too busy with my business to do more than attend half the time. Though I make sure I turn in all my assignments before they're due. No way am I going to tank my hard-earned 3.87 GPA.

Jonas practically lives in the lab. All his classes are upper level and require lots of lab time. On top of that, he's often in the lab three times a week until eleven p.m.

On the weekends he makes amazing meals for me and Collin, and during the week Collin and I take turns cooking. By the first week in February, we stopped apologizing for our lack of skill and finesse. Truly, I don't think Jonas cares as long as it's edible, filling, reasonably healthy, and we're there to eat with him.

Collin's been practically residing in the library working on his senior thesis. He's already taken on the disheveled appearance of an absorbed, dreamy college professor.

I swear, I'm more worried than Collin and Jonas put together waiting to hear from the schools they applied to for their PhD programs.

Big Pond Entertainment: It's happened. I've officially gone beyond my ability to keep up with all the work by myself. I'm a big word-of-mouth person, and start with the Old Ladies Club to find out if any of them know someone who has or knows of a great part-time administrative assistant. With them being as connected as they are, I get four recommendations within a week. I wind up hiring Ava's grandson's boyfriend, Jamie Frankel, who lives in NYC and works from home. Until party day, and sometimes the day before, almost all of what he does requires a computer and a phone. Big Pond's one of his three employers. The other two are tied to the arts, and already I'm seeing positive crossover connections and opportunities.

The part of my business I expect to slow down are the private college parties thrown by bored rich kids. I'll keep my finger in since where there are bored rich kids, there are rich, indulgent parents. To help with the private college parties for the rest of the semester, and to keep her ear to the ground for future opportunities in the Northeast college corridor, I've taken on an intern. I sat next to Charlie – Carlotta Peet – in my History of Photography class, and liked her immediately. A hippie-emo-fairy with blonde and pink hair, she's a freshman with loads of quiet energy, and eyes as big as saucers. She has an aesthetic that appeals to everyone, and she's friendly and keen.

After I shared all this with Grams, she *directed* me to contact her attorney, Gerald Faber, immediately to get someone to handle all the employment and tax stuff. Ugh. Of course I did it, and now, at the family rate, the accountancy firm Gerald recommended is handling everything for Big Pond Entertainment.

Jonas has started calling me mini-mogul.

Today, the last day of February, I'm opening the door to Jonas's place when I hear the sound of a cork popping. I walk in to find Jonas slapping Collin on the back and Collin punching his fists on Jonas's shoulders.

I slam the door and yell, "Which one?"

Jonas points at Collin.

I rush Collin, throw my arms around his neck, and jump up and down in his arms. He's smiling so huge his face must hurt.

"Does your dad and Aileen know?" He nods, and I can see the emotion in his eyes.

"I'm so, so, so proud of you. Columbia. An Ivy League PhD. Are you going to live in Morningside Heights, or at home?"

"Home. I've got to be careful with the money my grandfather left me. It could take seven or eight years to get my PhD, and then who knows how long it'll take to get a faculty position."

I slap his arm. "Pshaw." I pull out my phone and hit record. "I, Amy Stern, am making a five hundred dollar bet with Collin Dineen. I'm betting that directly upon completing his PhD, if not before, he'll be offered a faculty position at Columbia University in New York City." I send the recording to my email, Collin's email, and Jonas's email.

"When I win," I wink at him, "if you want, we'll use the five hundred you'll owe me toward the kind of party I know you'll like."

Collin pulls me to him and kisses my cheek. "Deal."

No matter what we had scheduled that night, we stay in, order pizza, and drink two bottles of Prosecco to celebrate Collin.

In an uncharacteristic move, the next day Collin leaves for NYC to celebrate with his family. Since spring break starts in four days, he's not really ditching much.

Starting tomorrow, Jonas and I are babysitting Skip and Sharon's dog, Milo. For the first time in Jonas's memory, Skip is taking a two-week vacation. Inspired by our vids from Costa Rica, and in desperate need of some rest, he and Sharon are going to Playa Negra to do lots of nothing.

Milo is a multicolored mutt who's twenty pounds of love. Discovered undernourished at a crime scene, where no one would be around to take care of him, one of the detectives brought him into the station. Sharon took one look at the shaggy mess and said, "Don't take him to the pound, leave him with me." That was two years ago.

Saturday morning, with Milo curled up in his bed in the well of the front passenger seat – in other words, between my feet – we drive down to New York to hang with Grams, who's delighted we're bringing a dog to the house. Gramps had died about six months before Maisy, their old Old English Sheepdog who went to sleep and never got up.

***

Thursday, March 16: Jonas couldn't ditch so we drove back to Boston four days ago. Two days ago, we brought Milo back to Skip and Sharon, who were tanned, relaxed, and smiling more than I've ever seen them smile. I'm sitting next to Jonas on a six-twenty a.m. flight to JFK. It's Grams's eighty-second birthday, and Saturday is my twenty-first. Grams has always considered me her best birthday present. For that, and thousands of other reasons, I'm on a plane at six a.m. Jonas doesn't seem to mind. In fact, at this inhuman hour, he seems way too mellow about sitting on a packed plane with a bunch of businesspeople.

Since we're now well-practiced at collecting a rental car, we're on the Southern State by eight-fifteen, and traffic is pretty light. Jonas turns on the oldies station and starts singing. I'm still grumpy and not really feeling it, but I force myself. And, as is always the way with singing, I'm feeling perkier by the song.

We stop to stretch and get a box of Dunkin'. Grams loves donuts but doesn't indulge often. But hey, it's her birthday. Today she gets to eat and drink whatever she wants. We pull up to the house to find her out front sitting on her gardening stool directing Ernie, her gardener for as long as I have memory. As I get out of the car, I see him giving her a salute before moving to the flower beds on the other side of the front door.

Grams is bending over a hoed row at the front of the flower bed with seeds in one hand and a bowl filled with seeds in the other. I march up and snap, "What are you doing out here in forty-one-degree weather?"

She smiles up at me and points to a thick scarf tucked into her heavy brown Mac. "What does it look like I'm doing?" She doesn't wait for my answer. "I'm planting the seeds we bought. The almanac and the Weather Channel say we won't have a hard freeze again, and you know I like to get the seeds in the ground as early as possible. There's lots to do to bring the garden back to its glory and time's a-wasting."

I drop my head and take a deep breath. "Ernie's here. Let him do the seeds."

"Ernie has other things to work on. It's not like I'm doing anything strenuous. I'm sitting on a stool dropping seeds into the ground. I won't even push the dirt over. Ernie'll come back and do it after I get done planting."

Out of the corner of my eye I see Jonas, who's been hanging back. But at the lull in the sniping, he steps forward, bends down, and kisses Grams on the cheek. "Happy birthday, Lilli." He holds out the Dunkin' box and her eyes light up. "I'll make you a deal. You go in the house and get breakfast going, and I'll get the rest of the seeds in the ground."

She taps his arm and smiles up at him. "You're a charmer all right." He helps her up and takes the bowl from her hand. "Swirl the seeds around every now and then so they stay well mixed."

"Will do." He gives my hand a squeeze, then says, "I'll bring in our bags after I finish up out here."

Gloria's in party prep mode. We're celebrating Grams's birthday on Saturday night, and she decreed we're including my birthday as well. Which means, along with all of Big Pond's parties, I've also been planning this formal birthday bash. Grams told me she and Gloria would handle the guest list since she knew I had a lot on my plate. I don't know who she invited outside the usual suspects, and they total around thirty-five people. Somehow, we're having sixty-one attendees, and I'm trying to figure out why so many.

The house can hold a crowd that size, but Grams wants a dance floor. So instead of being inside, we're having a sit-down dinner for sixty-one people in a large L-shaped heated tent. I talked her out of a live band, and she agreed only if I promised there'd be music from the 60s and 70s, and some of it had to be for slow dancing. I don't know what's gotten into her this year, but I acquiesced and booked my favorite DJ, who can and has handled similar requests.

The one thing we agreed on immediately was the caterer. Grams has been using Utterly Delightful Catering pretty much since she and Gramps bought the house. The founding owners' grandchildren run the business now, which has grown from a shop the size of a shoebox, Grams's description, to an enterprise in a building as big as a warehouse in Riverhead, a town about a half hour west of Sagaponack.

With everything party buttoned up – tables, chairs, linens, table settings, floral centerpieces per Grams's instructions – I don't understand why Gloria is in party prep mode.

Every available acre of counter space, with the exception of a sliver next to the stove, is taken up with Grams's best china. Service for thirty-two, and it looks like most, if not all of it, is out and being cleaned, along with glasses and silverware.

"What's all this?" I throw out my arm toward the kitchen and wave my hand at all the stuff on the counters.

"I invited the Di Caros and a few other out-of-town guests for brunch on Sunday."

I shake my head. "You know Alessandro won't let you cook. He'll do what he always does, he'll take us out for brunch."

"I'm not cooking. Utterly Delightful is bringing in a brunch buffet they'll set up in the kitchen."

I blink. Squint. Tilt my head, and blink some more to confirm, yep, my grandmother has an impish look on her face.

"What are you up to, Grams?"

"Can't a woman enjoy her *eighty-second* birthday without it being suspicious?"

"You're off menu."

"If you mean I'm deviating from the norm, well yes, I am. I haven't shaken things up in a while and I thought I'm due." She smiles. "It's fun."

Okay. Who am I to deny Grams her fun?

"We'll need to extend the seating capacity. Jonah and I will bring up the table from downstairs."

"Not necessary," she sings. "When the party supply folks come in on Sunday morning to pack up their stuff, a couple of their guys will bring up the table."

I want to tell her *Hello, it's my actual job to arrange things like that*, but I shrug and say, "Okie doke."

Something's up, and between now and Saturday night, I'm damn sure going to find out what the hell is going on.

I start with Sofia. "Yo," I say, trying to sound all cheery when, in fact, I intend to grill her like a kebab.

"Yo back. I'd love to talk, but I've got studio time booked, Alex is having a meltdown, as you can probably hear, and *Nonna*'s called like forty times because she wants to kill Aurora. Again."

Well, I understand about Ro. As younger sisters go, she's the snarkiest pain in the ass there is. Brilliant, but she'd cut you soon as look at you.

"Okay. Call me when you're not in crisis mode."

Next, I call Collin, who will surely buckle under my interrogation techniques. I get VM.

Just as I'm getting ready to call Elaine to run down the particulars to have her confirm something is off, Jonas walks into the sitting room, takes one look at me, and cracks up.

"What's so fucking hilarious?"

"You." He's still laughing. "You've got a face like thunder."

"Well." I cross my arms over my chest. "Something hinky's going on."

"Between Gloria and Lilli, Gloria and Ernie, or Lilli and Ernie?"

"Again with the jokes?"

He sits on the sofa next to me. "Okay, baby. Spill it."

This is the phrase he's adopted when he knows I have shit bottled up.

"Grams scheduled a catered Sunday brunch with the Di Caros and 'other out-of-town guests.'" I use air quotes.

"And this is hinky because…?"

"Because whenever the Di Caros stay over, Alessandro takes us out to brunch."

"Maybe Lilli doesn't want to put the expense or awkwardness of having other people at brunch be on him."

I rub my forehead. "With almost anyone else, I'd agree. But money doesn't factor, and he sure as hell doesn't do awkward."

"Regardless, Lilli wouldn't do that to him. Or anyone."

Shit. He's right.

"Well, what about her and Gloria doing the invitations?"

"I'm socially dense. You're going to have to explain that more fully."

"Grams gave me the party to organize, and then broke off pieces to handle on her own."

"You have a lot more parties lined up than you've ever had. Perhaps she wanted to take some of the pressure off."

"That's what she said."

"Then, there you go."

"You know, it's annoying you being so reasonable."

He grins. "Can't help it. Science brain."

"Do you ever wonder why we work?"

"Nope. Do you?"

"At times like these, yeah. You're linear and I'm—"

"My center. Some nights I'm in the lab trying to work out what seems to be a dead end, and I think of you and how flexible you are. How you reshape problems on the spot to make them non-problems. And it forces me to rethink how I'm doing what I'm doing." He leans in and kisses my cheek. "I don't need or want you to think like me. I need and want you to continue being you."

I tackle him and we make excellent use of the sitting room sofa.

***

I'm driving like I'm the family chauffeur. Grams and Jonas are sitting in the back talking loud enough for me to hear the conversation, but it's weird to interject. My words float around before landing in the backseat.

We're on our way to lulu's in Sag Harbor. It's one of Grams's favorite restaurants, and since it's her birthday, it's her call on where we eat.

Every time we go somewhere new, Jonas orders another unknown culinary delight he wants to replicate. I know Santa Monica and the whole LA area have lots of fantastic restaurants, but Jonas started high school right after he and his mom moved there. I figure between Elaine getting her footing in her new job, and Jonas having been yanked from everything he knew, he didn't get to experience many good restaurants until he started college. From what he's told me, he's done more food exploration in the summers when he goes back to California than he had in the four years of high school.

Jonas believes we're *beshert*. Destined to be together. That we belong to each other. I don't know if that's true since I've never been particularly philosophical. Growing up in a house that was a 24/7 shit show, survival took precedence over profound metaphysical thinking. But learning him, learning what makes him tick, and comparing the holes in his life to the holes in my life, I think of a line from the OG *Rocky:* "She's got gaps, I got gaps, together we fill gaps."

I'm embracing the idea of Jonas and I spending the rest of our lives filling each other's gaps.

***

There's something to be said for waking up every morning to a gorgeous nerd with a massive hard-on, especially 'cause he loves me. I'm a people watcher, and my observational research has led me to the conclusion that nerds do a lot of thinking. Many of them think about a whole host of subjects that interests them. My nerd spent a considerable amount of time fantasizing about what he'd do with me when he finally got me naked. Aren't I lucky the list is exhaustive.

This morning he turns me over, tells me to get on my knees and to grab on to the carved headboard of our sleigh bed.

"You move, Ames, and I stop."

Well, I never. And I mean that literally.

Since I'm me and rebellion is in my marrow, when he cups my breasts and starts tormenting my nipples, I wiggle my tush.

Bam! His hands disappear and I've got air where that wonderful massive hard-on had been pressing into the crease in my tush only moments before.

His breath tickles my neck when he whispers, "Testing me?"

Who is this guy? I'm getting ready to turn around to check when he fists his hand in my hair, holding me still as he moves his other hand leisurely down my body, brushing the skin on my torso, his hand moving side to side. He stops about two inches below my belly button before pushing his long fingers into my curls. Then he goes no farther.

"What'll it be, baby? Compliance or we stop?"

He has me in more way than one. If I give in to my mutinous nature, I don't get no nookie. Or I play the game, score, and plot my revenge.

I say nothing, since moving my lips might count against me.

He nibbles on my earlobe, then says in a husky voice, "Such a fast learner."

Staying still as his voracious mouth and talented fingers assail me is no easy thing. My hands are grasping the wood so tight I'm afraid we'll see sawdust soon.

Finally, he slides inside me and wraps me in his strong arms, holding tight as his hips start to piston. The sensation is so intense, my control so totally shattered, I'm gone in a flash.

He joins me moments later, groaning into my neck.

Still panting, he murmurs, "I love you," in my ear.

***

After my body recalibrated – yes, shower sex was equally inventive – and after Jonas and I ate a breakfast fit for sumo wrestlers, I thought we'd have a relaxing day with Grams. Maybe finish one of those thousand-piece puzzles. But, surprise, surprise, I have to rush out the door. Grams booked us for nine-thirty mani-pedis.

"We had to take early slots," she explains, knowing how I feel about morning appointments, especially when I don't have to be anywhere. "The salon is always so crowded on Fridays, which is why I usually come in on Tuesdays or Wednesdays."

I nod as I try to find a spot near the converted house since the driveway is packed. Grams loops her arm through mine and we walk into Matilda's Spa. Downstairs are the salon services: hair and nails. Upstairs are the spa services: facials, massages, salt rubs…you get the idea.

When I choose sea foam green for my nails and toes, Grams touches my arm. "Honey, why don't you put on the pretty pink you had on back in January?"

Typically, Grams doesn't care what color I wear. She's more interested in me getting a mani-pedi regularly, which I don't do. I endure this fussing only for her.

For whatever reason, today the color means something to her, and since I couldn't care less, I say, "Okay."

After our nails are done and fully dried after being under the UV nail curing lamps, Grams's stylist, Leticia, comes in with another stylist she introduces as Devon, who says, "C'mon, ladies. It's time to make you even more gorgeous than you already are."

See? See? Something hinky's going on. A mani-pedi is a regular thing we do. Getting our hair done? Together? Ah, no.

Eyeing him suspiciously, I sit in Devon's chair where he swirls on a lilac styling cape. When he lifts my hair to snap the button closed, he lets out a sigh. "So thick and healthy."

Yeah, yeah. I have pretty good hair.

"So, what are we doing today?"

I bend up the bottom of a hank of hair and have to admit, it's been a while since I had a trim. Maybe last August?

Using my thumb and forefinger, I hold them about an inch apart and say, "Only a trim."

The trim comes with shampoo, conditioner, a scalp and neck massage, and a hair masque. It's annoying that after he spends like ten minutes blow drying while using a huge round brush, my hair looks fantastic.

"We do this every six weeks, sugar, you'll be getting calls from L'Oréal and Clairol to be the star of their commercials."

Grams smiles with a knowing look when she sees me. My antennae have gone from quivering to tremoring.

Even with all the weird of the past twenty-four hours, of all the things I expect to be doing today, going with Grams to a vintage clothing store blows my mind.

I love vintage stores, but I know for a fact they're not Grams's jam.

She gets why I live on a strict budget. I would never take a penny from my parents. Grams pays for college, and that's all the money I'm going to take from her. I have a business, and from it, my own money. Not a lot, but enough to live on. Still, she doesn't understand why I would want to wear someone else's clothes.

I don't see it that way. I love vintage designer stuff, and out here in the Hamptons, the wealthy molt clothes daily. Expensive clothes. Most of the secondhand stores have more modern, trendy things than I like. But where we're heading to now is to a true vintage shop.

Apparently, Grams is hell-bent for leather to buy this Yves Saint-Laurent kimono-inspired jacket circa 1979. She read in the NYT Style section the look is coming back, and she's peeved she gave hers away to a charity auction about ten years ago. This store is supposed to've gotten one in.

While she talks to the saleswoman at the counter, I wander the shop looking for pleated slacks. I try on a couple of pairs of Calvin Kleins and buy them. They're comfy but professional looking. I like dresses and skirts, but when I'm working an event, they're not practical.

Grams looks pleased. "They got it in today. It hasn't been dry-cleaned, but she's bringing it out. I hope it's in good condition." I show her the pants. "These are nice, honey. Versatile. Good choices for work."

We're walking past a round clothing rack filled with an assortment of dresses, and Grams stops short. "Look at this." She holds up a cotton candy pink dress with a matching waist-length jacket.

The saleswoman comes out from the back carrying a black garment bag. When she sees the dress, she says, "Oh. What a wonderful choice. It's an Oscar de la Renta. I just put it out this morning."

"Try it on, honey. It's your color, and it's vintage."

"Nineteen seventy-one," the saleslady says. "A silk/cotton blend in perfect condition."

I know I'm being handled, but I go along with it because Grams is beaming,

Surprisingly, it fits well. No crushing on top, there's enough room for my girls, and the waist cinches, but doesn't pinch. The skirting hits my knees, and the jacket is comfy. It's made to wear open with a little hidden hook at the top. The sleeves reach my elbows, which is perfect. No restraint of movement. I suppose I could wear it to one of the fancy-schmancy parties I've recently been booking more of, and have Jamie do all the bending and last-minute rearranging.

I walk out barefoot and Grams lets out a sigh. "It matches your toenails."

"You look lovely…"

"Amy."

"I'm Marge. If you don't mind, I have a suggestion to add the right amount of oomph to the ensemble."

I wouldn't've thought the outfit needed oomph, but, "Um, okay."

She comes back with a belt made of two-inch crystal flowers going all the way around except for a silver clasp, which must go in the back.

"May I?" Marge asks, and I lift my arms away from my body and let her do her thing.

We all go over to a three-way mirror with a round stand in front of it. I step up and do a full slow spin for Grams.

"Oh honey."

This belt wouldn't've caught my eye, and never in my wildest dreams would I think to wear crystal flowers around my waist, but I have to say, it looks pretty.

Grams is wearing her dreamy expression, so I tell Marge, "I'll take it." She smiles. "And the belt."

After I'm back in my clothes and we're heading to the counter, Grams tells me, "My treat."

She does this way too often, but I don't have the heart to wipe that dreamy look off her face.

"If you insist."

"I most certainly do."

We're in the car when I realize Grams doesn't have the garment bag with her jacket in it.

"Hey. Where's the jacket?"

"Marge insisted they dry-clean it first. When it's ready, Gloria will pick it up."

We don't get far before Grams bullies me into stopping at a boutique shoe store. Today, I'm getting the top to toe treatment, literally.

Grams knows I refuse to wear ankle breakers, and zeros in on a pair of hot pink satin kitten heels with cutout sides and a sort of rosebud ornament over the front of the shoe.

Before I can comment, a tall, reed-thin woman about my age comes over and says, "The origami D'orsay kitten-heel pumps. They're divine."

Not a rosebud. Origami. On a shoe. In satin.

I try on a pair in my size, and I'm surprised they're comfortable. The pointed toe goes past where my toes are, so they're not being squished. The heel is no higher than my boots, and I don't feel wibbly-wobbly when I walk.

"We'll take them," Grams announces with a bright smile.

I'm gonna find out what the hinky is all about, 'cause I know something's going down.

Chapter Twenty-One

Big Fat Liars

Amy

Tonight's the party, and at seven p.m. our guests are scheduled to arrive. The most critical thing to a party's success, aside from great guests, is a meticulous timetable. At this, I excel. Three party rental trucks arrive at eight thirty a.m. People pour out of them and start unloading with the zest of circus acrobats. An hour later, two of the trucks leave the equipment and the set-up crew behind to do their thing.

The tent takes about four hours to put up, and that includes the lighting, the heaters, the generators, and the dance floor. Assembling the DJ stand, the two bars, the four waiter stations, the eight tables with all the linen and table settings, and the chairs, which will be slip-covered in white with pink bows, will take another three and a half hours.

They guarantee to be gone by five p.m., which is when the florist will arrive with the silver based forty-inch-tall crystal beaded trumpet vases filled with white, blush, and pink roses.

Weeks ago, when I saw Grams's floral order I asked, "What's with all the pink?"

"It's your birthday party too, honey. I know how much you love pink."

Now, with all the other indications something hinky is going on, I'm reconsidering her response.

The party rental people don't need me hovering. I'll check their progress once an hour, and they know where to find me if they have any questions.

The caterers are expected to take over the kitchen at three p.m. In anticipation of their arrival, Jonas, Gloria, and I move the seven-ton farmhouse table almost to the family room, and then we move all of Grams's china, silver, and glasses onto the table, then cover the whole shebang with a tablecloth.

Next, we set up the pool house with a couple of extra chairs and fill the fridge with water bottles for guests who might need a break or want to sit a moment before using the pool house's bathroom.

Back to the kitchen, where Gloria and Jonas put together Caprese sandwiches and a side salad for lunch that Gloria orders we eat at one-thirty. She insists the kitchen will be clean and ready for Utterly Delightful by two-fifteen.

I head upstairs to take out the huge toy box we keep in the closet of the smaller guest bedroom. Gloria's youngest daughter, Stacy, who's a junior in high school, has been conscripted to watch two three-year olds, Alex and Lia, Theresa and Ethan's daughter. Actually, Stacy will make a bundle. Don Di Caro will pay her, Matt will pay her, and Ethan will pay her. And believe me, she'll earn it. Alex has two speeds: sleep, and Mach 10. Lia is sweet, but sly. She's been known to encourage him to do naughty things, then steps back and watches when he gets in trouble.

Last chore before I head outside to check on the tent's progress is to get Jonas's suit – Grams insisted he wear a suit and tie. *It's a formal party, honey. You don't want Jonas to look schleppy, do you?* – and my black velvet pants to the cleaners for a quick steaming to get all the wrinkles out.

By the time we finish lunch, I'll be ready for a nap. And I'm going to make sure Grams takes one too.

***

Jonas is reading in the sitting room. I had to send him to the dry cleaner's with our stuff since I got stuck with the party rental people. We had to rearrange the table placement and move one of the bars. It wasn't a big deal, but they apologized like a hundred times. Parties in the Hamptons are the lifeblood of a lot of area businesses. Any company associated with parties that gets a bad rep folds in a heartbeat. Brutal, but true. I'm all too well aware since it's my business too.

"Hey." I kiss his mouth and plop down next to him on the sofa. He's clean-shaven and has been since January. His hair is longer, but the cut is so fly, he went from looking surfer dude gorgeous to roguishly sexy. Yeah, I'm stuck on him in a stupid gooey way.

"Hey." He runs his hand over my hair. "Lilli all set?"

"She's in the recliner watching a documentary about national parks. I give it about fifteen minutes before she dozes off."

"I hope so. She's been so jazzed about the party. What'd you guys do last year?"

"Dinner with a few of her friends in a restaurant in Montauk. There were eight of us."

"Sounds sedate compared to tonight."

"Yeah. This mega socializing is more in character with who she had been before Gramps died."

He takes my hand and says, "How about *we* socialize up close and personal?"

What starts out sweet and slow becomes wild and intense. Like we're chasing the high at the same time we're clinging to the sensation. I want more, yet I want to let go.

We're in a bubble, alone and completely wrapped up in each other. The outside world is far, far away. And it's only when we're shuddering in each other's arms, breathing each other's breath, that I begin to feel reconnected with our surroundings.

"What was that?" I whisper into his neck.

"Perfection."

***

We're in Grams's room, and she looks amazing. She's in full makeup and is wearing a knee-length long-sleeve scoop-neck ruby sequined dress, and velvet ruby tuxedo flats with crystal buckles. I haven't seen her this decked out in years. She's even put on her drop ruby and diamonds earrings with the matching wreath necklace, and her ruby and diamond cuff bracelet.

"Lilli, you're a vision."

She smiles at Jonas. "You're looking rather handsome yourself."

Actually, he looks exactly like he did in the GQ photo spread that accompanied an article about the Italian designer who made the clothes. According to Jonas, the designer loved the way his garments looked on him, and gifted him with the suit he's wearing, and a couple pair of slacks and three sweaters. I'm absolutely positive the designer was more interested in seeing Jonas without any clothes on at all.

He strikes a pose and gives Grams his Times Square smile.

I shake my head. "Show-off."

Grams motions me over and points to the bed. I sit, and she uncurls her hand. Inside is her curved diamond leaf hair comb. She pushes her fingers through the hair on the right side of my crown, and moves it all the way over to the other side of my head. Then, using the comb, she pulls up the hair over my left ear and anchors it and the swept hair up, a couple of inches above my ear.

Jonas, whose eyes had gone wide at the same time he'd grabbed on to the doorframe when I walked into our bedroom fully made up, dressed, and wearing the diamond studs Grams gave me for my twentieth birthday, says, "Wow some more."

I go over to the mirror and don't recognize myself. Girly and sophisticated at the same time.

He turns me, his hands wrapped around my upper arms, and tells me in his deep soothing voice, "You are so beautiful, Ames."

"I couldn't agree more," Don Di Caro states from the patio doorway.

I smile, go over to him, and kiss both his cheeks. He does the same.

"Jonas. Why don't you escort Lilli to the tent." Not a suggestion. "I need a minute alone with Amy."

We step out of the way as Jonas and Grams, with her arm through his, walk out onto Grams's private patio and head toward the well-lit tent.

Don Di Caro puts his hand on my cheek and says, "You're my third daughter. As much a part of my family as those of my blood."

My eyes tear up and I wave my hand in front of them. I have no idea why that works.

He smiles. "Such a soft heart." He takes my hand and holds it tight. "And a hot temper."

"Why do I feel like you're softening me up and warning me at the same time?"

"Because you're smart and intuitive."

"Oh boy. It's gotta be big if I'm getting the compliments too."

He chuckles. "I'm going to start by asking you not to be angry with your grandmother."

Damn. She's behind whatever the hinky is.

"I won't."

He nods and continues. "This is more than a joint birthday celebration."

"I figured."

"You're getting married tonight."

My hind brain must be controlling my rapid blinking response to amplify my hearing.

"Huh?"

"Lilli wanted to sure she was in control of all her faculties when you got married, and knowing Jonas will be getting his PhD, and you'll be working long hours to build your business, she was worried you'd wait too long."

"Oh." I mean, what else could I say: she's eighty-two and time is not her friend.

"She adores Jonas. She says he's a good man who loves you and will care for you. Right now she's telling him what I'm telling you. I feel confident he'll embrace the evening."

"He would've married me the day he asked."

"Lilli is of the same opinion." He squeezes my hand. "Would you have?"

I answer immediately. "Yeah. I guess I would've. I can't see my life without him in it."

"In that case, tonight is as good a night as any."

I'm about to say, *Let's get this party started*, when instead I ask, "Did Grams send out wedding invitations?"

He smiles, amusement dancing in his eyes. "She sent out 'You damn well better keep this a secret' wedding invitations."

I shake my head. "Jonas always says she's wily."

***

When we enter the tent, I see there wasn't really a problem with the bar that caused us to change the table arrangements. In place of the bar is a chuppah made out of white lattice with blush and pink roses twined throughout. Our rabbi is standing with Jonas beside him. Collin, handsome and smiling in his suit and tie, is standing at Jonas's side.

For a long moment Jonas and I stare at each other, and my heart swells. I feel his love, and hope he feels mine.

Sofia, Aurora, and Natalia materialize in front of me wearing slightly different tea length dresses, but in the same blush color. They grin as Sofia hands me a big bouquet of white, blush, and pink roses, then stands in front of Nat, Ro is behind her. All of them have smaller bouquets of white roses.

The tables were pushed aside enough to create an aisle. At the first table on the left are Helen and Art, Skip and Sharon, Theresa and Ethan, and Simon and Aileen. Sitting at the first table on the right are Francesca, Gio, Matt, Elaine, *Nonna,* and Grams, who are holding hands.

The first strains of the Brandenburg Concerto No. 5 begin to play, and Sofia starts to move down the aisle. Nat and Ro follow then break away to sit at the Di Caro table as Sofia continues on to stand opposite Collin under the chuppah.

Don Di Caro dips his head and asks, "Ready?"

I nod. "Totally."

He smiles, tucks my hand in the crook of his elbow, and walks me down the aisle to the man who broke through all my defenses so he could love me hard, and for a long, long time.

***

Jonas and I are laying naked and sweaty in a big bed in a plush room in a B&B that has only six rooms and is less than ten minutes from Grams's house.

"This is nice, but I like our room better."

He's lying on his side trailing his fingers up and down my back. "Yeah, but *Nonna* and Aurora are staying in the guest rooms. I doubt you would've screamed and begged knowing they were down the hall."

I flip to my side and narrow my eyes. "I didn't beg."

"Wanna bet?" He grins. "'Jonas, Jonas, now, now, fuck me now.'"

"That wasn't begging. I was giving you direction."

"I think I found all the right places all by myself."

"We're going to have to talk about your smug quotient."

"Keep talking math, baby. You'll get me hard all over again."

"Ha. It's," I lean over to look at the bedside clock, "four in the morning and we've been at it for three hours. Nonstop."

"True, but we've got only one wedding night. I plan to make the most of it."

At six in the morning, I'm lying on his chest when I tell him, "If there are positions we haven't tried yet, it'd be great to have something to look forward to."

He laughs and hugs me tight. "I'll admit to needing a short time-out."

"Okay. Tell me five of your favorite things about the wedding."

"Our first dance. Totally romantic. Great song."

"Slick Grams contacted the DJ behind my back and told him it was a wedding, so he added all the best love songs and knew 'At Last' is my favorite."

"Mine too." He kisses me long and deep. "Second was having our families there and watching them get along, being happy for us, and enjoying the celebration."

"That'd be my second too."

"What's your first?"

"The way you looked at me when you said your vows."

He smiles and cups my cheek. "Best words I've ever spoken."

I move up his body and kiss him, hoping he'll feel how much I love him.

"My sweet Ames."

I love when he says that. "Okay, number three."

"The opening line of your thank-you speech. 'I'm horrified to learn that everyone I love, everyone in this room, is a big, fat liar.'"

"They all laughed."

"You're funny, and they know you know they did it out of love. For you, me, and mostly Lilli."

"I know." I hug him tight. "Fourth favorite."

"When my gran, *Nonna*, and Lilli were dancing the hora."

"Yeah, that was a good one. All of them were so tipsy, they could hardly stand up."

"Fifth, I made a new friend in Gio. When I told him about all the medical crossover in the PhD program I'm most interested in, he was so into it we, to use your word, nerded out."

"He's really smart."

"I got that."

"You're smarter."

"You know what's really cool right now?"

I shake my head.

"I get to say 'my wife.'" I smile. "As in, it's great my wife's got my back."

"Well, yeah. It's part of the deal."

"You had my back before yesterday."

"Like I said, it's part of the deal. The I love you deal."

"A year ago this conversation would've been a fantasy."

"Welcome to reality, hubby."

An hour and a half later, with the most disheveled head of sex hair anyone, anywhere ever had, I tell him my numbers three, four, and five.

"Three. Everyone was genuinely happy for us. I felt nothing but delight and joy all night long."

"Yeah. I felt the same. The vibe was mellow and rad." My SoCal guy. "Number four?"

"Aurora was crushing on Collin."

"No."

"Oh yeah. She's nineteen and finishing her sophomore year at Barnard."

"Sister school to Columbia?"

"Bingo."

"How did Collin react?"

"Oblivious. He treats everyone the same. He's kind and patient. But I don't think he'd notice anyone crushing on him unless they did a painting of them kissing. Intensely. Like Gustav Klimt's "The Kiss.""

Jonas looks confused so I grab my phone and show him the painting.

"Damn. That's a hell of a kiss."

"Totally."

"Though the painting seems too contemporary for Collin, I get your point."

"It was probably just a one-night thing. He's too quiet and gentle for Ro, and she's too caustic and saucy for him."

"He dated this one girl for about a year when he was a freshman. I didn't know him then. He told me she was nice, but wanted to settle down, and he's not looking to get married."

"This is your second year rooming with him, right?"

"Yeah. Since I've known him, he hasn't dated anyone."

"One-nighters?"

He shrugs. "Not something we talk about."

Moving on. "Number five. When Claudia and Gwyneth near fell over when you took a picture with them."

"I never heard anyone screech that loud in my life. I recorded them promising me they wouldn't post the snap on social media or my agent and lawyer would come after them."

"Harsh."

"Truth. Anyone who in any way profits from my image with whom my agency hasn't contracted is in deep shit, in legal language."

"Good thing we're married or I'd have to dump the dick pics."

"You don't have any pics of my dick."

I grin.

He reaches over to grab my phone and forty minutes later I tell him, "You have impressive recovery powers."

"Let's shower and I'll show you how true that is."

The bedside phone is ringing as we're walking in from the bathroom at nine-thirty. Loong shower. I pick up and the lady at the front desk tells me she's sending someone up with a garment bag.

Grams packed fresh clothes for us.

In the Uber on the way back to Grams's, I ask Jonas, "Did you wonder about the marriage license?"

"No. Lilli told me it was taken care of."

I lower my voice. "Proxy marriage isn't allowed in New York. We were supposed to've applied and signed in person in front of the county clerk."

He raises a brow and leans in to whisper, "You know who walked you down the aisle, right?"

I nod.

"Well?"

"I guess it was taken care of."

When we walk into the house, every member of our combined family busts out laughing.

Gio shouts over the noise, "Damn. Not one wink of sleep. My man has skills."

Chapter Twenty-Two

Cruising

Jonas

We're back at school, and it's a bit surreal. A honeymoon is a back-burnered concept right now. We have six weeks of classes left, and a schedule to maintain. As we go about our daily lives, I realize we were married before we were married. Well, we didn't get fully intimate until Costa Rica, but since our first brunch, and except for the ten days I was away working, we've spent every night together, kept each other updated throughout each and every day, and became best friends.

After I'd interviewed at all three schools, I've checked the status of my applications via my portal for each school a couple of times. It's the end of March and I should be hearing something soon.

Amy doesn't ask, but I can tell she's anxious about me getting in since PhD acceptance rates are notoriously low. We've talked about what would happen if I got accepted to Carnegie Mellon and nowhere else. She's adamant we'll find a way to make it work, and that getting my PhD is priority one. While I'm sure she means it, I have no doubt she'd prefer for me to get accepted to WPI or Stony Brook. If Carnegie Mellon is my only yes, we're going to have to be creative about how we divide our time.

No way will I expect Amy move to Pittsburgh full time. Her business is in New York and New England, and while a lot of her day-to-day is done by Zoom, FaceTime, and emails, her clients expect real live-time face-to-face contact. And to grow her business, she needs to be seen by potential clients at all kinds of events.

Sure, it would suck large not to sleep next to her every night and wake up to her every morning, but we'll deal, and we'll make it work. Yeah, getting my PhD is really important, but she was wrong about one thing: priority one is us. Our marriage.

She came from a home where being married was a curse, and my parents split because their jobs came first. I'll never let anything like that happen to us.

It's Friday night and I'm heading home. Collin is holed up in the library so Amy is flying solo in the kitchen. She's solid with the basics, but she's not patient with multistep recipes. Part of the problem is she's hungry when she cooks. I keep telling her to put snacks or power bars in her bag, but she always forgets. I'm going to have stuff something in there every night to keep her level.

I open the door to "Shit. Fuck. Damn it," and the distinct odor of burned food.

Amy's standing at the stove scowling at the pot in front of her. She turns her head and looks at me while pointing at the pot. "I walked away to take a quick call and the bastard burned my homemade mac 'n cheese."

I'm not an idiot. I don't tell her she should always turn off the heating element when she's not in front of the stove. Instead, I say, "The fucker."

"Totally," she huffs. "I did a good job too. Three different kind of cheeses and the mac was *al dente*."

I wrap my arms around her. "Let's go out and get falafel in defiance of pasta."

While she gets ready, I send Collin a text.

J: Don't ask Ames about tonight's dinner.
C: That bad, huh?
J: A culinary mishap.
C: That's spousal diplomacy speaking.
J: I value your life.
C: Hahaha.

I dump the mess into the garbage and tie it up to take out. I put the pot in the sink, add dish soap and hot water. Tomorrow, I'll scrub it clean.

Amy's sitting cross-legged on her bed. I'm sitting with my back against the wall.

"I finally convinced Grams to combine our graduation party with the annual Memorial Day party."

"Makes better sense."

"That's what I told her like two hundred times."

I grin. "Rock, meet hard place. You get your stubborn from her."

"I'm not stubborn, I'm decisive."

"She said stubbornly."

When she sticks out her tongue, I tell her, "Bring that over here. I've got a few good uses for it."

I get a sassy glance. "Make me."

Game on.

She shrieks when I tackle her, and a few minutes later she's gasping and moaning.

I'm Superman with a little Tarzan thrown in.

We're sweaty and lying on our sides grinning at each other. She motions between us. "You think we're going to go at it like this when we're fifty?"

"Oh yeah. And way beyond fifty."

"I sure hope so." She lays her hand on my cheek. "You check your email today?"

This is her fishing for acceptance info.

"Not since lunch."

I don't make her ask again. I reach over, grab my phone, and see I have three emails waiting. First one's from Dad. He's old school. More of an emailer than a texter. He asks if I want to go to the BoSox game with him on April 15th. Next one's from someone named Raley Fitzhugh who's chairing the reunion committee for Santa Monica High School. The last one is from Stony Brook. I debate reading it myself first, but I can tell Amy's nearly jumping out of her skin. I turn the phone so she can see what they say the same time I do.

She bursts into tears and starts sobbing.

"Ames?"

"Ha...Ha... Happy tears."

***

Passover turns out to be more than recounting the Jewish slaves' freedom and exodus from Egypt during the reign of Ramses II. The family group text sent the morning after Amy and I celebrated and re-celebrated the Stony Brook news blew up our phones all day. Politely, I said thank you, and then deferred everything else to Amy.

We're having the first night Seder in a massive dining room – but not the biggest of the two formal dining rooms – in Alessandro Di Caro's home. There's seventeen of us. Mom, Gran, and Gramps flew into Boston, and we, including Collin, drove down to Connecticut – only an hour and change away, the Di Caros live near the Massachusetts border – in Dad and Sharon's huge SUV. Matt, Sofia, and Alex went in their own car.

Mr. Di Caro sent his private jet to East Hampton Airport to collect Lilli. She landed at the Worcester Regional Airport, only twenty-five miles from the Di Caro home, earlier this afternoon. She's staying over for a couple of days to visit with *Nonna*.

Amy arranged the catering, and she brought twenty new Haggadahs so everyone would be reading from the same book. Mismatched Haggadahs are famous at most family's tables.

What amazes me the most about this gathering are the Di Caros. Italian Catholic – and not in name only, they're devout, especially *Nonna* – they've been having Passover with Amy at Lilli's house since Amy was a little girl. They know the ritual, celebrate the story, and embrace the emotion behind it as if they were born to it. Aurora, the youngest at the table – Alex doesn't count, he's three – can recite the four questions, in Hebrew, almost by heart.

Collin's not as lost as I thought he'd be. The history part of studying art history means he covers a lot of cross-cultural ground.

When we get down to eating, the conversations are energetic, loud, and disorderly. Everyone talks over everyone else, and no one seems to care they get interrupted mid-sentence and headed off to another topic.

Mom and Gran fit right in, Gramps is talking business with Mr. Di Caro, and everyone is getting more than a little tipsy. Wine is a big part of the ritual Seder, and only Gramps and Mr. Di Caro have put their foot on the brakes since the first sip.

Dad's our designated driver. And I bet he *needs* to be sober. He's a big shot in the FBI having Passover in a Don's house. This is the perfect example of maintaining complicated relationships, which is a requirement in Dad's line of work.

We started the Seder about an hour earlier than sundown so we'd have more time together, but it's almost ten-thirty and we need to get back to Boston. Collin and I have to be at school tomorrow, and Dad, Sharon, and Amy have to work. Can you believe she planned a private second Seder event for one hundred forty people that includes a sit-down dinner?

Mom, Gran, Gramps, and I will be at Dad and Sharon's tomorrow night. It's cool. Mom and Sharon get along well. I wouldn't say they're besties, but they're miles closer to being friends than being merely cordial.

While I'd never say this out loud to anyone, I'm so fucking happy not one person even alludes to Amy's parents. For all the people at the wedding, and certainly for all our family, Victor and Monica Stern are dead.

On the ride home, Mom starts the post-game roundup with compliments, which invites Gran to add in her opinions. Sharon turns to ask Amy – who's sitting with me and Collin in the third row of the behemoth SUV – for the telephone number of the caterer.

All this chatter opens the door for Amy to say to Mom, "I saw you talking to Ro."

"What a bright young woman. She's still not sure of her career path, but she has plenty of time. Though it doesn't matter what she does, she'll be in charge and running the show before she's thirty."

Gran turns and says to Collin, "Didn't I see you and Aurora talking after dessert?"

Sharon, who never gossips, pulls down her visor and angles the mirror. "I saw them, and she seemed really into you, Collin."

I can feel Amy vibrating and I lay my hand on her knee. She looks up and I shake my head. She nods, and I shake my head harder.

Collin leans forward and stares at us. "What's wrong with you two?"

"Nothing," I say.

Amy shares, "We're having a silent disagreement."

"Oooo." Mom turns around. "About what?"

I squeeze Amy's knee, and she smacks my hand.

Collin, who's turning out to be a dark horse, says, "I think Amy wants to tell everyone Aurora flirted with me at the wedding, and I'm sure Ames thought I didn't notice."

"Well…" Amy starts.

"Well, my ass," Collin continues over Gran's laughter. "Aurora is exceptionally pretty and as subtle as a sledgehammer. It would've been difficult not to notice her moves."

"And?" Amy baits.

"And I didn't want to do anything but take in the wedding love fest. Can't say I've ever seen so many people invested in a couple's happiness. I've been around the two of you a while now, and you're the real deal. Everyone there that night saw it and supported it."

As Amy hugs Collin and clutches his hand, Gran says, "Awww," and Sharon adds, "Too true."

"So?" Mom asks.

"So," Collin responds, "tonight we talked. She's at Barnard, a college affiliated with Columbia, and I'm starting my PhD program at Columbia in September. She'll be working for one of her father's companies this summer, and I'll be in Boston working at the Museum of Fine Arts. We exchanged numbers with no plans, promises, or anything remotely leaning in that direction."

Gran claps her hands together. "I see good things."

Gramps shakes his head. "Woman, how can you see good things when the boy made it plain, they're in different places in their lives."

"*That's* what you took away from what he said?" She tut-tuts. "You disappoint me, Arthur."

"It sure as hell isn't the first time, and it won't be the last. I'll live."

Mom and Amy break out laughing, and even Dad joins in.

***

It's official, we moved in with Lilli, but came back to Boston for graduation, and it's a crazy day. Sofia's commencement ceremony at Tufts starts at nine a.m. and lasts two hours. BU's ceremony begins at one p.m. and lasts two hours. The core seventeen, as I've come to call us – and today add in Simon and Aileen – will shuttle been the two campuses. I don't bother to ask how everyone got tickets to both commencements.

Then, in a convoy of cars, we all go to the Di Caros' home for a mega party that lasts into the wee hours. Dad and Sharon leave around midnight to drive home. Collin, Simon, and Aileen leave after one to stay at a nearby B&B, and the rest of us crash at the Di Caros'. Amy and I called dibs the pool house for obvious reasons.

We barely have time to catch our breath when the graduation/Memorial Day celebration is upon us. There's a large open-air tent in the backyard, and the vibe is beach casual. Servers walk around with champagne, canapés, and other small bites. The rest of the food is set up buffet style, and there are two open bars.

This party has about thirty more people than were invited to the wedding, and the guests graze and drink until the sun goes down, when we all migrate to the fireworks. The Utterly Delightful folks are in Lilli's kitchen from nine a.m. until they clear out at ten p.m.

***

During Amy's last semester at BU her business took off. She hired a part-time admin assistant and took on an intern. By mid-April, she asked her admin, Jamie, if he wanted to work for her full time, and he said yes. At the end of April she asked Collin's sister, Aileen, if she wanted to work for Big Pond for the summer and got another enthusiastic yes. The intern is still at BU, but she'll get a finder's fee if she passes along requests for private parties.

Today, the last day of May, I received my final shooting schedule. I hunt for Amy and find her in the larger of the two downstairs bedrooms, neither of which has more than bare bones furnishings. We'd talked about space allocation and agreed she'd need the bigger room as her work space. The smaller bedroom is my office, and we decided the huge open space will be our den/entertainment center. For the most part, Lilli eschews TV and streaming vids, but Amy and I love movies, and look forward to having some time to catch up on some binge-worthy shows. We're still working through all the Jack Ryan movies, and there's a Jack Ryan series we haven't even touched yet.

Our wedding guests didn't bother giving us Cuisinarts and coffeemakers. All of them know us and Lilli well, and knew we'd move in here with her. Yet, they were overly generous. We're using some of the cash to decorate the downstairs and to buy a car. We chose a practical, electric SUV for me to go back and forth to Stony Brook, which is fifty miles from Sagaponack. Lilli gifted her car to Amy, who feels ridiculous driving around in a luxury sedan, but I remind her that her clients, most of whom are stupid rich and/or snobs, will think better of her for traveling in style.

"Ames. Why are you standing on the bed?" She holds out her hand to show me a tape measure. "I'm trying to visualize the room and I need measurements to match what I think I want with what'll fit."

"Baby, get down from there."

She plops down, then scrambles off the bed.

"Where's your phone?"

She digs into her messenger bag and pulls out an energy bar and her phone.

"You hungry?"

She shakes her head. "No. But you can stop making sure I'm stocked."

"Not gonna happen. Now focus. Follow what I'm doing."

I show her the tape measure and level in the phone's functions.

"Wow. I didn't know the phone could do that."

Not an idiot, remember? "There's lots of things it can do. I'll show you anytime you want."

She holds on to my shoulders to stretch up to give me a kiss. See what not being an idiot gets you?

"Here's something else that might interest you." I show her a few room design apps and she's dazzled. "Before you fall into a design rabbit hole, take a look at this." I hand her my shoot schedule.

"Holy shit. Almost all of it is in New York."

"Yeah. Big photo studios in Long Island City and Queens. Lots of CGI backgrounds make it look like we shot the winter wear on the slopes, or wherever. Also, lots of street shoots in New York. It doesn't matter if it's the middle of summer when you're standing in front of an old building in the city in a suit and a great coat. It looks the same in the winter."

"Then why are they sending you to Austria for five days?"

"It's one of those shoots to accompany an article. This time about the resort. They have snow in the summer so a winter shoot works."

"At least it's only five days. Then you finish off in New York."

The last five days I'll spend away from her.

"I have two weeks before I start. What's your calendar look like?"

We sit side by side on the bed and I can't believe what I'm looking at. We have ten contiguous days of nothing but time.

Her eyes are wide. "You want to go somewhere? I don't know. Do the honeymoon thing?"

"Nope. I want to buy a surfboard, surf, sit on the beach with you and eat food I made for you out of a picnic basket." I take her hand. "I want to dance with you on the beach at night, and I want to make love to you in the pool. Baby, we live in one of the most beautiful places anyone could imagine. Why would I want to go somewhere else?"

"You sure?"

"Tell you what, I have off from December twenty-second to January twenty-first. You carve out two weeks after the new year and we'll go somewhere warm. Deal?"

"Deal." She pulls me on top of her. "Let's break in this bed before we get rid of it."

***

It takes longer to drive to my shoots than to take the train. When Amy has to be in the city, we drive in together. I enjoy her colorful running commentary about people's driving abilities, but mostly, I just love spending time with her.

When I'm alone on the train, I read lots of research papers in my field of study, or use the time to reach out to some of my colleagues, as I've already identified the labs I'll join. Also, I've connected with my advisor. She's told me email is the best way to communicate, and she recommends we meet before the academic year starts.

Some days at work feel like weeks, and some weeks feel like years. The dichotomy of where my brain is on the train and what I'm doing to pay for my PhD is absurd. My patience wears thin when we have to wait for someone to stop whining because it's ninety-three degrees out with ninety percent humidity and we're dressed in wool turtlenecks and heavy outerwear. The concept of grin and bear it eludes some people. In my head I call them the hangry. Hungry to the point of being angry every single day.

A couple times I luck out and have three days in a row off. If Amy can, we hang out at the beach. We ask Lilli to join us, but it's too much for her. She prefers to work in her gardens or lounge on her patio. The one thing I know for sure: she's happy we're here with her.

Her love for Amy is quietly fierce. Sometimes I catch her watching Amy and I when we're sitting on the couch in the family room doing nothing more than talking. The expression on Lilli's face is a love letter to her granddaughter. The child she raised to become the woman I love is a gift I can never repay. But I try every day to let Lilli know, I've got this. Amy will always be loved, and I'll make sure she knows it.

July 25th and Amy's driving me to JFK and neither of us is happy about it. She's not even trying to make small talk or give me a brave face. So we sulk in silence and I imagine us behaving completely differently on the reverse trip home.

Five hours to London where I change planes to Salzburg. It's an hour layover, and an opportunity to FaceTime Amy. I almost laugh at how careful we were seven months ago when I was working. Texting a bunch of times a day, but never calling. I know now Amy didn't want me to think she was being clingy, and she didn't want to interrupt me at work. I didn't want her to know how I was counting the minutes until I saw her in Costa Rica. How breathing wasn't easy when she wasn't around.

I take my bag out of the trunk, then lean her against the car and give her a kiss that has to last for five days.

Her arms circle my neck and she presses her face into my chest. "I love you and I'll miss you."

"I love you and I'll miss you too, baby. Call me any time day or night."

"Okay."

I kiss her forehead and walk into the terminal.

My mental clock begins ticking off the minutes until I can hold her again.

Chapter Twenty-Three

Impact

Jonas

July 29th and I have one more day in this odd place. It's too perfect-looking, and the people are too homogenous. It's storybook with an evil queen, or some shit like that. It's eleven p.m. and I'm too wired to sleep, but I need to try. Tomorrow is a super early call, and then at two p.m. I'm leaving for the hour drive to Salzburg's airport where I fly to London, change planes, and head the fuck home. I'm getting in a little after midnight, but Amy doesn't care. When we talked a few hours ago, she was all about there being no traffic on the Southern State.

I'm getting into bed when my phone rings. It's Amy. I don't even get out, "Hey."

"Jo… Jo… Jo…" She's crying. Loud.

My heart's thundering in my chest. "Baby, what's wrong?"

"I… I…"

"Ames, listen to my voice. Try to find the words. What happened?"

"I… I came… Her recliner."

"What about Lilli's recliner?"

"She was sleeping too long."

"Did you wake her?"

"Can't." She's sobbing and my heart is breaking. "Can't wake her up."

I'm afraid to know, but I *know*. Still, I ask, "Is she sick?"

"Nooooo. She's cold. So cold."

"Baby."

"She's gone. My grams is gone."

"Amy. I'm on my way home. I'll make sure someone comes over to be with you."

"Don't," she screams. "Don't call the police. Don't call the police."

"I'm not going to call the police, Ames. We'll make arrangements for a Jewish funeral home to come over. In the meantime, I'll get someone, Sofia, her dad, to fly down to the small airport in East Hampton. They'll be there soon. Okay?"

"O... okay."

"I'm going to hang up for a few minutes and I'll call you right back. You go upstairs into the sitting room and lie down on the sofa. Can you do that for me?"

"Mmhmm."

"I love you, Ames. I'll call right back."

Disconnecting made my stomach ache. I call Sofia.

"Hey," she answers, all Sofia sweet. I'm about to ruin her happy for more than just today.

"Soph, this is super important. Please sit down."

"Fuck. What's wrong?"

"Lilli died. Amy found her in the recliner."

"Oh shit. Oh fuck."

The phone fumbles and I hear, "Who the fuck is this?"

"Matt. It's Jonas. Lilli died and Amy's in the house all by herself. We don't want the police because they'll send Lilli for an autopsy. We can't–"

"I know, Jonas. She has to be buried whole and right away. I'm so sorry, mate. So very sorry."

"I need to talk to your father-in-law. Now."

"Right. I sent over his contact info."

"I'll call you when I know more."

I hang up and call Don Alessandro Di Caro.

"Jonas." Of course he has my number.

"I need your help. Lilli died and Amy found her. She's all alone in the house and I'm still in Kaprun, Austria. Can you get to her right away? And can you help me get home?"

"I'll call you back in fifteen minutes."

He hangs up and I call Matt to update him.

Then I FaceTime Amy. I have to see her, and she *needs* to see me.

She picks up but doesn't say anything. Her eyes are red and swollen. Her cheeks are red, swollen, and wet.

"Ames. I spoke with Sofia, Matt, and Mr. Di Caro. Someone should be to you soon."

She nods.

"Baby, I'm on my way home. Until I get there, you won't be alone."

"I need you," she whispers, and snaps my heart into tiny pieces.

"I need you too. So, so much. Where are you?"

"In the sitting room like you said." She pulls her phone back a bit and I can see the couch and the throw wrapped around her legs.

"I have to pack, and you're going to walk around with me, okay?"

"Yeah."

I pull my bag out of the closet, throw it on the bed, and start pushing my stuff in.

"Everything's gonna get wrinkled."

"It does even when I'm careful. Poor technique, huh?"

"Only with packing."

This is so hard. I hurt all over. Literal pain in my chest, arms, and legs. I'm having trouble standing and my movements are uncoordinated. My Amy's alone in that house, and I'm devastated. Lilli is gone, and there's nothing I can do to change that. I'm trying to distract Amy with stupid packing when all I want to do is lie down and cry.

An incoming call beeps in.

"Baby, that's Mr. Di Caro. I'm going to put you on hold. Don't go away, okay?"

"Okay."

"Mr. Di Caro."

"There's a small airport called *Zell am See* about ten minutes from your hotel. A plane will be there in twenty minutes to take you to London where a private jet will fly you to JFK. A car will be waiting for you. I'm on my way to the local airport. I should be to Amy in an hour."

I can't help it, tears fill my eyes. "Thank you, sir."

"You're family. Now get going."

He hangs up and I click back to Amy.

"I'm heading out, Ames. I'm taking a plane from the local airport to London where I'm getting on a jet to come home."

"Hurry."

"I'm going now, baby. Mr. Di Caro should be at the house in an hour. You stay on the phone with me, okay?"

"But you'll be taking off soon."

"When I'm in the air, Sofia will be on the phone with you until her dad gets to the house."

She nods.

I get off the elevator and head to the front desk. "Send me the attorney's, Gerald Faber's contact info." I lean forward and whisper, "I need a taxi immediately."

The desk clerk nods, turns, and makes a phone call, then mouths, "Five minutes."

I mouth back, "Thank you," then see Gerald's info come through.

"Got it, Ames. I'm standing outside waiting for the taxi."

"You're wearing your jacket. Is it cold?"

"About forty-five degrees. Bet it's nice and warm at home."

"Yeah. I opened the windows in here. There's a breeze." Tears are streaming down her cheeks again. "I wish you were home already."

"I do too. Soon, baby. I'll be home real soon."

The taxi pulls up, and I tell the driver the name of the airport.

"Does everyone speak English?"

"This is a tourist destination, so most everyone."

"The hotel looked nice."

"It is. Really clean, and the staff is friendly."

"As… As friendly as Playa Negra?"

Her voice is breaking and she looks like she's going to start crying again. She's hanging on by a thread. I've gotta say something to distract her.

"Well, we were so very, very friendly in Playa Negra, I think it influenced our opinion."

"You have a one-track mind."

"Yeah, I do. I've had Amy on the brain for years."

That got me a little smile. I wish I could do more to make her feel better.

The taxi stops in front of a café attached to an air traffic control tower. On the tarmac is a small, sleek jet. I pay the driver, grab my bag, and walk toward the plane, turning my phone so Amy can see it, then I turn it back.

"That's taking me to London."

"At least it's a jet."

"Yeah."

Two men are standing on the tarmac. The one in a lumpy jacket must be some sort of customs official. He asks for my passport, gives it a quick look, presses a page between a seal clamp, then walks away. The man in a dark suit with an emblem on the jacket pocket says, "Mr. Vandenberg."

"Right."

"Mr. Di Caro sent us. We're ready to leave if you are."

I nod and follow him up the stairs. Small, but plush interior: there are four caramel-colored leather seats, two by two facing each other. I see another man in shirtsleeves sitting in the copilot seat. The guy who greeted me moves toward the cockpit, and over his shoulder says, "We expect to land at Heathrow in two and a half hours."

I show Amy the inside of the plane, sit, push my bag under my seat, and buckle in.

"At least you'll be comfortable."

"It's a short flight, and it brings me closer to you."

"Call me when you land in London."

"I will, baby. The minute we're wheels down."

Her eyes get watery. "I can't wait 'til you come home."

"I love you, Ames."

"Love you back."

I call Gerald Faber and tell him everything. He and his wife, Rose, are leaving for Sagaponack immediately.

Next, I call Sofia and tell her to call Amy. Then I call Sheree, my agent, and explain what's happening.

After the plane takes off, I put my hands over my face and cry so hard my lungs hurt.

***

The minute we land, I call Amy. Mr. Di Caro is there, Gerald and Rose Faber are there, and they dealt with the funeral home people who took Lilli's body. I'm so relieved Amy's not alone, and that Lilli is being cared for by the right people.

"Hey, baby."

"How was the flight?"

"Smooth. This whole private jet stuff beats the hell out of commercial flying."

"Spoiled already, huh?"

There's my Amy. Having people around is helping.

"It's certainly more civilized. I showed my passport to a customs official at a desk in a hangar, then I was escorted to the private plane by a woman in a dark suit with the same emblem as the guy who flew me to London."

I show her the plane, which is set up like a large living room. "Look at this, Ames. There are," I count, "sixteen plush chairs," they're recliners, but I won't be using that word anytime soon, "and a small couch." I keep walking and open the door to a private bedroom. "We're going to have to blow a wad on this at least once. It's the ultimate way to join the mile-high club."

"One-track mind."

"Amy on the brain, remember?"

A man in the familiar suit and emblem approaches. "Mr. Vandenberg, please take a seat and buckle up. We're in the queue to taxi."

I head for a chair, and as I'm sitting ask, "How long until we land in New York?"

"Six hours and twenty-five minutes."

"Thanks." I buckle in. "Hear that, Ames? I'll be home before you know it."

"I won't be right until I can wrap my arms around you."

"Me too, baby. I'll call you when we land."

"Okay. I love you."

"Love you back."

After the plane levels out, I go into the bedroom and crash. Between my heart hurting for Amy, and everything else aching because we lost Lilli, I need to recharge to be strong for my wife.

***

It's two a.m. in New York, and I'm in a limo speeding along on an almost empty Southern State Parkway. If I'm lucky, I'll get home before three-thirty. I hope Ames is sleeping. The next couple of days are going to be intense and draining.

Before I'm even out of the car, Amy is running out of the house. She slams into me, jumps up, wraps her legs around my hips, circles my neck with her arms, and buries her head under my chin.

Through her sobs I hear, "You're home. You're home. I'm so glad you're home."

"Baby."

I carry her into the house, head upstairs to our room, and sit on the bed with her still wrapped around me.

She's crying quietly now, and her tears run down my neck. "Grams is gone, Jonas. Grams is gone."

"I know, Ames, I know." I stroke her hair as I talk to her. "But think of this: She saw us get engaged, and she saw us marry. She knew I got into my PhD program. She saw us graduate. She got to know my family, and they got to know her. We partied together. We celebrated life together. We cooked together. We have tons of her recipes recorded, and we get to listen whenever we want. She knew she didn't have to worry anymore because she saw how happy we are, and will be for the rest of our lives. She left us peacefully. No illness, no pain. She took a nap, and went to Sam."

***

Amy fell asleep with me wrapped around her. I kept vigil for hours, making sure she rested soundly. A little before ten a.m. she wakes. We take a shower – a first, only a shower – get dressed and go downstairs to a full house.

My dad and Sharon, all the Di Caros, Gerald and Rose, Collin, Simon, and Aileen, and Gloria, who's directing the Utterly Delight staff in our kitchen. They're keeping the breakfast buffet fresh, and making food for lunch and dinner.

Hugs, cheek kisses, murmurs of love, and Alex, motoring at top speeds, reminding us life is for the living and we have to go on.

Gerald briefs us on the schedule. Tomorrow at eleven a.m., we're burying Lilli next to Sam in the Jewish cemetery in East Hampton. Our rabbi will officiate, and after, everyone will come back to the house. Everyone is the guest list from our wedding, and they'll sit shiva with us. Mom can't stay the whole week to sit shiva, but Gran and Gramps will stay with us for the duration.

This morning, Gloria covered all the mirrors in the house, and staff from Utterly Delightful will be in our kitchen until shiva ends.

Gerald concludes by telling us he'll read the will at his office in Patchogue on August 8. He takes Amy's hand and adds, "I know Lilli told you the terms of her trust. There are no surprises. It's a formality."

The funeral is sad, but not solemn. The rabbi tells a few Lilli stories that have us chuckling, and invites anyone who wants to speak, to do so. A number of friends and family tell wonderful stories from when Lilli was a young mother, and how over the years she helped so many members of the community. In every story we hear, it's clear how much she was loved.

With my arm around Amy's shoulders throughout, she leans against me, silent tears gliding down her face as she listens to words of love and comfort from the people who knew Lilli well.

With a never-ending buffet set up on the dining room table, people mill about talking and eating while sitting and standing around the pool, in the family room, and downstairs in the entertainment room. Sofia, Collin, Mom, Gran, and *Nonna* are never far from Amy's side.

At nine p.m., the rabbi presides over a twenty-minute minyan service, which signals it's time to go home.

Mom, Gran, and Gramps stay over. Most everyone else lives nearby or farther east on Long Island, and they go home. The Di Caros have taken over five of the rooms at the B&B where Amy and I spent our wedding night. Dad and Sharon are in the sixth room. Simon and Aileen go back to the city, and Collin sleeps on the sofa in the den.

No one goes in Lilli's room, and though I haven't checked, Mr. Di Caro told me the recliner had been removed from the house before Amy and I came downstairs yesterday morning.

The next day, Mom, Dad, and Sharon leave in the late afternoon. Collin hitches a ride back to Boston with Dad and Sharon. As word of Lilli's death spreads, members of the community come by to give their condolences, many bringing food. Between them and the caterers, there's enough to feed a battalion.

The ebb and flow of visitors keeps Amy busy, which is part of the purpose of sitting shiva. No one should be alone in their grief.

After the shiva week has passed, and the caterers have returned our kitchen back to us, Amy and I wander the house. Everyone has gone home. It's time to start getting on with our lives.

"It's so quiet."

"You're only noticing it because there were so many people here. Most of the time, it was this quiet." I pull her back against my front. "Lilli loved the quiet."

"She so did."

"You want to go into her room?"

"Not yet." She turns in my arms. "Did you know the recliner is gone?"

"Mr. Di Caro had it taken away."

"He would." She fiddles with a button on my shirt. "Did you have a chance to talk to Gloria?"

"Yeah. I asked if she could come on Mondays and Thursdays from ten to four. She said 'Of course.'"

"Good." She takes my hand. "That's a relief. Let's go outside. I want to see the gardens."

"Ernie's scheduled to come by tomorrow."

"Did you see the size of the pie his daughter baked?"

Every few feet Amy crouches to deadhead a flower or secure a tie. It's going to take a while for the familiar to become a comfort instead of a constant reminder of Lilli. I know with absolute certainty, we will live in this house until we leave this earth, and one of our children will do the same with their loved ones.

After we've made a complete inspection, I steer her to the pool house.

"I've been wondering if this couch is as comfy as it looks."

She hesitates, and for a moment I think she's going to balk. This past week has been filled with kisses, cuddles, and meaningful hugs, but too overwhelmed with grief, she couldn't reach for the intimacy.

I won't allow her to do it anymore. Not only because I miss our amazing sex life, but because when Amy hurts, she withdraws. And if left alone with it for too long, she'll start building her walls again, and that's never going to happen.

"One-track mind." She cups my crotch. "And aren't I grateful for it."

We get naked fast, and start out on the really great sofa, but end up on the floor. While we're still catching our breath, I scoop her up, carry her to the pool, and walk in with her in my arms.

I'm fucking thrilled we made up for lost time, but I'm nowhere near done.

Soaking wet, I pull her into the house and get as far as the slouchy sofa in the family room, where, after exhausting ourselves, we fall asleep, all wrapped up in each other.

Chapter Twenty-Four

Together

Jonas

We're getting ready to head to Gerald's office when Amy's phone rings.

"Huh. It's Gerald. Hey."

I watch the blood drain from her face, and tell her, "Put the phone on speaker."

She seems frozen in place, so I slide the phone from her hand, put the call on speaker, and ask, "What's going on?"

"Victor's lawyer called to inform me he and his clients, Monica and Victor Stern, will be attending today's reading."

"Can he do that?"

"I told him there'd be no need, but he stated since his client is his deceased mother's only surviving child, he has the right. Technically, he's correct. I can put up a fuss, but it would delay the reading."

"Well, shit."

"My sentiments exactly."

I kneel in front of Amy. "Are you okay with delaying the reading?"

"No. That's what he wants. They want. To fuck with me until I give in to make them go away."

"Okay." I tell Gerald, "We'll be there in an hour."

I hang up and hand Amy her phone.

"You should stay home."

"That's a non-starter, Ames. I'm going with you."

"No," she shrieks. "My parents will be there."

"And so will I."

"They're vicious and they're vile."

"One of the reasons I'm going with you." She opens her mouth but I get there first. "You're mine and I'm yours. Where the fuck else do you think I'd be?"

"Jonas," she snaps. "I don't want you to—"

"To what? See firsthand what I already know? You're special, and they're shit. That making your childhood miserable isn't enough, that they want to breach the four-year barrier you put between you and them so they can get off on fucking with you some more.

"Today of all days, I won't allow them to upset you. Get near you. They try anything, they'll have to deal with me. I'm not a violent man, but my dad is a hard-ass special agent in charge of an elite FBI team, and I've got a shitload of his genes. No fucking way are your parents going to be anything but civil and polite. I'll make fuckin' sure of it."

She pulls in a deep breath, then says, "I've heard you use that tone only once before."

"When?"

"Our first brunch. After the museum when we were back at your place—"

"And I laid it out for you."

"Yeah."

I smile. "Well, it worked then, so trust it'll work today."

She leans into me, wraps her arms around my waist, and looks up. "I trust you with my life. You're my one and only."

***

Gerald's reception area is exactly what I expect it to be: dignified and unpretentious. He comes out to greet us and takes us down the hall to his office, which is much the same, but with a desktop of a busy man.

There are two chairs in front of his desk, and a sofa against the back wall. I catch his eye and smirk. He's relegated the Sterns and their lawyer to the cheap seats.

He sits behind the wide desk and opens a folder. "Even though everything's electronically stored, I made copies of the will and trust for you and…them. As we discussed, there are no surprises. A few personal bequests to your grandmother's friends, and the rest goes to you."

Loud voices are nearing and I stand, my hand on Amy's shoulder, urging her to stay seated. Those motherfuckers get her back when they walk into the room.

Gerald doesn't get up, indicating his lack of respect and tolerance for the fiasco the Sterns intend to bring.

Victor Stern starts talking before he fully enters the room. "I told you the leech would be here. Bet he's salivating as he contemplates how much he's been able to whittle out of an old, deluded woman."

I bite my tongue, actually bite it, to keep from laughing. Lilli deluded is hysterical. Me being able to whittle anything out of her, really, really funny.

"Mr. and Mrs. Stern, Mr. Yancy, please have a seat on the couch." Gerald directs with an arm gesture.

"What? Has my daughter gone deaf and mute?"

I'm holding back my punch, but I have no problem blasting this asshole with my anger. Gerald gets there first.

"Mr. Yancy, if you cannot control your clients, you will all have to leave this office. This is not negotiable. You are on private property. I can and will have you removed posthaste."

Yancy turns, mutters something, and they sit on the couch, Monica with her pinched face, Victor with his flushed cheeks, and Yancy with his bright yellow pocket square.

Gerald gives me a small nod, and I sit and take Amy's hand, which elicits a grunt from Victor. Amy's right. They are vile.

"I'll read the terms of the trust and the will, then I'll provide a copy to Mr. Yancy and Mr. and Mrs. Vandenberg."

That gets another grunt, and it takes every molecule of willpower not to turn around and skewer the piece of shit.

Gerald begins, and there are no surprises. Lilli left the house to me and Amy. With the exception of gifts of select pieces of artwork to *Nonna*, and Allesandro and Francesca Di Caro, and one piece of jewelry to each member of the Old Ladies Club, everything else, all the house's contents, all the rest of Lilli's jewels, all her investments and holdings go to Amy.

"This is an outrage," Victor shouts.

Quietly, Gerald says, "Sit down and refrain from speaking, Mr. Stern, or I will call the police."

Yancy motions Victor down, then says, "When was the trust and will drawn?"

"With the exception of one change, the bequest of the house to both Mr. and Mrs. Vandenberg, which had been made to Mrs. Vandenberg alone prior to her marriage, you'll see the documents were signed and dated by Samuel and Lilli Stern eight years ago."

Amy's bat mitzvah.

Amy's eyes widen, and I have to hold back laughing. Again. Hard to make an argument about age and delusion when the bequests were made by Sam and Lilli eight years ago.

"Hand over those documents." Victor is up and heading toward Gerald.

I stand and block Victor from taking another step. I've got four inches and thirty pounds on him, and I'm a twenty-one-year-old surfer to his sixty-two. I look down at him and whisper, "Give me a reason."

Yancy comes alongside Victor and says, "Go sit down."

Victor holds my stare for another moment, then heads back to the sofa.

Yancy takes the documents from Gerald, and then motions to Victor and Monica to leave.

True to form, on the way out, Victor turns and hisses like the snake he is, "This isn't over."

I take a step forward, and that has him scurrying into the hallway. I shut the door and return to Amy's side.

Gerald shakes his head. "Unpleasant, but not unexpected."

"This guy Yancy have any brains?"

"He's competent. But he has a wounded client who's not going to let this go."

"He'll challenge the will and trust." Amy stands and runs her fingers through her hair. "I know him. He'll sue."

"Most likely. But he'll lose." Gerald hands the papers to Amy. "It'll slow down the transfer of the assets, and I'll have to block him from trying to remove you from the house–" Amy gasps. "He can do that?"

"Unfortunately, yes. But he won't win, Amy. You and Jonas go home. I'll handle whatever stupidity he files. I know all the judges in this county's Surrogate Court. Yancy's office is in Nassau County. He's not out this way very often."

"Thank you." I stick out my hand to Gerald and he shakes it, then, like my gramps does, he places his other hand over the top of mine and squeezes.

Amy kisses Gerald's cheek. "Everything will be fine," he says. "Go to the beach. It always clears out my head."

We're in the car for about ten minutes before Amy speaks. "She didn't say a word." She shakes her head. "Not that I expected her to countermand him, but she didn't even say hello."

"I've been around a lot of doped-up models, and Monica's eyes were droopy and glossy like a lot of the models'. She looked like she wasn't really there."

"She used to take a lot of Xanax. I guess she still does."

"Or something like it that's stronger."

"He was completely in character. A loud, bullying malignancy who thinks his shit don't stink."

"I guarantee, you'll never see them again." I reach over and grab her hand. "Gerald will get rid of them, Ames. You know he will."

She pinches the bridge of her nose. "But not before there's a public spectacle."

"I'm putting my money on Gerald getting a judge to throw the whole thing out before it becomes more than a few papers that cross the court clerk's desk."

***

Allesandro

"What?" Victor Stern snaps as I stop fifteen feet from his oversize desk. As is the way with people like him, he spoke without looking up. Without checking to whom he is talking. He probably thinks his secretary is standing in the middle of his obnoxiously large office waiting for him to deign her with his attention.

I don't answer. That's when he raises his head and all the color leaves his face. Perfect. We're off to a good start.

"You of all people…" He tries to sound fierce, but I can hear the tremble in his voice as he stands. Coward that he is, he keeps his place behind his desk, thinking what? Somehow the mahogany will protect him? "Know not to interfere in family matters."

What I wouldn't give to lose my temper right now. This *pezzo di merda* who never cared for his daughter, who left her with a shrill, bitter woman who took out all her frustrations on her only child, who abandoned his flesh and blood, has the nerve to call his nonexistent relationship with Amy *family*. This *stronzo* doesn't know the meaning of family.

"If this was a family matter, you would be correct." He opens his mouth to speak and I spear him with my glare. "Aside from a few days ago, when you had the unmitigated nerve to show up at the reading of Lilli's will, when was the last time you saw Amy?" He sputters and I save myself the time of him trying to look like he cares to remember.

"March twenty-first, seven years ago. You were home long enough to upset her so severely she fled your house and went into the cold night without a coat. She ran for who knows how long before she found a store where she was able to call her best friend, my daughter, Sofia, to ask if someone could pick her up."

He doesn't even try to respond. In this sliver of time, he's gotten smart enough to know better.

"The first time that child came to my home she was seven years old. I knew then you were a sperm donor, nothing more. You are not Amy's family. I am. All the Di Caros are Amy's family. Am I making myself clear?" He nods. "Good. I expect to see the evidence that the challenge to Lilli and Sam's bequests has been withdrawn permanently before the close of business tomorrow. I left my legal representative's card with your secretary. Have all the documents sent to my attorney's office.

"Also, I expect Amy to never hear from you, including legal filings, or see you or your wife again in any way, shape, or form. Never. Am I understood?"

He nods again and sits.

I turn and head out the office door. Tommie follows me to the elevators, where we stand until a car arrives to take us to the lobby.

After the elevator doors close, Tommie asks, "We going straight home, Don?"

"Let's take a detour and stop at Tiffany's so I can pick up a little something for *Donna* Francesca."

EPILOGUE

And so it goes…

Jonas

"Dr. Vandenberg, Dr. Di Caro."

Gio and I are ushered onto the main stage of the Staller Center for the Arts on Stony Brook's campus. We're here with our Australian counterparts, live on the screen behind us, to talk about our newest product, Detecto-Bots, which the FDA approved last month. The audience is packed with medical doctors, medical engineers, and robotics experts, all invited. There's press lined up against the side walls. No questions allowed, only filming.

I turn to Gio. "I'd rather be surfing."

He grins and starts the talk. "In conjunction with the original Australian team that created autonomous molecular machines, we took DNA nanobots one step further and developed swarm-bots that seek out disease, identify it, and send detailed data back to the patient's medical team. The Detecto-Bots can hunt down bacteria, viruses, and cancer cells inside our bodies.

"After the medical team's assessment of the information, enhanced Detecto-Bots will be introduced into the patient carrying a protein specific to the disease, and when they find a diseased cell, they assemble their proteins into a formation designed to eliminate the threat."

***

The house, pool, and yard are overflowing with people. Utterly Delightful has taken over our kitchen, and there's a huge tent with a long buffet table and two bars occupying one whole side of the yard.

Gio and I aren't even out the car when our kids and my two dogs rush us. Gio and Nat have three boys, sixteen-year-old Dario – who goes by Dare for good reason – fourteen-year-old Beniamino – Bennie for short – and eleven-year-old Isai, who insists everyone call him Isai.

Amy and I talked a lot about what our family would look like. Both only children, we decided we wanted our kids to have siblings. We started our family right after I got my doctorate. Boy, girl, boy, girl. We converted the sitting room into a nursery and were up to our ears in diapers for nearly ten years.

Naming the kids was easy. All four have our grandparents' names. We lost Gramps three years after we married, and Gran a couple of years after that. Sam is fourteen, Lilli is twelve, Artie is nine, and Helen, who goes by Lei-lei, is eight. Interestingly, or cosmically, all of them have the personalities of their namesakes. Lei-lei is our human tornado.

Right now, they're bombarding us with questions, and two of Sofia's three boys – it's a Di Caro thing – have joined in. Alex, who's twenty-two, isn't here. He's doing a Peace Corps year with Lia – they've been joined at the hip since they were babies – before both start law school next year. His brothers, Luca, seventeen, and Raffaello, fifteen, Rafe for short, are part of the pack, as we parents call them, which includes Theresa and Ethan's son Mikhail, who's nineteen and attending Yale.

In the space of a couple of hours – we had to suffer through a reception before we could leave – vid and commentary about our Detecto-Bots has gone viral.

Gio sticks his middle and forefinger in his mouth and blasts out a whistle that can stop traffic. "Yo, *famiglia*, give a man a chance to get a drink and some food, yeah?" He grabs Bennie around the neck and kisses the top of his head. The kid smiles up at him before taking off with the rest of the pack.

I'm stretched out poolside on a lounge chair, Amy's half lying on me. "Is it me, or are there more people at each successive party?"

"Not so much," she murmurs. "As the pack gets older, they're taller so they look less like kids. They skew the adult headcount."

"They each eat like three people."

"Says the guy with a surfer's body and a twenty-year-old constitution."

I bite her earlobe. "Says the woman who knows what to do with my surfer body."

"Yuck."

I don't have to look up. Only Lei-lei comments on Amy and my open affection in front of our kids.

"Problem?" I kiss Amy's neck, then turn my head to look at my dripping daughter with her hands on her hips, her head of strawberry blonde hair darkened by the water running rivulets down her arms.

"Well, yeah. There are people around. You're supposed to do that," she motions her hand up and down our bodies, "in private."

"Where's that written?"

She juts out her chin. "I say so."

"Are you in charge?"

She smiles. "Of course."

"Good. Do me a favor and drive down to the beach, then come back and tell me if it's still crowded."

She rolls her eyes. "You know I can't drive."

"Then you can't be in charge."

"Where's that written?"

"I say so."

Amy laughs and Lei-lei stomps off.

"Well played."

"I learned from her mother. Maybe you've met her. My fantasy come true."

"One-track mind."

"Still have Amy on the brain."

PLAYLIST

A Case of You – Joni Mitchell

Ain't Nobody - Chaka Khan

At Last - Etta James

Brandenburg Concerto No. 5 - Johann Sebastian Bach

Can't Help Falling in Love – Elvis Presley

Don't Know Much - Linda Ronstadt & Aaron Neville

God Only Knows - The Beach Boys

Let's Stay Together - Al Green

More Today Than Yesterday - The Spiral Staircase

My Girl – The Temptations

Nobody Does it Better - Carly Simon

Signed, Sealed, Delivered (I'm Yours) - Stevie Wonder

ABOUT THE AUTHOR

Elle Wright has been writing stories since she was a child, which led her to a career in journalism. She enjoys reporting life as much as making up a world she can control. She lives on the east coast of the United States where most of her large, noisy family resides. When she isn't in front of her computer, she loves to travel, garden, hang out with her dogs, and take in the brisk sea air that she's told is supposed to help calm her. She's been testing that theory for a while now.

CONNECT WITH ELLE:

Twitter: @ElleWright18

Instagram: @Elle_Wright_Writes

FB: /elle.wright.1460

www.BOROUGHSPUBLISHINGGROUP.com

If you enjoyed this book, please write a review. Our authors appreciate the feedback, and it helps future readers find books they love. We welcome your comments and invite you to send them to info@boroughspublishinggroup.com.

Follow us on TicTok and Instagram, and be sure to sign up for our newsletter for surprises and new releases from your favorite authors.

Are you an aspiring writer? Check out www.boroughspublishinggroup.com/submit and see if we can help you make your dreams come true.

Love podcasts? Enjoy ours at www.boroughspublishinggroup.com/podcast